The
Dirty Book Club

The
Dirty Book Club

Lisi Harrison

GALLERY BOOKS

New York   London   Toronto   Sydney   New Delhi

G

Gallery Books
An Imprint of Simon & Schuster, Inc.
1230 Avenue of the Americas
New York, NY 10020

First Gallery Books export edition October 2017

GALLERY BOOKS and colophon are registered trademarks of Simon & Schuster, Inc.

For information about special discounts for bulk purchases, please contact Simon & Schuster Special Sales at 1-866-506-1949 or business@simonandschuster.com.

The Simon & Schuster Speakers Bureau can bring authors to your live event. For more information or to book an event, contact the Simon & Schuster Speakers Bureau at 1-866-248-3049 or visit our website at www.simonspeakers.com.

Interior design by Davina Mock-Maniscalco

Printed and bound in Australia by Griffin Press

10   9   8   7   6   5   4   3   2   1

Library of Congress Cataloging-in-Publication Data

Names: Harrison, Lisi, author.
Title: The Dirty Book Club / Lisi Harrison.
Description: First Gallery Books hardcover edition. | New York : Gallery Books, 2017.
Identifiers: LCCN 2017003781 | ISBN 9781451695977 (hardcover) | ISBN 9781451696417 (softcover) | ISBN 9781451696424 (ebook) | ISBN 9781501166006 (export)
Subjects: LCSH: Book clubs (Discussion groups)—Fiction. | Self-realization in women—Fiction. | Female friendship—Fiction. | BISAC: FICTION / Contemporary Women. | FICTION / Humorous. | FICTION / General. | GSAFD: Humorous fiction.
Classification: LCC PS3608.A783573 D57 2017 | DDC 813/.6—dc23

LC record available at https://lccn.loc.gov/2017003781

ISBN 978-1-5011-6600-6
ISBN 978-1-4516-9642-4 (ebook)

For my Dirty Book Club:
Kelly Niemann Bailey, Michele Maniaci, Lisa Rodarte,
Shien-Lin Sun, and Rebecca Rootlieb, MD.
We've come a long way, baby.

The
Housewife's Handbook
on
Selective Promiscuity

CHAPTER

One

Pearl Beach, California
Friday, May 18, 1962
Full Moon

IF GLORIA GOLDEN were being honest, she'd say that Potluck Fridays weren't really about making the most of her newly renovated kitchen. Nor were they an excuse to connect with Dot, Liddy, and Marjorie, since best friends didn't need excuses. *Honest* Gloria would say their weekly get-togethers were the one thing she could rely on and that she was *tap-tapping* her fingernails on the countertop because if the girls stood her up, the number of things she could rely on would fall to zero. But a gal with a successful husband, a healthy baby boy, and a beach house with state-of-the-art appliances had no business being sour. Not when she's been told she bears a striking resemblance to a blond Ann-Margret. Not when children were starving in the Congo. So Gloria never said anything.

When the girls arrived (they always did) Gloria's *tap-tapping* was instantly replaced by the popping tops of Tupperware dishes and a Neil Sedaka record spinning on the Magnavox.

"'If you're feeling low down 'cause your baby's left town . . .'" they sang into serving spoons as they twirled across the Spanish tiles

3

like dancers on *The Ed Sullivan Show*. "'. . . Get out and cir-cu-laaaaaaaaate. . . .'"

Flushed and giggling after their big finish, Gloria checked the playpen in the living room. "Michael could sleep through an Elvis concert," she said of her tranquil son. Then, the telephone rang and he began to cry.

"Who is it?" Marjorie whispered, as if they were still freshmen at Pearl Beach High and not twenty-two-year-old grown-ups.

"Leo," Gloria mouthed. She found her reflection in the gas range. The ends of her honey-blond bob had wilted into *L*'s; she pinched them until they more closely resembled *J*'s.

Like rose petals in the sun, the ventricles of Gloria's heart unlatched for her husband. It didn't matter that he was calling from his office, fifty-five miles north, in Los Angeles. She could still see his caviar-black hair and denim-blue eyes, smell the bourbon that candied his breath, and feel the zing of his touch. That *touch*! How it filled her with orchestral crescendos and Technicolor joy, as if Walt Disney injected *Fantasia* straight into her veins.

"What does he want?" Liddy asked, raising those coarse eyebrows of hers.

Gloria shrugged, hopeful that eighteen months of Leo wheeling and dealing for Paramount Pictures had finally paid off. That he was being promoted to whatever it was that outranked his current job as producer. Then they could move to Beverly Hills, mingle with sophisticated intellectuals, and ride jumbo jets around the world. Not the way Marjorie was doing it—unattached and working as a stewardess for TWA—but the right way: with her wholesome family and Jackie Kennedy's wardrobe.

"Good news, baby," Leo said. He exhaled a gale of cigarette smoke. "I just lunched with the actress from *Breakfast at Tiffany's*, and you, my lovely wife, are now the owner of an autographed picture that reads: 'Best wishes, Gloria. Audrey Hepburn.'"

"Neat!" Gloria said, twirling the telephone cord around her finger. "And what time will you and my autograph be home for dinner? I'm making your favorite—"

"About that . . ."

Gloria's smile fell. *Not again*, she thought. *Please, not again.*

But Leo's hands were tied. The powers that be needed their golden boy to charm some stubborn young starlet into submission. Dinner . . . drinks . . . whatever it took to close the deal by Monday.

Michael's cries grew shrill, desperate.

"Does that mean another night at the Biltmore Hotel?" Gloria asked.

Leo struck a match, "I'm sorry, baby."

As usual, Gloria said she understood. Only after the line went dead did she stab her thumbnail in the thawing pot roast and brand it with a pout.

She wanted to tell her friends the truth: that Leo had not been home in two nights and she was lonely. Then they could smoke cigarettes and say all the right things until Gloria felt better, just like they had in high school when Leo was busy with water polo and forgot to call. But Miss Matrimony, the marriage columnist in *A Ladies' Life* magazine, forbade it.

Dear Wives, she once wrote. *Kindly remind all prying busybodies that husbands expect their private lives to remain private. If it's female* *support you're after, try the new Merry Widow by Warners. For $16.50 it will whittle your waist and give you a lovely lift. Available in white, black, and beige.*

"What's wrong?" Dot asked, her full, cherry Chap Sticked lips puffed to a sympathetic pout. "Is everything okay?"

"Leo was thinking about me, that's all."

Gloria managed a breezy smile. "You gals get started. I'll be right there."

Dot and Liddy took their platters into the sunroom while Marjorie, not keen on following orders, lifted herself onto the cooking island, leaned back on her hands, and crossed her bare legs. Her cleavage, upthrust and crevasse-deep, was like an oversized change purse positioned to catch pennies from heaven. "Now why did he really call?"

Gloria crunched down on a celery stick. "I told you."

Marjorie sighed. An auburn curl—one of the many to have freed itself from her too-loose-to-begin-with updo—stirred and settled on her cheek. "I know what will make you talk . . ." She was back on her feet, opening and closing cabinets. "Where do you keep the Smirnoff?" she asked, as if anyone would store liquor with the Lenox china.

"Vodka? It's eleven thirty in the morning!"

"Wow, motherhood has turned *someone* into a real drag," Marjorie reported to a studio audience that wasn't there. Then, glimpsing the clock above the breakfast nook, she clacked across the checkerboard tiles, removed it from the wall, and hung it upside down. "There. Now it's five o'clock. Might as well add some vermouth and olives while you're at it. I like mine dirty." She lifted her store-bought macaroni salad, bumped open the sunroom door with her shapely bottom, and slipped out.

The girls were seated at the Formica table in their usual spots: Marjorie at the head, Dot and Liddy on either side of her, with the butt, as they liked to call it, reserved for Gloria.

Typically, the sun burned through the marine layer by lunchtime, but that afternoon fog, silver as their rising cigarette smoke, blurred the palm trees that stretched above the vaulted glass ceiling and blocked their view of the outside world.

"Who's thirsty?" Gloria asked, as if offering Tang, not crystal martini glasses sloshing vodka and vermouth.

"Finally," Marjorie said. "Let's get blitzed!"

Dot gasped. "Before *Guiding Light*?"

Liddy pinched the crucifix she'd been wearing around her neck since her twelfth birthday. "You can't be serious."

"*Mon Dieu!*" Marjorie said, having just returned from her first transatlantic flight to Paris. "The French always drink at lunch."

Dot's pigtails wagged to differ. "Businessmen, not ladies."

"Everyone," Marjorie insisted. "But I guess you'd have to leave town to know that."

Dot stuck out her tongue.

Marjorie pinched it.

"Come on. Stop being such squares," she said, distributing the drinks.

Liddy slammed down her ice water. "We are not squares."

"You're wearing a pink kerchief on your head, for Christ's sake!"

"Why do you have to talk like that?"

Marjorie kissed Liddy on the cheek, marking her with a scarlet-red lip print. "You know I love you, Lids, but you're more buttoned up than Dot's blouse and Gloria's mouth, combined!"

Dot pinched her Peter Pan collar. "Buttoned up is the fad."

Gloria examined her lips in the blade of a butter knife. "What's wrong with my mouth?"

"It's girdle-tight."

"What do you know about girdles?"

Liddy and Dot purred with approval.

Conceived during their freshman year of high school, saying *purr* was their stamp of approval. It began with *the cat's meow*, which was shortened to *cat's*, then, *meow*, and finally, *purr*.

"It's become a real bore, Glo," Marjorie said, smacking a dollop of macaroni salad onto her plate.

"What has?"

"This whole, 'I can't confab about Leo' thing."

"We're married! Our leather anniversary is two months away."

"So?"

"*So*, being husband and wife for two years and ten months is different than going steady in high school. I need to respect his privacy."

"With us?"

"With everyone!"

"Says who?"

"*Whom*."

"Christ, Dotty, stop correcting me."

"Gosh, Marjorie, stop blaspheming *him*!"

"I'm sure he doesn't speak highly of me, either, Lids."

They purred.

"Fine." Gloria pushed her empty plate aside. "You want to know why Leo called?"

The girls leaned forward. Gloria surprised them all by taking a Marjorie-sized gulp of her martini.

"He got me an autographed picture of Audrey Hepburn and couldn't wait to tell me. That's why."

Marjorie placed a pitying hand on Gloria's knee. "Oh, honey, even *I* know what an autograph means and I'm in the clouds three days a week."

"Well, I don't."

"It means Leo isn't coming home tonight."

Gloria lit a cigarette.

"Every time Leo stays in Los Angeles for work"—Marjorie emphasized *work* with air quotes—"he gets you an autograph. Janet Leigh, Debbie Reynolds, Tony Curtis, and now Audrey. Do you want to know why?"

Gloria shook her head no.

"So he doesn't feel guilty about—" Marjorie connected her index finger to her thumb and then poked the hole with a cocktail weenie.

"Are you suggesting my husband is—"

"Marjorie is not suggesting anything," Dot said. "She's simply pointing out a pattern. Aren't you, Marj?"

"No, I'm suggesting."

Gloria put out her cigarette with a firm *How dare you?* stamp. "There isn't any *pattern*. Leo has to close a very important deal, that's all." She lifted the platter of deviled eggs and passed it to Liddy. "Now, let's eat before the mayo turns."

The platter made a full rotation around the table before it was returned to its original spot.

"So," Dot said with an enthusiastic clap, "*someone* has a date with Patrick Flynn tomorrow night."

Blotches formed instantly at the base of Liddy's neck. "It's nothing," she said, rubbing them redder. "He's just a friend from church."

"Well, I heard he's studying to be a pastor."

"Past-her sweater and under the bra," Marjorie teased.

"Just promise us you won't wear that old periwinkle thing," Dot said.

"What's wrong with my Easter dress?"

"All that pilling reminds me of Lenny Guzman's zits."

Purr.

"You're twenty-two, Lids," Dot continued. "Most decent men are already taken, and Patrick is a real catch. Whom, might I add, has made a believer out of every spinster in town. Did you see how full those pews were last Sunday?"

Liddy folded her arms across her ivory sweater set.

"Hold the phone!" Gloria hurried into the house and returned with her *Ladies' Home Journal*. "What about this tangerine shift? Jackie wore something exactly like it on her visit to India."

Liddy palmed the scarf around her short brown hair. "A peekaboo back?"

"Foxy, isn't it?"

"He's a man of God, not a nightclub owner."

Dot grabbed the magazine, studied the photo. "It's a cinch to make. I could scallop the neckline if you want."

Marjorie shuddered. "Don't scallop the neckline, lower it. Show some skin and he'll never look at another spinster again." Then with a wink, "Besides *moi*, of course."

"Patrick doesn't want skin."

"Honey, every man wants skin."

"Tell that to the good book," Liddy said. "Timothy 2:9–10."

"Doesn't sound like a good book to me," Marjorie said.

Dot reached into her straw bag and pulled out a tome, thick as the American history text they used to lug home from school. The cover looked like a wedding invitation—glossy white with gold script that read, *Prim: A Modern Woman's Guide to Manners*, by Alice Eden. "This is *my* bible." She flipped to one of the dog-eared pages and began reading with a faint British accent, though both she and Mrs. Eden were American. "And I quote: 'A girl should don her prettiest dress on a date, something modest and suited to her age. A boy wants to see her as he remembers her, not as an over-dressed older woman of thirty, nor as someone his friends might assume is easy.'"

"You carry that brick in your purse?" Marjorie asked.

"Robert and I are engaged." Dot said, her deep-set blue eyes wide. "I have to know things."

"Jesus!" Marjorie made a show of pulling out her own hair. "The Bible, *Prim* . . . They're rule books, not good books."

"I like rules," Liddy said.

Dot and Gloria agreed.

"Rules don't inspire people, *expériences* do." Marjorie lifted her martini above her head. "*Viva la France!*"

"What's so great about Frahn-ssss?" Gloria asked.

"French women don't worry about going to hell, being gossiped about at Crawford and Sons Grocery, or becoming spinsters. They do what they want, when they want, with *whom*ever they want and they're only 5,652 miles away." Marjorie lit a Gauloise. Raw and dark, the tobacco's stench was more Lawrence of Arabia than Marjorie of California. "Even their cigarettes are unfiltered."

Liddy fanned the air.

"I've got a transatlantic flight on Tuesday. Come with me! I'll prove it."

Liddy reached for her crucifix. "I'm not going *there*."

Marjorie turned to Dot. "What about you?"

"I'm engaged."

"And I have a baby," Gloria added, wondering if Leo would even notice she had gone.

"Then, I'll wait."

"Wait?" Gloria asked. "For what?"

"For your kids to grow up and your husbands to die. And when they do we'll move there together."

"What if we die before our husbands?" Gloria asked, her tongue heavy with vodka.

"Impossible," Marjorie said. "Men come first, men go first. It's a fact."

They paused to consider her logic.

"Come on, girls, who's with me?" she asked, her green eyes crackling with hope.

Dot gazed up at the overcast sky. "There's a full moon tonight. That's why you're acting all crazy, right?"

"She's not *acting*," Liddy said.

Gloria giggled. "I mean, if we really do become widows someday, maybe France would be nice."

The others nodded, deciding that a plan B was better than no plan at all.

"Fab! Let's make it official," Marjorie said.

Without waiting for their response, she put four Lucky Strikes between her lips, lit each one, and quickly doled them out before anyone could object.

It had been that way since the sixth grade. Whether she was debasing an innocent game of truth-or-dare, encouraging them to glug the Dewar's from her father's liquor cabinet, or stuffing socks in their bras before a dance, Marjorie was their pied piper of mischief; *You'll never get caught and you'll thank me a lot*—her seductive tune.

"I, Marjorie Shannon," she began, "hereby call secret pact number thirty-three into being. On this day—"

"Wait!" Dot quickly flipped to the notes section of her address book. "Pact thirty-three was to not like the Beach Boys. This is thirty-four. Start again."

"I, Marjorie Shannon, hereby call secret pact number thirty-four into being. On this eighteenth day of May, in the year 1962, we promise to move to France when the kids grow up and the husbands croak. All in favor inhale."

The girls drew on their cigarettes.

"May this smoke deliver pact thirty-four to the secret spaces inside our souls so it dwells within us forever." They held their breath for fifteen seconds (the amount of time it takes a pact to find a secret space), then exhaled.

Four sabers of smoke crossed and rose as one.

"Pact thirty-four is sealed," they said together.

"Time for presents!" Marjorie announced, never failing to bring them something from her travels. She reached inside a TWA airsick bag and handed every girl a chain—each with a different key hanging from its center. "I swiped one from every hotel I stayed at."

While they gushed and fussed with the clasps, Marjorie slapped a thin green paperback on the table like a winning hand. There were no glossy photographs or formal typography on the cover, just: *The Housewife's Handbook on Selective Promiscuity* by Rey Anthony, written in modest, black letters. "Now, this, my friends is what I call a good book."

"What is it?" Liddy asked.

"A little something I picked up in Paris."

"Syphilis?"

They purred and then leaned past the Lenox china to get a closer look.

"It's an autobiography about a young girl named Rey who had loads of questions about sex and no one to ask so she hides out and reads dirty magazines."

"Then what?" Dot asked.

"She masturb—"

"Marjorie!" Gloria hissed, pointing at the Smoots' house next door. "Not so loud."

"Does she ever get caught?" Liddy asked, the tips of her ears reddening.

"No. She becomes a sex maniac. Listen to this . . . 'I kissed his body, his stomach, his penis, his testicles—'"

Dot snatched the book and wrapped it in her *Prim: A Modern Woman's Guide to Manners* cover. Then she shyly raised her hand. "Question."

"Yes?"

"Did her husband *want* to be kissed in those places?"

"Her husband didn't know about it," Marjorie said. "She was doing that stuff with her doctor. Rey didn't believe in monogamy. She thought it was unnatural to stay with one person for the rest of her life, and I agree."

"She circulates," Gloria said, quoting Neil Sedaka.

"She's vulgar."

"It's just sex, Lid," Marjorie said to the lipstick that was still on her cheek.

"Exactly. She should keep it to herself."

"That's how I feel when you girls swap recipes. I mean, what's the point of going public with that?"

"To find new ideas."

"To know if we're doing it right."

"To get better."

"Same reasons I read about sex." Marjorie lit a cigarette. "It's not like you three are going to teach me anything." Then to Dot, "If you think Robert would rather have you read about table settings than"—Marjorie closed her mouth around a Kosher dill and poked it against the inside of her cheek—"you're more blitzed than you look. And, Gloria, try what Rey does on page 126 and Leo will never stay at the Biltmore again." Then to Liddy, "Rey even does it with women."

"Why do you always look at me when you talk about lesbians?"

"I don't know." Marjorie smirked. "Why do you always get so defensive?"

"What else does Rey try?" Gloria asked. Because what if Marjorie was right? What if this book could teach her things, things that would bring Leo home more often?

Marjorie raised an eyebrow. "I could read it to you, and if you like it I know where to get more."

Liddy reached for her crucifix, accidentally grabbing the room key instead.

"How many more?" Dot asked.

"One for every full moon from now until we board that airplane to France. We can start our own secret club."

"Robert would not approve."

"It's a dirty book club, Dot! No one would approve," Gloria said, imagining what old Mrs. Smoot would think of a mother who reads about sex while her baby is napping.

"That's why rule number one should be: tell no one."

Eyes closed, lips nibbling on a prayer; Liddy seemed to be saying an act of contrition—preemptively repenting for the sins they were about to commit.

"And rule number two is: a husband's right to privacy cannot and will not be respected," Marjorie added. "We have to talk the way we did in high school."

"I thought you were against rules," Dot snipped, as she wrote them all down in her black notebook.

"Not my own, honey," Marjorie said, with a playful wink. "Never my own."

Dot flipped to a fresh page. "So what are we calling pact thirty-five?" Her pen hovered anxiously above the margin.

"The Dirty Book Club," Marjorie said, with a credit-where-credit-is-due nod to Gloria. Then she lit four Lucky Strikes, sealed the pact, and began reading *The Housewife's Handbook on Selective Promiscuity*; starting a fifty-four-year tradition that would save them all.

Fear of Flying

CHAPTER

Two

M. J. STARK opened her Sub-Zero: a fridge named as much for its self-contained cooling system as the amount of food she kept inside. She reached for the bottle of prosecco and began the 3,500-square-foot trek across her hardwood floors, shuffling in fuzzy socks past barren bookshelves and a neon No Regrets sign that had never been turned on.

Poor prosecco, M.J. thought as she curled into the corner of the sectional and muted *Project Runway*. Light, sexy, and full of sparkle, this effervescent wine didn't come all the way from Italy to be lit by the glare of a flat-screen TV or chugged by a woebegone woman wearing a bleach-spotted hoodie and some ex-boyfriend's silk boxers. It was meant for glitter-dusted models during Fashion Week. Boating on the Mediterranean. Giggling girlfriends and their summery perfumes.

But Fortune's wheel didn't give a shit what prosecco was *meant* for. It spun when it wanted to spin and stopped where it wanted to stop. And prosecco would have to deal with the outcome just like everyone else.

And so, with a cynical smirk, M.J. lifted her ill-fated companion to the heavens and drank. Charging the alcohol to haul away her pain like a wounded soldier from the battlefield—hands under armpits, heels scraping along the dirt—until its agonizing cries were no longer heard.

Then, the jiggling sound of someone tampering with her locks. Holding her breath, M.J. strained to listen above her jackhammering heart.

Logic pointed to the neighbors in #5F who were constantly jamming turquoise envelopes under her door filled with offers to purchase her apartment. Though M.J. refused to sell, their persistence made a case for buying stock in Kate Spade stationery.

"Hello?" M.J. called, her voice strained and small.

Then, *click*.

The lock turned. The door creaked open. And then an abrupt jolt. The chain.

Hands shaking, vision coned, M.J. palmed the cushions for her phone. *9-1-1*, she thought, as if Siri could read her mind and make the call.

"The police are on their way!" she managed.

"It's me," called a familiar male voice.

Dan?

M.J. kicked off her socks, hurried to unlatch the chain, and then clung to her boyfriend's firm torso. A log in a torrent of raging white water.

"What the fuck are you doing here?" she asked. His T-shirt carried the stale smell of economy class. She kept clinging anyway.

"I didn't think you should be alone tonight."

"So . . . what? You just hopped on a plane?"

"It was more like a dash," he half smiled, with a superhero's attempt at modesty. "But yes."

"I look like a homeless undergrad. Why didn't you tell me?"

"You would have told me not to come."

He was right. "What if I wasn't home?"

"I'd have gone to your office."

"What if I was out with friends?" she tried, though they both knew there weren't any friends, not anymore.

Dan, glimpsing the half-empty bottle of prosecco on the coffee table, gave her a lucky-guess shrug, then presented her with her usual box of See's butterscotch lollypops. He knew better than to ask why she wasn't tearing off the foil wrapper the way she normally did.

Taking his hand, M.J. guided him to the couch. Adrenaline made it hard for her to stand still and reacquaint herself with his California tan and the gold bursts in his hazel eyes. That, and the awkwardness that always seemed to spritz a mist of shyness onto their reunions. It was one of the drawbacks of their long-distance relationship. Eight months of daily conversations, weekend visits, a carpal tunnel's worth of texts, and, still, that feeling of always having to start over was impossible to shake. But it was worth it. *He* was worth it.

Tonight, though, the mist was thicker than usual. Coagulated by Dan's surprise visit and M.J.'s assertion that this night, above all others, was to be endured alone. Even if she had been appropriately waxed and plucked, she couldn't swing the primal, make-up-for-lost-time sex he was used to. She could barely eke out a genuine smile. But she had to do something. Because when a tanned thirty-four-year-old general practitioner on the verge of opening his own medical practice spontaneously flies across the country to be with his pasty, probably anemic, workaholic girlfriend on the third anniversary of her family's death, she should, at the very least, unzip her hoodie and show some cleavage.

"Is that the journal?" he asked, indicating the leather-bound notebook on the cushion beside her.

M.J. nodded, feeling the heated pinch of mobilizing tears. Like the prosecco, that journal was meant for better things; story ideas, half-baked characters, and the musings of a thirty-one-year-old aspiring author. She bought it back when she was a copywriter at *City* magazine, barely making rent on her studio apartment in Hell's Kitchen and sleeping with guys who wore silk boxers, back when everything was how it should have been. When M.J.'s handwriting was fat and happy and she was still using pens.

Now, knees to chest, she flipped past those old entries and entered the zone where those well-fed letters were now pencil gray and wan.

"It looks like you were possessed when you wrote that," Dan noted.

"I was."

Shoulders weighted in alcohol, M.J. told Dan about Dr. Cohn, her grief therapist, who was shiny-eyed with relief when she finally agreed to write about March 31. "He gave me his cup of special pens and said I could use whichever one I wanted."

"And you asked for a pencil, right?"

"Yep," M.J. said, instantly warmed by how well he knew her. "Of course, he thought I was messing with him until I told him I hadn't used a pen since the accident."

Dan closed his eyes and slowly shook his head from side to side. "Poor guy probably wanted to retire."

"You have no idea. I thought he was going to bludgeon me with his *You Can Be Right or You Can Be in a Relationship* mug."

Dan laughed harder than he needed to, probably capitalizing on the last bits of levity before M.J. turned herself over to the anguish, as she always did on March 31, and read her entry.

"I can't believe you came," she said, trying her best to sound appreciative, since what she really felt, ungrateful as it was, was a tinge of resentment toward his surprise visit. Because that screaming pain at the base of her belly was all that remained of her family. Feeling that was feeling them. And now that Dan swooped in with his anesthetizing hugs, the pain would fade—*they* would fade—bringing her that much closer to them being gone for good.

"I want to help you," he said, brushing a lifeless strand of hair from her cheek.

M.J. thanked him, as if helping her was even possible. But they both knew that Fortune spun her wheel and this is where it landed. And short of bringing them back, Dan, her savior, would have to accept that there was nothing he could do to help. Because in the end, M.J. didn't want to be saved; she wanted what she once had. And that was gone. So she accepted her fate—yet again—and for the first time in three years, read the entry Dr. Cohn made her write.

Remembering March 31, 2013

I'm getting off the subway. Heat, stale as morning breath envelops me like a drunk's hug. I emerge from the tunnel on Prince Street to the putrid smell of trash and an ambulance siren. I wonder if that's what it felt like to be born. To go from one extreme to the other, with no time to prepare for the sudden change.

I arrive at Cipriani twenty minutes before our reservation and sit at the bar. I write in my journal—this journal—while I wait for my parents and sister to arrive. They are driving in from Long Island to celebrate my big news: after years of circulating proofs, balancing trays of coffee, and pitching articles that other, more "experienced" writers got to write, I am going to be published in <u>City</u> magazine.

"It's called 'Dial-Up Parents in a High-Speed World,'" I say once we're seated. "Inspired by your struggle to keep up with technology."

Mom pinches a bread crumb from Dad's beard. "I can't help taking this personally."

"Because it is personal." I remind her of the e-mail. The one where I told her I was in bed with the flu, and she wrote back: LOL.

April laughs that phlegmy, rolling laugh.

Mom scrunches her curls. "I thought it stood for _lots of love_."

"I rest my case."

April says, "You have to include the time dad texted me to say I left my phone at his house."

She reaches for a handful of my fries.

I smack her hand. "You have your own!"

"Oh," she gasps, as if just noticing her plate. "When did those get here?"

We laugh and tease one another through a bottle of Veuve Clicquot and all the way into dessert. Dad orders a latte. I check my phone.

My best friend Katie is around the corner at the Mercer Kitchen and wondering what's taking me so long. She has four tequila shots and eyes on a "hot Malcolm Gladwell." She tells me to get my ass over there before some slut with brains clubs him over the head and stuffs him in a taxi.

Dad signs the check. I stand. Mom motions for me to sit back down.

"We have something for you."

That's when she gives me the empty Montblanc box.

I glance at April and roll my eyes as if to say, "What is wrong with these people?"

"A great writer deserves a great pen," Dad says.

"Um." I wave my hand through the empty box with a Vegas magician's flair; Look, folks, nothing inside...

"We thought you'd enjoy picking it out yourself," Mom says. "The store is just around the corner."

I appreciate the gesture. I really do. But I thought celebrating my first big break at the Montblanc store with my parents would be depressing.

So I lie. I say I'm tired and ask if we can go Sunday after our weekly brunch instead.

They smile, trying not to look hurt. April says she has to miss brunch. She's going to some fitness convention. I tell her it's no big deal. I'll see her next week.

We hug good-bye on Greene Street. I feel flushed from champagne, the promise of Hot Malcom, the love of my family, and a career that is about to take off. The feeling: that life doesn't get any better than this, propels me to the Mercer Kitchen and lights me from within.

Katie is right about Hot Malcolm. And Hot Malcolm says I look like an average-sized Elle Macpherson, so we hit it off instantly.

Between shots, Katie is making out with her boyfriend, and Hot Malcolm is telling me the stories behind his assortment of silver rings. We're contemplating a karaoke bar when my phone rings. The number is blocked. I send it to voice mail. I order another round of shots.

My phone rings again.

I do a shot.

It rings again.

I finally answer.

There's been an accident... Long Island Expressway. A truck driver was texting... He hit Dad's junky old Audi... it spun... slammed into an SUV... no airbags... everyone killed instantly.

If only I went to the Montblanc store.

If only I bought that pen...

If only... If only... If only...

M.J. closed her tear-soaked journal, curled into the corner of her couch, and sobbed like it happened yesterday. Dan rubbed her feet with his warm doctor hands, injecting compassion into her bloodstream with his magical medical touch. M.J. didn't know if she should unleash on him for crashing her pity party or write a romance novel about it. She did know that, Dan or no Dan, it hurt like hell.

CHAPTER

Three

TWO MOANS AND it was over.

Ahhhhweeeeuhhh. Ahhhhweeeeuhhh.

There was a time when M.J. would have turned inward for hours and searched for the best way to describe the sound of concert tickets ribboning through her paper shredder. Car tires spinning on ice . . . Shouting, "Are we here?" into a kazoo . . . A sheep passing a kidney stone . . . But these days she flatly referred to it as "another set of complimentary tickets she was too busy to use."

Thirty-five floors below her office at *City* magazine, brake lights strobed to the beat of start-and-stop traffic. Yellow cabs honked. Buses screeched to a lazy stop. New Yorkers rushed, dined, danced, traded, designed, debated, and created. And M.J., a ghostly reflection in her window, floated above it all.

"Delegate!" said Nicole from graphics as she passed by the open door.

M.J. swiftly raised her middle finger above the rising towers of submissions and proofs that crowded her desk like the Gotham City skyline. It was a playfully pat response to her coworkers' needling reminders that M.J. had a competent staff and a sentinel of interns at the ready. She didn't have to do it all.

But she did.

Work was her escape. Deadlines were her lifelines. When she was editing other people's stories she forgot about her own. That was Dr. Cohn's explanation, not hers. M.J. didn't have time for explanations. A hoisted middle finger would have to do.

"Guess where I am?" Dan asked, minutes later over Skype. Bare-chested and dressed in butter-yellow surf trunks, he was perched on the railing of an outdoor deck holding a bottle of Dos Equis; the emerald-colored bottle green as the ocean behind him. A pair of mirrored aviators resting on top of his head.

"Spring break?" M.J. tried, though she didn't have time for games. Truth? She assumed he was calling to wish her luck on her soon-to-be-official promotion and that's why she accepted the call. His thoughtfulness was irresistible; one of the few things that could tear her away from her prospectus on the future of *City* magazine. Not that anyone was expecting it. But they would. And when they did, she'd be ready.

"Nope. Guess again."

"Dan, I—"

"The cottage," he said. "We got it! I closed escrow today."

M.J. softened. Whether Dan genuinely considered his accomplishments theirs, or he used *we* to keep her from feeling alone in the world, didn't matter. His use of inclusive pronouns gave M.J. a sense of belonging that made her smile out loud.

"Congratulations, Dr. Hartwell!" she beamed. "I can't wait to see—"

A woman, age twenty-eight or maybe thirty-four, wearing a black sports tank and Lycra leggings in performance pink, bounced into frame. "I can't find my keys!" She tipped over the railing to check the sand. Her suspiciously thick Victoria's Secret hair spilled forward as if helping her search.

Dan, respectfully avoiding eye contact with her high-definition ass, offered to check the kitchen. "Hold on a sec," he told M.J. as he set down his iPad. A prop plane dragged a banner through the optimistic blue sky: REGGAE AT THE OASIS!

M.J. snuck a quick peek of herself in the chat box. Her complexion was pigeon gray compared to their radiant California glows. Summoning the poor girl's blush, she pinched her cheeks and accidentally scratched the left side of her face.

"Found them!" the woman announced while M.J. applied pressure to the wound with a coffee-stained Starbucks napkin.

"Who was that?" she asked when Dan finally returned.

"Britt Riley. My Realtor."

"Well, Britt Riley is going to get a yeast infection if she keeps wearing her exercise clothes to work."

"They're moisture wicking!" Britt called as she left.

Dan winced.

"Sorry," M.J. mouthed, cheeks hot.

"Are you okay?"

"Well, I just insulted your Realtor—"

"No, you have a scratch on your face and . . . when's the last time you ate?"

"Does toothpaste count?"

"Come out here. Let me take care of you."

"Next Friday," she reminded him. "Well, technically Saturday. I have to take the red-eye because I'm doing an interview for the *Times*."

"That gives us . . . what? Like a day and a half?"

"I know, but I'll be back for my birthday, then you'll be here in June and—"

"That reminds me," he said with more enthusiasm than she would have preferred. "Randy just confirmed our surf trip. It's June thirty-first. We're doing seven days in Java."

"June only goes up to thirty."

"Really?" Dan rubbed the back of his neck. "I could have sworn he said the thirty-first."

M.J. quickly googled Java on her phone. "Indonesia? What if there's a terror attack? Do they even have cell service? What if you drown?"

"I'm going with two other doctors and a pro surfer," he said. "We'll be fine."

"Randy is a retired pro surfer," she said, while making a note to fill that week with time-consuming meetings and late-night photo shoots.

"Anyway, I wasn't talking about a visit and you know it. I was talking about you coming here to live." He smiled, boyishly. "With me."

M.J. sighed, tired of defending her choices.

"I know we've only been together for eight months, but so what? We'll get a dog, go on hikes, spend Monday through Friday together. You could start writing again."

"Dan, I'm not a writer anymore. I'm about to be named editor in chief of the most successful monthly magazine on the East Coast." Something inside of M.J.'s stomach took flight when she said *editor in chief*. After two and a half caffeinated years of sweat-shop discipline and unwavering dedication it was happening. Really, really happening.

Dan drained his beer and set it down on the railing with a decisive *thunk*. "Tell them you don't want the job."

"I can't. I'm about to sign the contract in, like, two minutes."

"Can't or won't?"

A calendar reminder popped up on M.J.'s computer screen. It was time.

"Both," she said. "I have to go."

"Have to go or want to go?"

She rolled her eyes. "Stop."

"Fine. Skype me from the cab on your way home. I'll give you a tour of the cottage."

"That's it?"

"I love you."

"How about 'Good luck, M.J.'?"

"Luck is the last thing you need. Actually, this promotion is the last thing you need."

"Meaning?"

"Running that magazine isn't going to make you happy."

"What?"

"All those e-mails, and meetings, and articles you're always editing . . . they're excuses."

"Thank you, Dr. Cohn. Same time next week?"

"I'm serious, M.J. It's been three years since the accident. It's time to start giving a shit again."

"I give a shitload of shit."

"About your job, yes. Not about—"

"It's not a *job*," she snapped, because it wasn't. *City* was so much more than corporate perks and cinematic views. It was a playground for the ambitious with rules that made sense. The more she worked, the more she achieved. No surprises, no unexpected calls from blocked numbers. Why was that so hard for him to understand? "Dan, this place saved me."

"It's a place, M.J. . . . . It can't save you."

Her heart began to rev. "Why don't you move to New York and open a clinic here instead?"

"I just bought a house."

"And I own an apartment."

Eyes locked, nostrils flared, chests puffed, they glared at each other. Two soap opera characters enduring the awkward, lingering silence. They had arrived at this impasse many times before. How could they build a life together when neither of them would sacrifice what they had built when they were apart? And now with Dan's new cottage and M.J.'s soon-to-be-signed five-year contract, a solution seemed further away than ever.

"What do you want me to do, Dan? Move to the beach and work at an organic juice bar?"

"Sounds kind of nice, doesn't it?"

"It does," she admitted, if things were different, if she was different—but they weren't.

———

ANN ROSE-COOKE WAS seated at the twenty-six-person conference table, shuffling papers and setting out pens, when M.J. entered. Standing, Ann welcomed her with a *Let's get it done* handshake and a *Thank God it's Friday* smile. No one had to tell this president of human resources how to commix business and pleasure into a single greeting. Ann made a career out of professional etiquette. She knew.

"I just love daylight savings. The extra hour of sun makes all the difference."

M.J. glimpsed the bank of floor-to-ceiling windows with a concurring nod, though she had grown to resent the amenable weather conditions other New Yorkers so desperately craved.

While perfect for those who wanted to toss a Frisbee around Central Park or linger at an outdoor café, blue skies and balmy nights did nothing for workaholics but underscore their tragic condition.

"Are we late?" Gayle asked, blowing into the conference room like a nor'easter.

We? M.J. thought. And then Liz Evans, president of marketing and the Queen of Happy Hour, followed Gayle through the open door.

"What up, May-June?" Liz asked, in her ongoing effort to annoy M.J. by using her full name.

"Liz and I just had a very productive lunch meeting with Rafferty Witt," Gayle said, shooting a chummy wink at Liz as she settled into her seat at the head of the table.

When had Gayle West—current editor in chief, soon to be CEO of Pique Publishing Group—started winking chummily at Liz? Crass humor, trashy style, and gold selfie sticks hardly seemed to be her thing.

Liz muffled a burp. "Sorry," she said, fanning the air. "Sauvignon blanc."

Gayle wagged a finger. "I told you not to order that third glass."

"I didn't," Liz boomed. "That was *you*."

"Ha! You're right."

"Why don't we get started?" Ann suggested.

"Let's." Gayle clapped. "Liz, you begin."

"Sorry, but am I at the right meeting?" M.J. asked, tapping through her schedule.

"Of course." Gayle grinned, meeting M.J.'s eyes for the first time. "I thought you'd want to hear the good news before we get to the great news."

"Sure. Yes. Totally," M.J. said, cheeks burning and still confused.

"And now . . ." Liz drumrolled her bloated fingers on the table. "For the first time in advertising history . . . Witt Holdings have pulled their ads from *New York* magazine and are making *City* their new home. And now back to you, Gayle."

M.J. drew back her head. "Does that mean . . . ?"

"Everything!" She beamed. "Restaurants, boutiques, art galleries, even their luxury condos."

It was the first time M.J. didn't want to smack the smug look off her coworker's face. In fact, she could have kissed it. The score was impressive and the skank deserved to be proud. Witt Holdings would bring millions of ad dollars to the magazine. The additional revenue would placate the board members and maybe even reverse their position on shutting down *City*'s print division. Not to mention the personal win for M.J.: her first year as editor in chief would be the most successful one on record. "Incredible job, Liz. How did you do it?"

"I took Witt himself to see Laser Floyd: Dark Side of the Moon and we had a blast."

"People still do that?"

"They sure do," Gayle bellowed. "I've seen that show at least ten times."

M.J. furrowed her neglected eyebrows.

"Yes, honey, black people like Pink Floyd, too," Gayle teased.

"This isn't about you being black," M.J. insisted. "It's about you being—"

"Forty-seven?"

"No."

"Female?"

"No."

"Claustrophobic?"

Laughing, M.J. said, "I didn't know Rafferty Witt was a fan of Floyd," because there was no respectful way to say she thought Gayle was more sophisticated than that.

"The tequila shots and steak dinner didn't hurt," Liz added.

"Well, it's quite a win, Liz," Ann said. "But I'd really feel much better if we could take the focus off alcohol and—"

"God." Gayle sighed. "I'm really doing this, aren't I?"

"Doing what?" M.J. asked.

"Stepping down as editor in chief to become the CEO of Pique?"

"Are you having second thoughts?"

"More like pangs of nostalgia." Gayle dabbed the corners of her pooling eyes with the sleeve of her tastefully sheer blouse. "I'm going to miss this place, but I know it will be in capable hands." She went on to laud M.J.'s leadership skills, her tireless quest for perfection, the innumerable weekends and holidays she worked, and the magazine's circulation, which was up 43 percent.

M.J. gripped the two gold wedding bands on her thumb. Her parents would be so proud. "*City* is everything to me."

"Same," Liz boomed. "Shit, I seriously can't imagine a better partner."

M.J. thanked her with a humble grin. "I will be leaning on you and your marketing team a lot, especially during the first few months."

"Ha!" Liz said.

"What's funny?"

"That was a joke, right?"

M.J. looked from Gayle to Ann, then back to Liz. "No, why?"

"As of Monday I won't have a marketing team," she said. "We're the team now, May-June."

"I'm sorry but I don't get what's happening here."

Gayle fingered the layered chains around her neck. "Didn't you read the e-mail?"

"What e-mail?"

She made *ch-ch-ch* sounds as she thumbed through her phone. "Here we go. Sunday, April 17, 2:13 AM. Subject: Exciting Changes."

"Never got it."

"Shoot," Gayle said. "It's in my drafts folder."

Ann began to straighten her already straight row of pens.

Liz popped a Mentos.

"Will someone please tell me what's going on?"

"In a nutshell?" Gayle was suddenly alight with corporate enthusiasm. "I've formed a coalition."

Liz bobbleheaded in agreement.

"I still don't . . ."

"You and Liz," Gayle said, as if they'd discussed it hundreds of times. "Coeditors in chief."

"Co?"

"Yes," Gayle said, delighted by her own ingenuity. "You run *City* in here, and Liz runs it"—she rolled her wrist toward the windows—"out there."

"I'm sorry, but what does that even mean?" M.J. glared straight into Gayle's eyes, suspecting that maybe this wasn't Gayle at all. The Gayle she knew wouldn't gaslight her like that. That's not how they worked. That's not how they *were*. They were open and honest and collaborative. Gayle knew how hard M.J. worked. How capable she was. How she gave every ounce of her neglected self to this magazine. She knew!

"You look a little . . . ashen. Do you need a moment?"

M.J.'s heart began to pound like a fist at a protest march. "A moment? I'll need more than a moment to understand why my new position has suddenly morphed into a . . ."

"Coalition," Liz offered.

"Gayle, can I speak to you for a minute?" M.J. managed.

"Great idea," Ann said. "Would anyone like coffee?"

"Depends where you're going," Liz said. "Sixbucks or the commissary?"

"*We're* going to the commissary," Ann insisted.

Liz stiffened. "Oh, right." Then with a wine-scented whisper said, "Don't worry, May-June, you got the better office." Then she and Ann left the boardroom.

"This is insane," M.J. hissed once they were alone. "You know that, right?"

Gayle extended her hand toward M.J. "I hate that it was sprung on you like this. I assumed you got the e-mail."

"And what? You thought I loved the idea so much I forgot to mention it?"

"I'm trying to do what's best for the magazine."

"And this is how I find out? Here, in front of everyone?"

"It was stuck in drafts." Gayle flashed her screen as proof. "I didn't know."

"Oh, I think you did. I think you knew exactly what you were doing."

Gayle folded her arms and sat back in her chair. "Meaning?"

"Meaning, I think you knew I'd freak out and you were scared."

"Scared?"

"Yes, scared. So you did that whole 'break up in public so she doesn't cause a scene' thing. No, wait, what you did was worse. You broke up with me in public and invited your new lover to watch."

"I'm hardly breaking up with you, M.J., I'm giving you my magazine."

"You were giving me your magazine. Now you're co-giving it to me and I have no idea why." Tears, hot and sudden, blurred M.J.'s vision. She blinked them back.

"Fine. You want to know why I did it?"

M.J. nodded.

"You're no fun."

"Excuse me?"

"You get free tickets to every club, gallery opening, and concert in Manhattan and you never go. When's the last time you took a client to dinner or came in late because you got the junior editors drunk?"

"When was the last time I left the office before midnight?"

"I get it," Gayle continued. "I hate people, too. But Liz? She lives for that crap, and our advertisers can't get enough of her."

"I agree. She's great. I'll give her a raise and a promotion."

"I considered that," Gayle explained. "But—"

"But what? Liz has no idea how to run a magazine."

"That's why I need you."

"I know, but why do you need her?"

"Liz has more cache as an editor in chief and more cache for Liz means more cash for us."

M.J. recoiled. "So that's what this is about? Money?"

"This is a business. You know that."

"And I gave this business everything. Every holiday, every idea, every everything! And now you're giving it to Liz!"

"She's a strong spice, yes, but she'll carry half the load and that will mean less pressure for you. You'll have more time to see Dan and daylight and who knows? Maybe you'll start writing again."

"All I want is what you promised me."

Gayle exhaled sharply. "Trust me, okay?"

"And if I don't?"

"Meaning?"

"What if I refuse to share the position?"

"M.J., I know you're disappointed but—"

"Disappointed?" This wasn't disappointment—it was another death. Only this one wasn't an accident. It was premeditated and carried out in cold blood.

"It's not personal, honey."

"Well, it's sure as shit not professional," M.J. said, as she pushed back her chair and began moving toward the door in strides that felt both swift and sluggish and not entirely her own. Scenes from a life not yet lived flashed before her—a life where she had no career, no reason to wake up, nowhere to hide from her pain. They came to her in fragments like flying shards of glass after an explosion.

"At least consider it," Gayle insisted. "Take a few days off. Think about it. I'll hold the announcement for a week. What do you say?"

M.J. wanted to come back with something so poignant and crisp that it would silence the busy streets below and echo through the empty chambers of Gayle West's heart for years to come. But her throat was too dry and her words were spinning and colliding and impossible to grasp.

"Wait!" Gayle tried. "Where are you going?"

Without looking back, M.J. replied, "To the fucking beach!"

CHAPTER

Four

Pearl Beach, California
Sunday, May 1
Waning Crescent Moon

SUNSHINE SPILLED INTO the bedroom, waking M.J. like a messenger with urgent news.

She rolled over onto Dan's pillow and listened to Gayle's latest voice mail. It was a reminder, her third, that it wasn't too late to go back to *City*. But unless Gayle rescinded her offer to Liz, it most certainly was.

M.J. pitched the phone onto the tangle of sheets, stretched lazily across the bed—*their* bed—and gazed out at the wraparound deck. Dan was there, lying on a yellow-and-white-striped chaise reading *Emergency Medicine* magazine. The tiny muscles in his shoulder twitched when he turned a page. She wondered what the birds were singing about, why the sky was so freakishly cloudless, and where that chaise might have come from, because it sure as Chanel wasn't there yesterday.

Pressing a sheet against her naked body, M.J. padded onto the deck and took in the view: blooms of colorful beach umbrellas, cliffs that jutted like buckteeth over the curving coastline, and the blue-

42

green ocean that really did sparkle. Maybe unemployment wasn't so bad. After months of memorized airline schedules and long weekend visits that never felt long enough, their Sunday wouldn't end with a tearful curbside good-bye at LAX. Sand had finally stopped slipping through the hourglass. It stood still now and stretched on for miles, theirs to be strolled in barefoot and enjoyed.

M.J. checked her watch; a 1974 Timex with an olive-green strap. "How did you let me sleep until three?"

Dan removed his mirrored aviators, greeted her with smiling eyes. "Is that still on East Coast time?"

"It's not East Coast time. It's August Stark time. My dad was wearing it the day he was murdered, and I want it to stay exactly the way—"

"Hold on a minute—" Dan tossed his magazine. It landed with a smack. "Your dad—"

"Stop! I don't want another lecture on the difference between murder and manslaughter. I already know. But intent or not, someone took his life and—"

"No." Dan chuckled. "I didn't know Augie was short for August."

M.J. plucked a loose thread from the strap. She envied the old watch. How it ticked merrily along as if nothing ever happened.

"So your mom was January, your dad was August, your sister was April, and you're May-June?"

"We were named after our birth months," she said, a proud member of this exclusive club. "I was born at midnight on May 31, so they gave me June, too." M.J. sat on the edge of the cushion. "Now I have a question for you: where did you get this chair?"

Dan hitched his thumb toward the bungalow on their right.

"They just gave it to you?"

"Not exactly. I'm kind of borrowing it until we get our own. Curtis said they're on a cruise and won't be back for another week or two."

"Who's Curtis?"

"The UPS guy."

"You know his name?"

"Of course."

M.J. had lived in the same building for almost three years and didn't know the daytime doorman's name. She didn't remember the names of the couple in #5F who wanted to buy her apartment and never bothered to read a single barista's tag. But now? Her schedule was wide-open. She could make room for pleasantries. Meet the people in her neighborhood. Sprinkle them with glee.

Dan invited M.J. to sit with a *pat-pat* on his cushion. "I still can't believe you live here," he said, as she settled onto his warm chest and found her reflection in his sunglasses. It was amazing how one week without computers, deadlines, and Ambien could brighten one's face. What was once pigeon gray was now bronzed and vibrant, as if her electricity had been restored after months of unpaid bills.

"It's so-real," Dan said.

"You mean, sur-real?"

"Whatever."

There was that dismissive tone of his. The one that said, *I am a man of science and medicine. Words are not, and need not, be my thing. When's the last time you set a broken bone? Yeah, thought so.*

"Are you happy?" he asked.

"When you talk in typos? I'd say mildly charmed at best."

Dan slid his hands under M.J.'s sheet and playfully squeezed her ass. "I'm talking about you being here. Are you happy?"

"I don't know, Dr. Hartwell. What are the symptoms of happiness?"

He folded his hands behind his head and lifted his chin toward the endless stretch of blue sky. "Sleeping until noon, dressing in bedsheets, tying me to a bed and having your way with me."

"You liked that didn't you?"

"Yes. Yes, I did. Until you played the girl-on-girl porn."

M.J. blushed at the memory of her previous night's blunder. "Most guys love that shit."

"Most guys don't have lesbian mothers and four younger sisters!"

"I know. I'm sorry. I forgot," M.J. said, cheeks burning. "Hey, we should go up to San Francisco tomorrow. I'd love to meet this family of yours."

"I can't." Dan indicated the unfurnished cottage, where boxes and bulging suitcases seemed to whimper like neglected puppies. "I'm scouting locations for my new clinic tomorrow and I don't even know where my shoes are."

"Right. Well, leave the unpacking to me," she chirped.

Like the birds that now woke her in the morning, M.J. would whistle while she worked. She would flit joyfully about in a state of meditative mindfulness as she discovered the pleasures of living a simple life. Molt her city skin and start fresh. Smell roses, smile at strangers, walk the beach five mornings a week, get a wax.

She kissed the top of Dan's head. His hair was hot from the sun.

"Where are you going?"

"To look for your shoes."

Dan flashed a dubious smirk. "You're really going to unpack?"

"Indeed I am."

"Not a team of professionals or exploited interns?" he asked. "*You?*"

"Corrrrect."

"And when that's done? Then what?"

M.J. yanked the sliding glass door that opened into the living room. "I'll start decorating," she said, then stepped boldly inside to embrace her wondrous future.

———

"WHAT ARE YOU looking at?" M.J. asked, weeks later.

"A faded tan, bloody cuticles, and the same bathrobe you've been wearing for the past two weeks," her opponent would have answered. But it was a cardboard box. So M.J. kicked it.

Twice.

Once for being rude and then a second time for signifying the end. Because after this last box was unpacked, they'd all be gone. M.J. would be an empty nester. And then what? More naps? More googling Liz Evans? More silence?

There would definitely be more silence.

Except for that damn ocean. It never shut up.

CHAPTER

Five

IT WAS FOUR o'clock in New York. The weekly editorial pitch meeting at *City* was probably wrapping up. Within the hour, Liz would be sending an e-mail with her favorite ideas, and M.J., who was still on the distribution list, could read (and judge) them all.

With an open laptop balancing on her thighs and a glass of bubbly in her hand, she leaned against the propped-up pillows on her bed and watched her in-box, waiting for the starting gun's *ding*.

"You're writing!" Dan said, from the open doorway.

M.J. snapped her laptop shut. "What are you doing home?"

"I thought I'd take you to lunch."

His skin color seemed more espresso than cappuccino when he wore his black T-shirt, his hazel eyes more green.

"You're handsome."

"And you're still in that bathrobe."

"Ugh! You sound like that stupid box."

"What box?"

47

"The one in the living room."

"It talks?"

"Only when I'm bored." M.J. kicked off the sheets. "Forget it."

"Like hell I will!" Dan cracked his knuckles, then dashed off to confront her corrugated bully; his heroic gesture only to be undermined by the sissy slaps of his flip-flops.

"I had no idea this was here!" he called, too busy ferreting through landfill amounts of San Francisco Giants mugs, socks, plaques, pendants, trading cards, and ticket stubs to notice that M.J. had traded her bathrobe for a sleeveless silk dress. "So much awesomeness."

She knew Dan rooted for the Giants, but had no idea his devotion ran so deep, or that he said *awesomeness*. It made M.J. wonder what else she didn't know. Was he a Disneyland lover? A tax evader? An Adam Sandler fan? What if he drank milk with sushi?

"My parents must have slipped this into the U-Haul when I wasn't looking. They couldn't stand the team's colors." Then, in a high-pitched attempt to impersonate his mothers, he said, "Orange and black is a putrid combination, Danny. If Halloween happened more than once a year, trust us, Pantone would intervene." Sitting cross-legged with a scrapbook of yellowed newspaper articles, Dan looked as he must have when he was cutting and pasting these clippings for the first time. "I lived for those games with Uncle Ollie." He placed a child-sized Giants cap on his head. He looked like Elmer Fudd.

"Uncle Ollie, your Moms' best friend?"

"Yep."

"They met freshman year at Stanford, right?"

"That's the one."

"Sperm donor Uncle Ollie? First Sara . . . Then Marni . . . Then Sara. . . Then Marni . . . Then Sara? *That* Uncle Ollie?"

"Yes, that Uncle Ollie," Dan snipped, clearly frustrated that she was missing the point. But it was he who missed the point. Not only had M.J. recalled the name of the Hartwells' sperm donor, but to whom his donations were allocated, and in which order. Take *that* insecurities! "Did your sisters go, too?"

"No," he said with a scoff.

"Not into sports?"

"The opposite. They were hard core. Joan played softball. Margaret was a black belt, Serena was a track star, and Norma dated two quarterbacks. But no one seemed to notice that stuff. It was always: *Take care of your mothers, Danny. Protect those beautiful sisters of yours, Danny. You're the man in the family, Danny. Be the man, Danny.* It was this constant—" He stiffened his fingers into an arthritic claw.

"Pressure?"

"Yeah."

"No wonder you loved those games so much."

Dan looked up at M.J., eyes wide and ready to receive.

"No one to take care of," she clarified.

He considered this. "Probably."

M.J. sat. Her knee joints cracked on the way down. They needed a couch. "I'm surprised you became a doctor. You know, since taking care of people is kind of the whole point."

Dan snickered, as if just clueing into the irony. "Maybe it was that earthquake."

"What earthquake?"

"October 17, 1989," he said. "It was the third game of the World

Series, Giants versus the Oakland A's. Twenty minutes before the game started I felt this shaking . . . I thought it was nerves, or maybe too much soda, until everyone started screaming, '*Earthquake!*' Popcorn was flying, people were slamming into one another . . . it was intense. Uncle Ollie was dragging me toward the exit, pulling my shirt so hard I could barely breathe. And I was crying my goddamn eyes out."

"I'm sure," M.J. reached for his hand. "You must have been terrified."

"Only that we were going to miss the game."

"They played?"

"No." Dan grinned at the memory of his younger self. "It was chaos. It took us six hours to get home. Of course my family thought I was dead and I thought they were dead but everyone was fine. They were all . . . fine. And something about that—"

"Set you free," M.J. said flatly, without judgment, the way Dr. Cohn would have.

Dan's eye lit on her.

"They didn't need you to save them. They were fine and that pressure was lifted."

"Exactly!"

M.J. sat taller. Is this how psychologists felt? Part God, part psychic and pure genius? She kept going, "But there were people out there who needed to be saved for real. Not because they were born female, but because they were wounded and sick. Because their traumas were legitimate, not borne from hypothetical conjecture or male chauvinism. And that's what made you want to become a doctor, right?"

"No," Dan said. "It was the surgeon who gave us a ride home because we couldn't get to Ollie's car. He had this tricked-out Mercedes with a surfboard strapped to the roof and a smokin'-hot girlfriend, and I said to myself, I want to be this guy."

"What?" M.J. gave him a playful smack on the arm.

Dan grinned. "And maybe a bit of what you said, too." He kissed her softly above the right eye in deference to the day they met. "I'm a sucker for a hot mess."

M.J. giggled at the memory.

She was in Pearl Beach for a corporate retreat at the five-star Majestic Resort and Spa. Enjoying some downtime, M.J. was lounging poolside and marking up a piece about a communal living trend in Queens. Her chest was starting to burn. She sat up, reached for her aerosol body-mist sunscreen, shook the can, and—*thwack!*—pegged herself right above the eye.

When she came to, there was a hazel-eyed doctor with caramel sea-salted skin holding an ice pack to her eyebrow. He had been at the outdoor bar, meeting with a potential partner for his clinic, and saw the whole thing. Potential Partner was ready to respond, but Hazel-Eyed Doctor insisted he stand down. He had been watching Hot Loner all afternoon. This one was his.

A petite blond with a sticky southern accent said they made a beautiful couple. M.J. corrected her, saying they had just met. The blond insisted that it didn't matter, they were destined to be together. She knew this because she was the resort's *Liaison of Love*. A professional expert on amour. And as it turned out, she was.

Dr. Dan Hartwell took M.J. to dinner that night so he could monitor the wound. Though it was healing well, he quickly learned that M.J.'s pain went far deeper than an accidental blow to her supraorbital foramen. And he'd been trying to save her ever since.

"Do you pity me?" M.J. asked, while returning his souvenirs to the box soon-to-be marked GARAGE.

Dan stood. "Why would you ask that?"

"Because I'm fucked up."

"Everyone is fucked up." He handed her a white paper bag. "Happy Friday."

She peered inside. Three regional magazines, a black Moleskine journal, and a pencil peered back. "What is this?"

"It's me *not* pitying you." He cupped her shoulders, and with a sympathetic bedside-manner sigh, said, "It's time for you to get out of the house."

"I'm acclimating."

"I know. And I know you're crushed and scared and pissed off. But arguing with boxes and drinking in bed?" He tucked her hair behind her ear. "You're losing your fight, M.J. Burn the bathrobe. Write. Think about your next job."

Job.

There was that word again, M.J. thought as she sat out on the deck later that afternoon and flipped through the pages of *Pearl Beach Living*—which were tragically similar to those in *Orange County Today* and *West Coast* magazine. She didn't want a job. She wanted a career that doubled as a lifestyle. She wanted a bottomless pit of culture and innovation with a glut of keen writers who could find compelling angles, then sharpen them to a cutting edge. She wanted what she had at *City*, and Pearl Beach was not the place to find it. Here the pit was more like a puddle dedicated to restaurant reviews, medical spa openings, and socialites who were heavy on social and lite on style. All those cruise-ship corals and purplish blues. No credible magazine would allow that. And as long as they did, fetal was the only position M.J. would take.

Beyond the wood railing, children squealed with joy as the breaking white water chased them up the beach. The briny smell of the Pacific Ocean seasoned the breeze. A hummingbird zipped by. M.J., suddenly exhausted, laid back, and remembered a time when she was inspired by things like that.

***

"AH-HA!" SOMEONE CALLED.

M.J. woke with a jolt to find a chic older woman glaring at her from the deck next door; a deck that suddenly seemed uncomfortably close to her own, now that it was occupied. Wide-legged linen pants and an ivory blouse billowed around the woman's narrow frame. An old-fashioned key lay flat against her clavicle. Big and tarnished, it was probably a gift from a grandchild—something only a relative could love.

"Gotcha!" she said, with a mosquito-killing kind of clap.

M.J. sat up and shielded her eyes from the late-afternoon glare.

"I'm sorry. Have we met?"

"No, but I see you've acquainted yourself with my patio furniture."

"Your what?"

The woman pointed a manicured finger at the chaise longue.

"Oh my God!" M.J. jumped to stand as if the yellow-and-white-striped cushions had sprouted fangs. "I'm so sorry. Dan took them, I mean, he borrowed them. He should have asked first, I know, but you were out of town so he figured—"

"And Dan lives . . ." She indicated the cottage.

"Just moved in."

"And you?"

"New York." M.J. shook her head, "I mean, here, I guess I live here now. With Dan."

"And he is your . . ."

"Boyfriend."

"So you just threw your boyfriend under the bus?"

M.J.'s cheeks burned. "I think so."

"Smart." The stranger winked, then offered her hand. "I'm Gloria Golden."

"M.J. Stark."

A warm, spicy blend of amber and powder perfumed the air as they shook. It smelled like a hug.

"Are you wearing Coco Chanel?"

Gloria flashed a row of white teeth as well preserved as the rest of her. "You too?"

"My mom did. But only on special occasions."

"Honey, every day we're alive is a special occasion," she said as her gaze drifted to M.J.'s pile of discarded magazines.

"I had a little downtime."

"That's what friends, martinis, and stalking your adult children on Facebook are for, right?" Gloria exhumed a dented pack of American Spirits from a potted plant, struck her lighter, and shakily connected its flame to her cigarette.

"You smoke?"

"No." Gloria inhaled. "They're my husband's. His cardiologist says his arteries need Liquid Drano, so he pretended to quit and I pretend I don't know about his hiding spot." She exhaled. "Every now and then I indulge."

"What if he sees you?"

"I told him I was hosting a town hall meeting tonight and he couldn't get out of here fast enough. It's what I say when I need a little alone time with my girls." Her eyes narrowed as if straining to find a fading memory. "It's a funny thing . . . Back when Leo worked, I was desperate to have him home. And now that he's retired I want him out." She laughed to herself. "Isn't that the way?"

"How many daughters do you have?"

"No daughters. Four boys. David, my baby, is almost thirty-seven."

"Oh. When you said girls I thought you meant—"

"I was talking about my friends. When you've known someone since high school they seem young forever."

A car pulled into her driveway. Then three doors slammed.

"Speak of the angels." Gloria snubbed out her cigarette on the rosy cheek of a ceramic garden gnome. "A gift from my daughter-in-law, Kelsey. A real bitch, that one. Anyway, it was nice meeting you, M.J."

"You too," she said, meaning it. "Oh, and Dan will return the chair as soon as he gets back from the Realtor's. He's trying to open a medical practice here and—"

"Please, it can wait until tomorrow. And if he works weekends and can't do it for a few days, so be it. My Leo worked so many Saturdays I started telling people he was a rabbi. You'll bring it when you bring it."

As Gloria left to greet her girls, M.J. tried to imagine growing old with the friends who knew her when she was young. To share a lifetime of memories, inside jokes, and milestones. To know who will be pulling into her driveway when she is Gloria's age. All she saw was darkness.

M.J. gathered her things and went inside. "Mom, Dad, April?" she said, eyes closed, hands together in prayer in front of the open fridge. "I'm looking for a sign here. It doesn't have to be big. Just a little something to show me the way, because things are pretty fucked right now and—"

The doorbell rang. She hurried to answer.

"May-June Stark?" said the FedEx deliveryman as if serving a summons and not a package.

Heart pounding, she nodded.

"This is for you."

"Thanks, Curtis," she said, while signing his electronic signature pad. "Oh, and call me M.J."

"Only if you call me Neil."

"Neil? Why Neil?"

"Because that's my name. Curtis works for UPS."

"Of course he does," M.J. muttered to herself. Her family was probably dying all over again laughing at her blunder.

With the door still open she pulled the cardboard tab across the envelope and read the document that was tucked inside. A document that instantly transformed her from a spiritual skeptic into a woman who believes in signs.

CHAPTER

Six

M.J. RELAXED HER gait and loosened her hips in the manner of a carefree maiden on an aimless Saturday-afternoon stroll, who also happened to be casually swinging a bottle of Tito's vodka by her side. To see her was to think she was the trope of small-town spontaneity; to be her was to grapple with the urge to turn around and run home.

This whole "pop by the neighbors' for a visit" thing had been Dan's idea—another attempt to set M.J. up with a life before he opens his clinic and is gone all day. But M.J. wasn't a "popper." She needed an invitation; nothing formal, just an overall sense that she was welcome.

"It's what locals do," Dan assured her. "They think it's rude if you keep to yourself."

"No, what's rude is taking their outdoor furniture without permission."

"Hence, the apology vodka."

The gesture would have felt a lot less invasive if Dan had gone with her. But he had a lunch meeting with a retiring doctor; a local hotshot in search of someone to take over his practice. So M.J. had to play first lady and handle the social outreach alone. It was either that or spend another afternoon sunning solo on her deck and judging the mothers who let their teenaged daughters wear thong bikinis to the beach.

"Well, hello there," said the man in Gloria's garage. He was rubbing soapy circles into the hood of a cranberry-red Aston Martin, a cigarette dangling from his mouth. His MacBook-colored hair, still thick as a teenager's, was weekend-morning wild, his tan was retirement deep. He was a picture of old-school machismo, even as Barbra Streisand's "Stoney End" blared from his boom box.

"Mr. Golden?"

He straightened his posture and smoothed his side part. "Call me Leo."

M.J. went limp with relief. While it didn't erase the fact that she called Neil "Curtis," getting this one right was encouraging. "I'm M.J. I live next door."

"So I've noticed." Leo turned up the good-time glint in his navy-blue eyes as he bridged their forty-year gap with a lingering handshake. Then, aiming his cigarette at the bottle that was now slipping from M.J.'s sweaty palm, he asked if she would care for a glass.

"The vodka is for you and Gloria. From Dan and me to thank you for not arresting us," she said, with a nervous giggle. But why? M.J. was a street-smart woman, and Leo was at least seventy. Yet his unwavering eye contact made her squirm.

She took a tiny step back.

"Dan returned the chair, right? This morning, before his meet-

ing? Not that he works on Saturdays. He doesn't. Not usually . . .
Anyway, he'll be home at three. We're going couch shopping." Embarrassed, M.J. shook her head. Why was she telling him this? She
sounded like a schoolgirl with a teacher crush. Even Lolita was more
composed.

"You know who you remind me of?" Leo asked. "A shorter Elle
Macpherson. Not to say you're short—"

His phone dinged. He glanced at the screen and then returned
his attention to M.J., who was wishing she had worn something less
revealing: a maxi dress and Birkenstocks instead of denim cutoffs
and a boxy T-shirt that offered peekaboo glimpses of her flat midriff.
"Is Gloria home?"

"She will be in exactly"—he glanced at his screen again—"four
minutes and six seconds."

"Are you sure? I can always come back."

Leo chuckled as if recalling a joke. "Oh, I'm sure. That woman
has been giving me five-minute warnings for the last fifty years.
Which means we better hurry if we want to—"

"Want to *what?*"

Leo approached the life-sized cardboard cutout of Marlon
Brando, reached behind the rose on his lapel, and removed the box
of American Spirits that had been taped to the back.

He lit two cigarettes, offered one to M.J.

Though M.J. didn't smoke, she accepted it on behalf of her fidgeting hands that desperately needed something to do.

"So tell me, M.J., are you an actress?"

"No. But your wife obviously was."

She indicated the back wall, where dozens of framed headshots
hung in evenly spaced rows. Audrey Hepburn, Mia Farrow, Elvis,

Faye Dunaway, John Travolta, Jessica Lange, Diana Ross, Goldie Hawn, Harrison Ford . . . There were at least thirty, and they were all addressed to Gloria.

"Those came from me," Leo said proudly. "I was a producer at Paramount for forty-eight years. Back when people who loved films made films." He took a deep *Those were the good old days* drag of his cigarette. "Today, executives have their heads so far up their own bottom lines, I bet half of them don't even see the movies they make. But me? I cared." He snickered. "Too much, Gloria would say." His smile melted into a closemouthed fatherly grin. He flicked his ash. "Make sure that boyfriend of yours doesn't make a habit of working weekends. It's a hard one to break, and like most bad habits, it'll catch up with him in the end."

A horn honked.

Leo released his cigarette into a sudsy puddle. It died with a quick hiss. He signaled for M.J. to do the same.

"There's my queen!" he announced as Gloria emerged from her Mercedes sedan.

"Save the ass-kissing for your cardiologist," she said, slamming the car door. The key around her neck knocked clumsily about her collarbone as she charged toward him. "You're out of refills. You have to see Dr. Winters first thing Monday morning or else—"

Leo gripped her slender shoulders, then kissed her firmly on the mouth. "God, I've missed you."

Gloria gave him a playful shove. "I'm serious. This is seri—" She raised a professionally arched eyebrow at the cigarettes floating beside his sandaled feet.

Leo pointed at M.J. "They're hers!"

M.J. laughed. It was something her father would have said. Gloria, however, was not amused.

"Call Dr. Winters," she insisted. Then, with a sharp tilt of her head, she ordered M.J. and the Tito's to follow her inside.

"This is why you look so young," M.J. said as a blast of frigid air greeted them in the front foyer. "The temperature is set to cryogenic."

"We have Leo to thank for that. He says the cold keeps his cranky arthritic friends from stopping by." Gloria turned up the thermostat. "I say it's the reason I stopped wearing lingerie."

M.J. instantly warmed. "You and Leo really seem to love each other."

"Love, my dear, has never been our problem."

The sweet almond smell of macaroon cookies censed the bungalow, which, on first glance, seemed as elegant as Gloria herself. The white tufted furniture was chic yet comfortable, the accents a timeless palate of flax and gold. But a closer look revealed porcelain monkeys, a mirrored wall, bamboo floor lamps, and a coffee table book called *Prim: A Modern Woman's Guide to Manners*. If a person who valued style could overlook such outdated pieces, what else, M.J. thought, might she fail to notice?

In the kitchen, Gloria held a silver cocktail shaker against the door of her fridge and deftly caught the avalanche of ice that rumbled forth. "If only a ready-made martini came out next," she laughed. "Now that would be something."

"To new neighbors," Gloria said with a sharp hoist of her glass.

M.J. hoisted back, then she drank: one sip to keep from spilling, a second to lubricate her rusty social wheels, and a third because the martini was just the right amount of dirty.

From there, they sat on opposite sides of the cooking island and began to chip away the top coats of their colorfully painted pasts, careful not to expose the dark details that lay hidden underneath.

"This doctor of yours must be something," Gloria said. "Getting you to leave New York City for Pearl Beach." She listed toward the window above the sink, indicating the surfers and sunbathers that animated her view. "This place must feel like a retirement village to you. Everyone tooting around in electric golf carts. Restaurants close at nine. And the constant *smack* of those unsightly rubber things. Oh, what are they called?"

"Flip-flops?"

"Yes," Gloria paused for a quick sip. "My dear friend Marjorie used to date a Frenchman named Philipe Follop."

"You're lying!"

Gloria raised her right hand. "On my life. Soft, cheap, and unsupportive, Marjorie used to say; just like the sandal."

M.J. laughed. "They're for broken toes and pedicures if you ask me," she said, leaving out Dan's fondness for the "unsightly rubber things."

Gloria clinked M.J.'s glass in a show of solidarity. Then, the brightness behind her eyes dimmed, as if setting the scene for something more intimate. "I admire you."

M.J. laughed again.

"I'm serious, "Gloria said. "I've lived in this town for seventy-two years. Appliances and hair colors are the only things I've ever changed. But you? You had a glamorous career in the most exciting city in the world and you walked away from it all. Now you're starting a new adventure in a sleepy beach town with a man you barely know." She topped off their drinks, and then with a slight slur said, "You have a big braload of courage. I envy that."

"Thank you," M.J. said, because Gloria's assessment wasn't *entirely* wrong. M.J. joined an improv group in college. She bungee jumped off a rotting bridge in Cancun. She even occupied Wall Street. To call her courageous wasn't inaccurate, just slightly outdated. But what was she supposed to do? Tell the truth? Admit that she hadn't walked away from anything, that she'd run like a petulant child. No, but the truth was no way to make a good first impression.

Still. If M.J. accepted praise she didn't deserve, she'd be no different than Liz. And Liz was the antithesis of courageous; she was corrupt.

"I didn't leave New York because I'm adventurous," M.J. admitted. "I left because my ex-boss gave fifty percent of my promotion to a glorified sorority girl and I was pissed." But there was more. Though the development was less than one day old it weighed on M.J. as if fully grown. And the vodka in her dirty martini wanted to talk about it. "I got an offer from that ex-boss yesterday."

Gloria's eyebrow shot up. "What kind of offer?"

"I have enough unused vacation days to take the entire summer off, with pay, so she'll call my resignation a leave of absence if . . ."

"If what?"

"If I go back in the fall."

"And the sorority girl?"

M.J. twisted a finger around the frayed denim hem of her shorts. "She'll be there."

"And you're okay with that?"

M.J. sighed. "Two weeks ago I would have said *no way*. But now?" Her eyes fluttered closed.

"What does the handsome doctor think?"

"He found the FedEx envelope in the trash, which he promptly moved to the recycle bin, and then asked why my ex-boss, Gayle, was reaching out."

"What did you say?"

"That my old coworkers sent some good-bye cards." M.J. pressed two fingers against her throbbing temple. "It's the first time I ever lied to him."

"Does this mean you're accepting her offer?"

M.J. shrugged. She didn't sign the contract, but she didn't tear it up, either. She hid it in one of her suitcases, buried it under the black cashmere sweaters that had yet to find a place for themselves in her sunny new world.

Gloria reached for her hand. "There's no shame in leaving your options open."

"I know, but I should tell Dan. And I will. Today. After we buy a couch." M.J. looked at Gloria and frowned. "It's just that he's so proud of me for taking a stand and we love living together and—"

"You can't do that."

"You're right. It's cruel." M.J. reached for her purse. "The decent thing would be to tell him now, before the couch. Before he spends another second believing I'm all in."

"No, you can't do that."

"What?"

"Tell him. Not until your bags are packed and your flight is booked."

"But—"

"Trust me. Wait until you're sure."

"I can't wait. Gayle wants an answer by the end of July."

"Do you have one?"

"No.

"Exactly, so why rock the boat?"

"To be open and honest."

"Sometimes honesty causes more problems than lies. And openness?" Gloria leaned closer. "Honey, do you think Leo and I stayed married for fifty years because we're open? Christ, we wouldn't have made it past the honeymoon if we were. This is the kind of stuff you figure out with your best friends first. Then you tell Dan."

"But Dan *is* my best friend."

Gloria lowered her fist like a gavel. "Now *that's* a problem."

———

MARIPOSA LANE SEEMED more vibrant than it had when M.J. first arrived at Gloria's. The bougainvillea, the palm fronds, the lemon tree, the cloudless sky . . . It was as if a jewel-toned filter had been added to the lens through which M.J. saw her neighborhood. Her vodka-soaked senses were heightened, her bloodshot eyes amazed.

Stumbling toward home, she wondered what Dan would think of his day-drunk girlfriend with the cigarette-scented fingers.

Her stomach roiled.

Was she really going to stay quiet about Gayle's offer? *Could* she? Honesty had always been a source of pride between them. They swore they'd never become one of those couples who lied. Though, technically, this was more of an omission than a lie. Lies were sharp and incising, and this was blunt, pliable. An omission might poke their hymen of truth, but wouldn't break it.

"Nice meeting you, Leo!" M.J. called toward the garage.

If he answered, she couldn't hear him over Barbra's optimistically upbeat "Time and Love."

She called to him again.

Still nothing.

Perhaps he was on the deck, or maybe the beach.

But the water . . .

What once snaked down his driveway, now rushed.

M.J. kicked off her shoes and padded upstream back to the garage. There was Leo. Sitting against the fender of his Aston Martin, his spouting hose unmanned. "Good thing there's no drought," she teased. "I mean it's not like California is in a state of emergency or anything."

If Leo appreciated her sarcasm, he didn't show it. He just sat there; legs splayed, shoulders slumped, chin to chest.

"Don't worry. I won't report you," she said, though Leo didn't seem the least bit worried. His lips were slightly parted and the lines on his forehead were smooth. If anything he looked relaxed, almost serene.

"Hey." M.J. gave him a nudge.

"Bug off, lady, I'm sleeping," Leo seemed to say as he tipped toward the oil-stained concrete and landed stiffly on its side.

CHAPTER

Seven

THE BLAST OF cold air that had greeted M.J. on her previous visit to the Goldens' bungalow had been replaced by a pall of coffee-scented sorrow.

There was a rabbi in the living room leading the well-preserved congregation in some unintelligible prayer, and like respectful theatergoers who arrived during the first act, M.J. and Dan waited by the front door until he was done. It would have been longer, if M.J. had her way.

It didn't matter that she had known Leo for only a few hours, or that his death, while sudden, wasn't tragic. She found his lifeless body. She heard Gloria's primal cries. It was another unexpected loss. The simple act of being there popped a stitch in her slow-healing wound.

"I can't do this," she whispered to Dan.

He bowed his head and began mumbling along with the others.

"What's wrong? Are you having a stroke?"

"Hebrew," he mouthed, then lifted a stern finger to his lips, the way her mother had when she and April would giggle in church. "It's the mourner's prayer."

The Pyrex dish in M.J.'s hands almost slipped from her grip. *Dan could pray in Hebrew?* Gloria was right. M.J. did move in with a man she barely knew: a man who might have a wife and kids or a connection to a terrorist organization or who might not be a man at all. Maybe he was a Stanford-engineered robot designed to administer experimental drugs on an orphaned girl no one would ever miss.

Dan hooked his arm around M.J.'s waist and pulled her toward him. Whoever he was, whatever his intentions, that simple gesture shattered the panes of her worst-case scenarios and restored her faith. Besides, they had only lived in the same zip code for a few weeks. New details were bound to present themselves, right?

There was a tap on her shoulder.

"What is that?" asked a heavily hair-sprayed woman, her pinched nose trained on M.J.'s foil-wrapped dish.

"Homemade garlic bread," M.J. lied, because she was trying to pass off one of Mama Rosa's appetizers as her own.

"At a *shiva*?"

"It was Leo's favorite," Dan offered.

"My brother ate garlic? With *his* stomach?" She rolled her pale blue eyes. "No wonder he had the GERD. That bread is probably what killed him."

The service was over and a sudden burst of chatter woke the room. Black-suited men greeted one another with somber smacks on the back, while the women, like videos unpaused, seemed to pick up their conversations right where they had left off. Uniformed waiters balanced trays of champagne while children chased one another though the labyrinth of legs. And Gloria was at the center of it all talking to a fit, silver-haired couple who could easily play the role of "sexually active old people" in a Cialis commercial. Her bright smile suggested she hadn't begun to feel the impact of her loss. And she wouldn't. Not until everyone went home and she returned to her daily routine: a routine that would be forever stripped of its rhythms, patterns, and distinguishing marks. Where the once familiar would be foreign and Gloria would be left to wander aimlessly through it all, wondering who would zip her zippers and fasten her clasps.

"Why are we even here?" M.J. asked. "We didn't even know Leo."

Dan kissed her on the forehead. "Because it's the right thing to do."

"According to whom?"

"My Jewish guilt."

"Is it Jewish guilt or Dan guilt?"

He lowered his watery gaze. "Both."

M.J. wanted to pull him in for a hug, but the damn Pyrex dish. "Dan, this isn't your fault. Even if you were home when I found him there's no way you could have—"

He smiled weakly. "It's not your fault, either."

M.J. drew back her head. Had she told Dan about her superstition—that every time she lost herself to a moment of fun, someone died—or was that a lucky guess? "It's not my fault, *either*? What does that mean?"

"It means we both need a good therapist." Dan nudged her forward. "Come. I bet there are dozens in here."

A baby-faced waiter approached M.J. with an empty tray and a full agenda. "How about I take that to the sunroom," he said, reaching for her dish. "The buffet is already set up, so I can just slide it on in there . . ."

"That's okay," M.J. said, eager to delay what was sure to be an emotional encounter with Gloria. "I'll take it myself."

"Awesome," the waiter said. "The sooner the better, though, if you don't mind. I mean, it smells rad to me but some of the old folks are complaining." He leaned toward her ear and from the side of his mouth muttered, "You know how they are."

The sunroom was a glass-walled reprieve off the kitchen that was teeming with plants, thirtysomethings, and small talk. Hips were jutted, champagne glasses were swinging, forks were clanking, and friends were greeted with open arms and high-pitched squeals. The only thing they seemed to be mourning was the lack of vegan options.

"Dr. Hartwell!" rasped a woman. She waved him over with a tanned, bare arm, which absolutely did not jiggle, not even around the tricep. Something about the thick dark hair that spilled past her shoulders was familiar to M.J., like she had seen it before, maybe on a commercial for TRESemmé.

"It's me, Britt Riley."

Prickles of humiliation began to metastasize inside M.J.'s body. Britt wasn't a hair model, she was Dan's Lycra-loving Realtor, the one she accused of having a yeast infection. And now she had a mustard stain on her white blouse that M.J. was trying not to look at.

With a casual step toward the buffet table, she began shifting homemade lasagnas, casseroles, and salads to make room for her contribution. She found a spot by the lox but continued to fuss because there was no way she was turning around—not until her burning cheeks cooled and her heart stopped beating Morse code for *awkward*.

"I brokered the deal on your cottage," Britt told Dan. "Maybe you don't recognize me. I cut bangs." She scissored her fingers for emphasis.

"I know who you are," he said. "It's the Dr. Hartwell part that threw me. You've always called me Dan."

Britt flicked her hair toward the two women behind her and with a subtle hitch of her thumb whispered, "Single girls like single doctors. Work with me here."

"Not single!" M.J. blurted, having no time for pronouns.

"This is M.J.," he said, steering her into the conversation. "My girlfriend. You were actually introduced a few weeks ago over Skype."

The dimple just below Britt's bottom lip deepened and softened, deepened and softened while she strained to remember. Then her whiskey-brown eyes widened. "Ah, yes."

"I'm from New York," M.J. explained, in lieu of an apology. "I didn't realize it was normal to dress like that until I moved here. I'm sorry if I offended you."

"Dress like what?" Britt asked, forehead crinkled, thirsty for Botox.

"You know . . ."

"I don't."

"The whole activewear thing. New Yorkers wear that stuff to the gym, but then they change. I like it, though," M.J. tried. "I mean, if anyone can pull it off—"

Dan cleared his already clear throat.

"Well, I'm from New York, too," Britt said. "And I always wore activewear. Tons of people did."

"*You're* from New York?" M.J. asked, willing to forget all about the woman's *Just Do It* approach to style. Finally, someone who understood her longing for food delivery and people who don't check CAUCASIAN on a census. "Which part?"

"Brooklyn."

"Where? Prospect Heights, Park Slope?"

"Flatbush."

M.J. giggled. "My old friend Katie used to call her pubic hair Flatbush when she took off a pair of tights: 'Next Stop, Flatbush Avenue,' she'd say, just like the announcer on the five train."

"So, Britt," Dan interjected. "How do you know Leo?"

"My husband did the Goldens' landscaping for years."

M.J. cut a look to the tangle of vines outside the glass walls.

"It's been a while," Britt said. "Paul has been so busy. Anyway, he's around here somewhere, I'd love to introduce you—"

"There she is!" A blond, swizzle stick of a woman approached Britt; arms splayed, professionally whitened teeth bared. "You can run, but you can't hide," she bellowed. "And this summer I am not taking no for an answer. You are joining the Downtown Beach Club. Trust me, your kids will ab-so-lutely love it."

"My kids are going to sleepover camp."

"Well, then you and Paul."

Britt looked past the woman's shoulder and into the kitchen, where a shaggy-haired man was eating chicken nuggets off his twelve-year-old daughter's plate. "Maybe."

"Promise you'll think about it, m'kay? The rooftop bar has been totally renovated, the library has been converted into a hot-yoga studio, and need I remind you, no *tourists*."

Dan lovingly smoothed the back of M.J.'s hair. "Maybe you could join."

"Me?"

"It sounds like a great way to meet people."

"Not if you like tourists," M.J. said.

Dan laughed.

The woman evaluated M.J.'s black slip dress with a quick flick of her eyes. "Are you a local?"

"She is," Dan boasted.

"Why don't I know you?"

"I just moved here," said M.J.

"From New York," Britt added, with an air of *Look at what the hoity-toity cat dragged in.*

"How fortuitous," the other woman said. "The DBC is having a new-recruits luncheon next week. I could drop off an invitation if you're interested."

"That would be great," Dan said, before M.J. could stop him. "We live right next door."

"Easy enough," she tittered. "I'm sorry, where are my manners? I've been so thrown by this whole Leo thing I forgot to introduce myself. I'm Kelsey Pincer-Golden, Michael's wife."

"You gave Gloria that garden gnome, right?" M.J. asked.

Kelsey raised her right hand. "Guilty! I mean how darn jolly is that little guy?"

"Incredibly darn jolly," M.J. said, thinking of the gray ash smudges that pocked his dwarf head like bullet holes. "She loves it."

"Phew." Kelsey dragged a hand across her wide forehead, wiping away sweat that wasn't there. "Because I just ordered another one. You know, to keep Gloria from getting lonely."

M.J. twisted the gold wedding bands on her thumb. "I'm sure that will help."

"Right?" Kelsey mouthed, then turned her attention to the buffet table. "Beach season is coming, ladies! I better get some food in me before I lose my curves." She lifted a plate from the bottom of the stack and surveyed her options.

"Try my bread," M.J. said, hoping to placate Dan with her attempt to socialize.

"Garlic?" Kelsey raised an overplucked brow at buttery round rolls. "Michael did just bury his father, so it's not like he's going to get frisky tonight, right?" She took an investigatory nibble, swallowed, and paused, as if evaluating a fine wine. Then with a suspicious squint said, "Is this from Mama Rosa's?"

"How did you know?"

"Round bread, roasted garlic, and real Parmesan," Kelsey said. "It's a small town, M.J. You can't get away with anything." She tilted her plate and released a piece back onto the dish. "They have a gluten-free option. You know that, right?"

"Ha." Britt's lips curled into a vicious smile. "Now *you* have a yeast problem, too."

"We should say hi to Gloria," Dan suggested. This time M.J. agreed.

They found her in the living room, sitting on a love seat between two women who flanked her like bookends as they pored over her wedding album. There was young Leo licking icing off her finger during their wedding reception, the happy couple in a chauffeur-driven Paramount Pictures golf cart. The sign on the back bumper read, MARRIED: TAKE ONE.

Gloria smoothed the air bubbles in the plastic sheet that bound the faded images to the cardboard page. "We made it, my love," she sniffled.

The bookends held her close.

"We should come back another time," M.J. said to Dan, feeling morbidly voyeuristic peering down at them like that. She never could stand the hot, heavy burden of being watched while she cried. The sympathetic pouts, the frustrated sighs, the wishing aloud that there was something, anything, the watcher could do. But of course there was nothing. And so M.J. would stop her sobbing midstream and their pained expressions would soften with relief. It was a selfless gesture. One that ultimately meant M.J. would have to pack up her emotional blue balls, endure their throbbing while she searched for a private moment to empty herself out. And why put Gloria through that?

But Dan didn't shy away from the awkward or infirm. He injected himself into the main artery of the moment with a syringe's precision. "I wish I could have been there for him," he said, hugging his way into their intimate huddle.

Gloria lifted her glistening eyes and surrendered to Dan's professional embrace. "I'm so sorry I wasn't there," he said, holding her while she shook. "So, so sorry."

"Aortic aneurism," she told the wet spot she'd left behind on his dress shirt. "The coroner said it happened fast. There was nothing you could have done."

"The flowers are beautiful," M.J. said, for no good reason, as she hugged the widow.

"Did you tell Dan about Gayle's offer?" Gloria whispered into her ear.

M.J. shook her head, surprised that she had the wherewithal to remember their little secret, let alone concern herself with it at a time like that.

"Good." Gloria winked and then motioned for her friends to stand. "M.J. and Dan, meet my girls."

The one on the right was Liddy Henderson. Tall and broad with a gray pixie cut and red-framed glasses, she had a no-nonsense way about her. Dotty Crawford, however, was the opposite. Dressed in a tunic and leggings, she had the merry plumpness of a grandmother who never grew tired of licking the bowl.

"Dotty's responsible for the flowers," Gloria said. "She's the florist at the Majestic Resort."

"Well, I won't be for long if I don't return those vases," she said, palming the back of her grayish-blond bob.

"You stole them?" Liddy asked, punctuating her inquiry with a melodramatic gasp.

"Borrowed. I promised Jules I would have them back by three."

"Why so early?" Gloria pouted.

"Anniversary dinner."

"Congratulations." Liddy beamed. "How long have you two been dating?"

"The dinner is for our guests, smart-ass," Dotty said. "Jules and I are curating it."

"And what? The *Liaison of Love* can't set a few tables without you?"

"She's allergic to flowers."

"Wait," M.J. turned to Dan. "We know her!"

"We do?"

"Yes, the blond with the Southern accent. She was there the day we met, remember? She sprinkled glitter on our heads and said we were going to be together forever."

"That would be Jules." Dotty beamed. "The last of the true romantics."

"Shhh, look, it's the surgery sisters," Liddy interrupted, her red-rimmed glasses fixed on two women in the front foyer.

Dotty squinted. "Is that Daphne Bic?"

Liddy pulled back her cheeks until her mouth morphed into bulbous fish lips. "We can't be sure without her dental records."

Gloria covered her mouth to suppress a giggle. "It was kind of her to show up."

"What about Betty Bic?" Dotty said. "One more facelift and she'll have a beard."

They made a purring sound, then laughed.

M.J. watched as they tried to compose themselves, amazed by Gloria's lightness during such a dark time. Were her friendships that strong, or had her relationship with Leo been that weak?

She glanced at Dan, wondering if their giddiness surprised him, too. But his attention was on a text message from his old surfing buddy Randy.

"Be right back," he said, phone pressed against his ear.

"I'll go with you."

"Stay," Gloria insisted, taking her hand. "There's someone I'd like you to meet."

"Is it Kelsey, because I've already—?"

"No, this girl I love. She's like a niece to me. The two of you will be fast friends."

They found Addie Oliver creeping out of the hallway bathroom like someone who didn't want to be associated with whatever she'd left behind. She was dressed in a Ferrari-red wrap dress—exuding more confidence than one would expect from a curvy woman in a beach town of size zeros—with a plunging neckline that vouched for her commitment to sunscreen. There wasn't a single freckle or spot to distract from her voluminous cleavage, only the bronze wing pendant on her necklace, which could hardly compete.

"Addie, darling, I'd like you to meet M.J.; she just moved here from—"

"Hey," Addie said, as she smoothed her cinnamon-colored hair like a Miss America contestant preparing to take the stage. "Well, nice meeting you. I'm sure I'll see you around sometime." She turned so quickly she generated a breeze that, any stronger, would have blown the family photos straight off the wall.

"Adelaide!" Gloria snapped.

Addie stopped with a jolt that jiggled her cleavage and revealed the gaping cups of her black lace bra. Were her straps undone?

"Where are you rushing off to?"

"Where am I rushing off to?" Addie repeated, louder than M.J. thought necessary considering Gloria showed no signs of hearing loss. "I'm not rushing off anywhere, Gloria, I'm staying right here outside the bathroom door and talking to you."

She must have been on drugs. The nervous restlessness, the blotchy cheeks, the disheveled appearance—the younger set at *City* wore these warning signs like badges of honor. They'd swallow, snort, or smoke anything in the name of getting ahead. And poor Gloria was too seventysomething to see it.

"You two get to know each other and when I get back I'll take you into Leo's closet," Gloria said, then with a deprecating grin, "You're not afraid of a few skeletons, are you?"

"Excuse me?"

"I'm kidding. He's got some to-die-for cashmere sweaters I'd like you both to have. Ralph Lauren, Purple Label, they're worth a fortune."

"What about your sons?"

"You mean the four ungrateful boys I raised who never call me? They can have the itchy wool from Macy's." Gloria turned the knob on the bathroom door.

"What are you doing?" Addie asked, still too loud.

"Going to the restroom," she said, and then slipped inside.

Cactus-green eyes darting, Addie began biting her thumbnail.

"Did you grow up in Pearl Beach?" M.J. asked.

Addie nodded, her attention fixed on the door.

"Do you work around here?"

Another nod.

"Where?"

"Women's health clinic," she answered. Then, as if seeing M.J. for the first time, said, "You don't have regular periods, do you?"

Shocked, M.J. brought a hand to her chest, which looked like a tarmac compared to Addie's. "How did you *know* that?"

"You're too skinny and—"

The bathroom door flew open and out walked Gloria, followed by a sexy Australopithecus, a type whose prominent brow bone, long limbs, and hunched shoulders harkened early man. "Look who I found hiding in the shower! It's my son David."

With a forced smile, M.J. peered past Gloria's shoulder and down the hall. *Where the fuck was Dan?*

"Hey," David grumbled with a stoner's lazy drawl. He had Leo's navy-blue eyes, tanned skin, and the kind of magnetism that gets a man funeral-fucked.

"Do I need to remind you that this is your father's shiva?"

"No, Mom. I'm quite aware."

Gloria inhaled, preparing for a lecture, but was interrupted by a guy, roughly M.J.'s age, waving a manila envelope that he promptly gave to Gloria.

"Who's that?" M.J. muttered to Addie, taking in his pin-striped suit, black-framed glasses, and fedora.

"Easton Keller," she said, scenting his name with the smell of scotch. "He manages Liddy's bookshop. And yes, he really does dress like that."

"It arrived last night," he told Gloria. "While I was closing up the store."

Addie and David began sneaking away. Gloria was too busy running her finger across the postmarked Republique Francaise stamps to notice. "Did Liddy see it?"

Easton pointed out the top line of the mailing address, "It's addressed: 'To the DBC care of Gloria Golden.'"

It was hard to imagine Gloria being a member of the Downtown Beach Club, or any organization that would voluntarily place her in the same room as Kelsey. But like so many well-off women her age, she probably took it on as a charity project, and in the name of doing good, learned to tolerate the bad.

Gloria cut the seal with her fingernail, reached inside, and pulled out three Air France tickets that had been tied together with a black ribbon. While most people would have tossed off the ribbon and ripped open the envelopes, Gloria took a moment, the bounty balanced in her palm.

"What is it?" Easton asked just as a postcard of the Eiffel Tower slipped out and drifted toward the floor. It read:

Pact #34
MEN COME FIRST, MEN GO FIRST.
See you soon!

All my love and air miles,
—M

Much like stubbing a toe on a coffee table, there was a brief delay before the impact was felt, at which point Gloria leaned against the wall of family photos and muttered, "My God."

———

"YOU'RE BACK!" DAN said, relegating his laptop to the floor like a lumpish cat. He was sitting inside the blue-taped border that was meant to be their couch, back against the wall, as if laying claim to the coveted L seat.

"Seer'sly?" M.J. slurred, the champagne from Gloria's having gone straight to her tongue.

"I was just about to call you."

Why? To tell me about the boy band you joined? M.J. might have said to the unbuttoned dress shirt that pooled around his pelvis. But only the Jaws of Life could pry her sense of humor from the wreckage of that afternoon. So Dan got M.J.'s bitchy face instead, followed by her wild-eyed insistence that a phone call was not what she had needed; anything short of an emergency airlift would have been a waste of his time.

"Dan, that wasn't a funeral, it was a fever dream," M.J. continued, "and you left me there." She forced the back strap of her sandal over her heel as if it were a Madden, not a Moschino. "So next time you want to feel Jewish guilty about something, feel Jewish guilty about *that*."

He lifted his gaze to her swaying torso. "I do; I feel terrible. It's just that Randy called and—" A gust blew from his nostrils. "You're not going to believe this—"

M.J. cocked her head, an invitation to motherfucking try her.

Face suddenly wide with hope, or maybe it was fear, Dan stood and took her hands in his. "Wanna go to Java?"

"Coffee?" M.J. withdrew her hands. "I'm not drunk, Dan, I'm pissed."

"No." He laughed. "Java the island."

"In Indonesia?"

He nodded.

"I'm confused."

Pacing, Dan admitted that he had also been confused. Not about the date of the trip—he was right about the thirty-first—it's the month he got wrong.

Panic smacked. "May thirty-first?" M.J. shrieked. "As in forty-eight hours from now?"

"If Randy hadn't called to make sure I got the water filters . . ." Dan sighed with his entire body. "The point is, I messed up. We're supposed to leave on your birthday."

"'Supposed to'?" M.J. asked, following Dan to the fridge, where he removed a beer, twisted off the cap, and tossed it in the sink where it landed with a hollow *plink*.

"I'm not going," he mumbled into the bottle.

"Can't change your flight, huh?"

"Actually, I can," he said.

"Oh." M.J. reached for his beer and took a swig as a tsunami of insecurity crashed over her. One she had always associated with teenage hormones and thought she'd outgrown decades ago. But being away from Dan, and alone in Pearl Beach, would be unbearable. Was unemployment the new PMS? "So why aren't you going?"

"I can't leave you on your birthday," he said with a pitying pout. "We could fly up to San Francisco so you could meet my family. It'll be fun. Of course, Randy won't be there, but you'll meet him some other time. Unless . . ." He reclaimed his beer and drained it. "You come with me."

"On a guys' surf trip?"

"Why not?"

"For one, I'm not a guy, and for two, I don't surf."

"And for three, Java is insanely gorgeous, so who cares? We can travel around Jakarta, check out the temples."

"Aren't you going to be surfing?"

"Not *all* day."

Dan lifted himself to sit on the kitchen counter and began knocking his ankles against the cupboard where pots and pans would go if they had any. "And when I am, you can explore. Check out the volcanoes and the rain forests, learn to surf. Actually, I can't think of a single reason why you shouldn't come."

"I can," M.J. wanted to say, because the boards she favored met in climate-controlled conference rooms; sharks wore suits, waves were greetings made in passing, and *surf* was an outdated term for trolling the Internet. And what about pride? She'd have to recuse herself as an independent woman, at least until she stopped living Dan's life and learned how to live her own. She'd read enough Judy Blume novels to know that.

"So?" Dan asked. "Whadd'ya say?"

M.J. opened the sliding glass door and gazed out at the restless ocean. On the beach, couples were taking lazy all-the-time-in-the-world strolls under the dusking sky. It was time for rosé on the deck, chips, dips, and perfumed conversations about where to go for dinner. Not *this*. "I don't understand why you have to go all the way to Java when there are perfectly good waves right here."

"It's an adventure."

M.J. stepped onto the deck and lifted her face to the setting sun, a sun that could just as easily make her feel lonely as it could feel loved. It depended what was inside her when the light hit, what it illuminated. And in that moment it shined on a dozen good reasons to give Dan her blessing and let him have that adventure with his friends. But a dozen wasn't enough.

"Count me in."

CHAPTER

Eight

IF BIRTHDAY CAKES were supermodels, this one would be Kate Upton.

Rich, professionally frosted, and hardly the type to be picked up at a grocery store, the curvy, butter-colored treat was not what M.J. expected to wake up to. How had Dan managed to checker-jump over today, land in tomorrow, and still find her favorite: vanilla pudding in the center and covered in fresh berries? And the card: *Thirty-four years ago my future was born, thirty-four years from now I will still be grateful. You are the most beautiful, elegant, intelligent, goof-ass I will ever know. I love you, Dan.*

His words expanded behind M.J.'s ribs like the grow-in-water dinosaurs she and April used to submerge in the bath. If it had been written in Dan's woozy doctor's scrawl, the surge of adoration might have made her burst. But the tidy rows of block letters suggested the hand of a different kind of professional. One who answered the phone at Pearl Beach Bakery, took dictation, then neatly transcribed the long-distance caller's sentiments onto the back of the shop's promotional postcard. Still. At some point between Los Angeles and Hong Kong or maybe Hong Kong and Jakarta, Dan made it happen.

M.J. tried to thank him with a call, a text, an e-mail, a Skype, but if it was close to noon in California, it wasn't her birthday anymore where Dan was. He had circumvented the occasion, left it somewhere over the Pacific Ocean, where it now hung in hindsight, meaningless as an empty threat.

She should have been lying beside him, nestled inside his warm, croissant-shaped embrace. Their naked bodies swaddled in coarse three-star hotel sheets, their skin carrying the floral scent of complimentary soap. But while booking her ticket, M.J. realized that her passport was still in New York.

"Maybe this is a good time for you to fly back and get the rest of your stuff," Dan said after she insisted he go to Indonesia without her.

"Not a bad idea," she said, because it wasn't. The trip home, the packing, the purging, it would keep her occupied while Dan was gone. But the possibility of her moving back to New York was still too strong. And the only thing more maddening than schlepping one's entire wardrobe across the country was schlepping it back. So M.J. left it at that, knowing that she'd have ten days to manufacture a good reason why the trip just wasn't in the cards.

Now, braless and barefoot wearing one of Dan's unlaundered T-shirts she was staring down the barrel of day one without a single activity in sight. Only a kaleidoscope of blues that shifted from one lonely image to another: the fog outside her windows known as June gloom, the L-shaped tape that outlined the corpse of their futon couch, her birthday cake on the kitchen counter, no candles, one fork.

M.J. hooked her finger around the hair elastic on her wrist and *snap!* A hot sting radiated up her arm. It was a tactic she'd inherited from her mother. "When you want to bite your nails, pull the rubber band," Jan had said. The goal was to trick the mind into associating the bad habit with pain so she'd stop doing it, and M.J. was not going to feel sorry for herself. She would celebrate the life her parents gave her. Celebrate the boyfriend who wanted her to feel loved on her birthday. Celebrate this sleepy, uninspired town; her grim existence.

Snap.

M.J. would not think about the contract at the bottom of her suitcase or how easy it would be to sign it and return to the place where honking horns and screaming ambition drowned out the mewls of her mental anguish—anguish that poor Gloria would be stuck with for the rest of her life now that Leo was gone.

Snap.

Then a revelation: Why not share the cake with Gloria?

On her way out, M.J. noticed a black envelope wedged under her front door and immediately thought of her neighbors in #5F; their endless attempts to buy her apartment, and her refusal to sell it. How could she when it was bought with her parents' life insurance money? Selling the apartment would be like selling them and—

Snap.

Cake box balanced in her open palm, M.J. picked up what appeared to be an invitation to the type of party that required a Latin password and a mask. There was a gold seal on the back flap with the letters *DBC* stamped into its waxy center; hardly the anchors and starfish she expected from the Downtown Beach Club.

"No, thanks," she muttered as it landed among the to-go cups and magazines in the recycle bin. She promised to give Pearl Beach a chance but not Kelsey Pincer-Golden. If only she had her paper shredder.

Snap.

NO LONGER BRALESS, but still barefoot, M.J. scampered across the asphalt of the Goldens' driveway, wishing that trail of cool soapy water was still trickling down from the garage.

She rang the bell, stepped back onto the bristly WELCOME mat, and waited. If Gloria's afternoons were anything like M.J.'s in the weeks that followed the accident, she was caught in the grog of last night's sleeping pill, trying to remember where she left her leg muscles.

The door yawned open.

"Britt?"

"Oh, hey," she said, eyeing the box. "I didn't know Mama Rosa's made cakes."

"It's my birthday," M.J. said with a rise-above-it grin. Because Gloria didn't need a catfight. She needed compassion and kindness; someone to mind her while she wandered around her bungalow as if searching for lost keys, someone to hold her when she realized that what's really missing is gone forever.

"Thirty-six?" Britt snipped.

"Thirty-two," M.J. lied. "Anyway, I thought Gloria might want some cake," she said as she stepped into the foyer, which was now a balmy seventy-six degrees. The macaroon cookie smell had been re-placed by a putrid combination of gardenia-scented candles and ammonia, the living room, stripped clean of its dated tchotchkes. "Is she here?"

"No."

"Do you know when she'll be back?"

"Thanksgiving."

"You're seriously not going to tell me?"

The dimple below Britt's lip twitched. "I just did. Gloria moved to Paris. Dot and Liddy picked her up in a Lyft two hours ago."

The cake became heavy. M.J. placed it on the foyer table beside a ceramic peacock business-card holder. "Are you sure?"

"Positive." Britt plucked a card from the peacock and offered it to M.J. "I'm listing the house."

"She didn't say good-bye."

"Sorry," Britt said, a bad actress trying to care. "Were you close?"

Snap.

"I guess not," M.J. muttered, vision coning as she stepped back out into the gray afternoon, leaving her birthday cake and all hope for companionship behind.

M.J. RETURNED HOME to a garden gnome. Cocksure and squat, it stood on the front porch mocking her with his jubilant smile and whimsical swimwear. Had a friend with an ironic sense of humor delivered him, M.J. would have kissed his cherubic cheeks and positioned him on the deck with a view of the ocean and a permanent seat for cocktail hour. But the sky-blue card lodged between his chubby knuckles suggested a different kind of messenger: one who legitimately thought this smug little bastard was cute.

As suspected, he was a "gifty" from Kelsey, there to invite M.J. to the Downtown Beach Club's new-recruits luncheon on June 16.

"Then tell me, lass," she imagined the gnome saying, and with a leprechaun's Irish accent of all things. "If I brought tidings of the Beach Club luncheon, what was in that black envelope you chucked in the rubbish?"

"Good question, Smug Little Bastard," M.J. told him. Then she hurried inside, rummaged through the recycle bin, and pulled out the answer.

Dearest M.J.,

    *I am currently en route to what I hope is no longer called
"Gay Par-eee," since I am unattached for the first time in fifty-
one years and have a suitcase full of lingerie (black, of course,
because I am mourning).*

    *My Leo is gone and my boys are grown, so I'm going to live
the rest of my life with the women who have helped me brave it.
One of whom once said, "Men come first, so men go first," and on
May 18, 1962, had us promise that when the last of our husbands
"croaked" we'd move to France. Of course, we didn't believe her
prediction would ever come true. But she was right. We're all
single now.*

    *The weight of my sorrow is crippling. When Leo died, he
killed us both. Everything I have ever known is gone. And yet, I
have to keep going and doing because there's a young girl inside of
me, tugging on my pant leg, reminding me that she's in there and
that her story isn't over. I need to start a new chapter—one that's
all about her this time—and I need to start it now. Because every
moment wasted is another blank page falling away and one less
chance for her to leave her mark.*

    *M.J., I will miss the secrets and martinis we could have shared
had I stayed. I will miss giving you unsolicited advice about your
love life the way Liddy, Dot, and Marjorie gave unsolicited advice*

about mine. Most of all, I will miss watching your story unfold. As it does, don't ignore the young girl tugging on your pant leg, help her become the woman she wants to be. Start by showing up at:

The Good Book
Saturday, June 4
7:00 PM

The key will get you in; discretion will keep you in.
That's right: don't tell anyone. Not even the handsome doctor.

Au revoir,
Gloria

The enclosed key had been the one Gloria wore the evening they met. Bronze, with an oval bow and two wards jutting from the shaft, it hung from a tarnished chain that smelled like pennies and Coco Chanel.

M.J. lowered it over her head and gently positioned it in the dip between her clavicle.

You are so not wearing that in public, said the young girl inside her, tugging.

"I won't," M.J. promised as she held the key against her chest like a hug from someone she didn't want to let go.

CHAPTER

Nine

Pearl Beach, California
Saturday, June 4
New Moon

SLENDER, WITH A white door and solid black facade, the shop's exterior resembled a nun's habit, the gold block letters on its sign a King James Bible. Nestled between an ice-cream parlor and the sea glass–colored caftans in the window of Misty's, the Good Book was an ebony bead on a rosary of Swarovski crystals.

What if Gloria wasn't really Jewish but rather a Christian missionary heaven-bent on luring lonely, unemployed, out-of-towners into her frankincense-and-myrrh-scented trap? Or maybe this was a surprise party, set up by Dan, who wasn't really in Java. And maybe Gayle was there, too, forked tail between her legs with a cake shaped like a giant apology.

M.J. inched toward the entrance. Then—

Oof.

The door flew open; a man, sharp-boned and smelling of waxy hair products bashed into her.

"Sorry, miss," he said, smoothing his shellacked side part. "I didn't see you there." He placed a placard that read CLOSED FOR A

PRIVATE EVENT firmly on the sidewalk. "We open tomorrow at ten."

"Easton, it's M.J., we met at Leo's *shiva*."

He stroked a goatee that wasn't there

"I'm not here to shop. Gloria invited me."

His suspicious, brown-eyed squint lowered toward M.J.'s unadorned chest.

"Oh, right." She reached into the pocket of her denim dress and flashed the ancient key.

"Follow me."

The shop smelled dank and earthy, like Manhattan after a midday downpour. Over time, moist air must have penetrated the wood rafters and seeped into the cracks between the uneven floorboards.

"So, what exactly is this private event?" M.J.'s fingers stamped quotation marks around the words she needed him to define. "Is it a . . . Christian thing?" she asked, taking in the labeled bookshelves that stretched toward the back of the narrow space, even as church pews. There were seven: PRIDE, ENVY, GLUTTONY, LUST, WRATH, GREED, SLOTH—one for every deadly sin. A pulpit furnished with a cash register faced them all.

"*Christian* thing?" Easton's sharp Adam's apple shook as he chuckled. "You obviously don't know Liddy. That framed first edition of *Are You There, God? It's Me, Margaret*, is as religious as she gets." He parted his velvet sport coat and patted the inside pocket. "This letter should explain everything. Not that I read it. It has a wax seal, so I couldn't, even if I wanted to."

The soles of M.J.'s feet itched with anticipation. "Can I—"

"'Fraid not." Easton buttoned his sport coat. "All four of you have to be together. You're the third to arrive so it shouldn't be much longer." He indicated the walkway between Gluttony and Lust. "Why don't you put on that necklace and go back to the lounge. The staff room pantry is fully stocked, so think it and ye shall drink it." Then with a backward tilt on the heels of his Oxfords: "I graduated bartending school last week."

"Do you have prosecco?"

He did.

"Could I get it in a rocks glass?" M.J. tapped the tip of her ski-jump nose. "It doesn't fit in a flute."

"As you wish." Easton pivoted and headed for the door behind the pulpit marked HOLY WATER.

Assholes, M.J. thought as she ran her hand across the mess of signatures and cartoonish doodles that defaced splintering bookshelves. Was Liddy too strapped to replace them or too stubborn to let the vandals win? Either way, the Sharpie-wielding hoods had her beat. There was Stephen King, whose pretentious inky loop wrapped around his name like a lasso, the bulbous-nosed monster drawn by Maurice Sendak, Maya Angelou, *Angelou* underlined. She passed Shaun Tan, Kate DiCamillo, Dorothy Allison, Jonathan Tropper, Jeanette Walls, Adrienne Rich, and hundreds more.

They're autographs! said the young girl inside M.J., tugging. *Who's the asshole now?* She began turning M.J. in every direction, begging her to touch the names of her favorite authors, poets, and illustrators—the ones old M.J. forgot how to love.

Eventually, she emerged from the stacks and entered the lounge—a chandelier-lit reading area with black upholstered couches and red beanbags that faced the fireplace. Decorating in the devil's colors was a nice sardonic touch. But the hearth—a mosaic of artfully burned book covers—was a masterpiece. *Catcher in the Rye*,

To Kill a Mockingbird, Lolita, The Joy of Gay Sex, The Grapes of Wrath, Forever, The Color Purple . . . All of them titles that had once been banned. It was an installation befitting the Museum of Modern Art.

"This place is Las Vegas for librarians."

A closemouthed, Pillsbury Doughboy giggle trickled out of the petite blonde in the polka-dot dress who was sitting stiffly on the edge of the couch. "So true, so true," she said, then uncrossed her ankles and stood, right arm extended. "I'm Jules, Jules Valentine," she announced with a honey-coated drawl. Her hand was cold and her bones were delicate, but her grip was firm.

M.J. introduced herself and tried to place what it was about Jules that seemed familiar. Wide blue eyes that blinked innocence, pursed lips, a sun-shaped face too big for her girlish frame . . . was it Tweety Bird?

"I guess you got Gloria's invitation, too," M.J. said, noticing the dangling key around Jules's neck.

"Gloria? No, mine came from my coworker, Dotty Crawford."

"That's how I know you!"

Jules stiffened even more.

"You work at the Majestic. You're the, oh, what's it called, the—"

"Liaison of Love?"

"Yes! You were there when I—" M.J. pointed out the smile-shaped scar above her eyebrow.

"That's right! You bonked yourself on the head with a beer can."

"It was sunscreen, actually."

"Then, a handsome prince appeared from out of the fog and rescued you with true love's kiss."

Fog?

M.J. would not have been using sunscreen if there was fog. And Dan didn't kiss her until later that night, which had more to do with tequila than true love. But correcting a liaison in the middle of her liaise was probably like waking a sleepwalker. What if she lashed out?

"Y'all are still together, right?"

"We are." M.J. beamed. "I moved out here to be with him. Left my career and everything." She edited out the whole Gayle-bifurcating-her-promotion part and how she'd still be in New York had that not happened, in favor of painting herself as the type of woman who gives it all up for the security of a man. Because M.J. built a career on knowing her audience and at the moment Jules's Tweety Bird blues were thumping emoji hearts. "And we owe it all to that magical love dust of yours."

"Don't I get any credit?" rasped a woman from the Wrath aisle. "I found the prince and princess a reasonably priced beach house in the height of the market."

Shit.

Britt shuffled into view: hair damp, skin tone uneven, eyes screaming for Visine.

"Y'all know each other?" Jules asked, wilting at the prospect of being left out.

"We've interacted," Britt said, adjusting the built-in bra inside her maxi dress. Then to M.J., "Before I forget . . ." She began ferreting through her *My Other Bag Is a Birkin* tote and pulled out something round and black with a winged logo stamped in its center. "My daughter almost swallowed it." She tossed the thing to M.J., who made no attempt to catch it. It was probably one of those gag gifts that squirted fake blood. And unlike Britt, M.J. was wearing dry-clean-only.

"Take it," Britt insisted. "It's yours."

"What is it?"

"A car key."

"It's not mine. I don't drive."

"Well, I found it in your cake."

"Y'all had cake?" Jules asked.

"No," they both answered. Then Britt lifted the key off the floor, handed it to M.J., and told her to return it to the bakery because some poor pastry chef was probably going crazy looking for it.

The three women, now settled into the couches, began to fidget like strangers in the waiting room of a gynecologist's office.

"My babies left for sleepover camp today," Britt eventually said. "Eight weeks!"

"Sneezes H. Crust," Jules gasped. "They're only eight weeks old?"

"No, they're twelve. They'll be *gone* for eight weeks. Margot and Jasper. They're fraternal twins."

"I was just playing." Jules winked. "Gosh, I couldn't be away from Destiny for that long."

"Dan's on a surf trip in Java for ten days and I'm losing it," M.J. said, trying to relate.

"Well, they love it, so . . ." Britt checked her phone. "Apparently, they're having too much fun to text." She lifted her gaze to the thicket of bookmarks that had been strung from the ceiling, taking a moment to watch them twirl in the air-conditioned breeze.

"Is Destiny your daughter?" M.J. asked, wondering where Easton was with that prosecco.

"She is. Turned fifteen years old last month. We're closer than two coats of nail polish."

Easton charged into the lounge, a scientist with a life-saving antidote. "Who's thirsty?" Three hands shot into the air. He went straight to Jules. "You and I should take up juggling," he told her, setting down his tray on the coffee table.

"Why juggling?"

He crossed one leg revealing a blue-and-white polka-dotted sock, the same pattern as Jules's dress. "Because we're very coordinated."

Britt and M.J. exchanged a horrified glance while Jules tittered with delight.

"What a pistol you are."

"If I'm a pistol, what does that make you?"

"The Liaison of Love at the Majestic Resort and Spa," she said, deciding that the flirting was over. "I coordinate weddings, proposals, vow renewals, and flowers, now that Dotty is gone. As my husband always says: Cupid is as Cupid does."

Easton glimpsed her right hand. A gold band, fine as baby hair, glimpsed back. "Husband?"

"Brandon. We were high school sweethearts." She beamed. "Married fourteen years."

Britt cocked her head. "And Destiny's fifteen?"

"Yeah, well, we kinda ate supper before saying grace," Jules said with a shoo-fly swipe of her hand. "But everything worked out. And things will be even better just as soon as he gets here."

Easton asked where he was.

"An hour south, in Oceanside. We moved there twelve years ago when Brandon got into MiraCosta College. One day I'm a wedding coordinator for the local church and the next, *poof*! The Majestic offered me a job and a garden view villa. Brandon's been trying to get here for five months, but his clients are having the hardest time letting him go."

"Is he a therapist?" Britt asked.

"No, a personal trainer."

"So where does that leave you?" Easton asked.

"Ashley Madison," said the curvaceous redhead as she emerged from Pride, her kimono dress straining to conceal her plus-sized cleavage. She wore a bronze-winged necklace, but no key.

"Welcome, Ashley, I'm Jules."

"It's Addie."

"I'm sorry." Jules blushed. "I thought you said 'Ashley.'"

"I did. Ashley Madison is a website for married horndogs who want a little extra on the side. Since your husband isn't around I thought—"

"Too late," M.J. said, remembering an old article in *City* magazine. "The site was hacked and its client list was exposed. It's done."

"Oh well." Addie shrugged. "Hey, E, can I get a Macallan?"

"Sure." Easton handed her a key necklace. "As soon as you put this on. Gloria said I should give it to you in person because you'd probably throw it out."

"She was right. It's hideous. I will take that scotch, though. In a to-go cup if you can."

"You have to wear the necklace."

"Ew." Addie winced. "Why would I do that?"

"It says so in the invitation."

"I get lots of invitations—can you be more specific?"

"The one I slid under your door last week."

"Never saw it."

"If you didn't get the invitation," M.J. asked, "why are you here?"

"I saw the PRIVATE EVENT sign and thought I'd score a free drink before I went out."

"She lives in the apartment upstairs," Easton clarified. Then to Addie, "You have to stay if you want a drink. Those were my instructions."

"Stay for *what*?"

Easton removed the black envelope from his blazer. "Everything will be explained in this letter."

Addie reached for the envelope. Easton offered her the key.

"Those two aren't wearing one," she said.

Britt and M.J. quickly put on their necklaces.

"You'll get me that scotch?" she pressed.

Easton nodded.

"Fine." Addie coiled the chain around her wrist and committed to the edge of the coffee table.

"Finally!" Jules snatched the envelope from Addie and popped the wax seal with her French-manicured nail. Then she inhaled herself into perfect spinal alignment, cleared her throat, and read, "'Dearest Easton, stop hovering and give the girls some privacy. They'll holler when it's time for you to return.'"

Easton bowed and backed out of the lounge. "As you wish."

When the sound of his footsteps faded, Jules blinked back a tear and whispered, "That's what Westley says to Buttercup in *The Prin-*

cess Bride. It's my favorite line from my favorite movie of all time and he just said it."

"Nobody gives a shit," Addie said. "Read the letter."

Dear M.J., Britt, Addie, and Jules,

Question: What's dirty, wet, and comes every fifteen minutes?

Answer: Our martinis!

So forgive the sloppy penmanship. We're at a bar in Canal Saint-Martin where the croque monsieur is to die for and so is Thierry, the bilingual (and single!) sixty-six-year-old owner. Think iron footbridges, food markets, restaurants, boutiques, and the movie *Amélie*. And it's only a five-minute walk (ten with Dot's bursitis) from our *magnifique* full-floor penthouse.

We thought vodka would make writing this letter easier. We were wrong. Nothing will make it easier. Because we have a fifty-four-year-old secret; a secret that contains hundreds of other secrets that contain hundreds more, and we are about to trust you with them all.

If the old saying is true and we are what we hide, then the four of us became who we are on Friday, May 18, 1962—the day Marjorie persuaded us to read *The Housewife's Handbook on Selective Promiscuity*. The book was all about the author's sex life and, well, it was so explicit, her publisher was sent to jail for selling pornographic literature. And if we, the good girls of Pearl Beach were caught reading it? Oh my. Gloria would have been banned from the PTA, Liddy excommunicated, Dotty left at the altar, and Marjorie's bad reputation would have gotten a reputation. But did that scare us?

Damn straight it did.

So we wrapped the book inside the cover of *Prim: A Modern Woman's Guide to Manners* and read it three more times. Why? Because the author, Rey Anthony, wrote about everything we felt and nothing we were allowed to admit. She had the same needs, curiosities, frustrations, and desires that we had. Turns out we weren't sexual deviants after all; we were repressed! And that little green book of Marjorie's set us free. So we wrapped and read hundreds more just like it and called our secret the Dirty Book Club.

We gathered every month, on the night of the full moon, in what we called "G-spots" because they're the places that most husbands don't bother with—the middle school roof, our Little League snack shack, the grocery store parking lot. While they thought we were at town hall meetings, we were naming their penises, copping to our fantasies, and whispering about the erotic passages in our forbidden finds. We weren't exactly burning our bras, but we were buying sexier ones. It was progress.

Today, sex is no longer taboo. The words *testicles* and *clitoris* won't cause giggle fits. And you certainly don't have to hide your erotica like we did. Today women are encouraged to "own" their sexuality: "Welcome to Bed Bath and Beyond. Interested in masturbating with us today? Then check out the new handheld MuscleProbe back massager on sale now in the wellness aisle..."

So what can the DBC teach you that you don't already know? You'd be surprised.

A dirty martini will make you admit things to other people, but a dirty book? That will make you admit things to yourself. Real things, honest things, things you wish you didn't feel but you do. Each time you uncover one of these truths, a brick falls from the facade you've built around yourself and leaves a hole for the light to shine through. Men are wonderful, but wood alone can't cultivate that light. You need fire. You need girlfriends. Who are yours?

Our secret letters, our forbidden library—they belong to you now. Why have we named you the beneficiaries of our bawdy pasts? Let the bricks fall where they may and you'll figure it out.

Welcome to the Dirty Book Club.

The Ten Tenets

1. Trust each other.
2. Share everything when together; share nothing when apart.
3. Gather every full moon.
4. Wear your key.
5. Close each meeting with four lit cigarettes. Inhale and say: "The smoke entering our bodies carries secrets that will stay locked inside us forever." Then turn the key around your necks and exhale. Four beams of smoke should cross, blend, and rise up as one. (Is it schmaltzy? Yes it is. We were kids when we wrote it. Forgive us. And about the cigarettes: light a goddamn

smoke once a month. One puff won't kill you. We're still here, aren't we?)

6. We had a rule: Whoever chooses the book, writes about the meeting. We thought it would be neat to read the notes when we were older and then burn them during some dramatic ceremony in the desert. Then we got older and realized we didn't want to relive our pasts and the desert is too hot. Besides, everyone we were hiding from is gone. So the letters are yours. You could add to them by writing your own, but we know how anti-paper you modern girls are, so we'll let this one go. All we ask is that you start each meeting by reading them aloud.

7. Your books are with Easton. (In boxes, of course.) Make sure the seals have not been broken. He's a curious one.

8. Membership is optional, substitutes are not. If one of you quits, all of you quit.

9. Once you have agreed to the above, Easton will bring the first box.

10. We saw Thierry first. He's ours!

Times have changed, women have not. You'll see.

—The DBC

ADDIE UNRAVELED THE key from her wrist and slammed it on the coffee table. "I'm out."

Jules's eyelashes fluttered. "You're leaving?"

"There is no DBC. The club, the secrets, the whole sisterhood-of-my-traveling-aunts crap—it's bullshit. They made the whole thing up."

"Why would they do that?" M.J. asked with a pinch of irritation.

"Isn't it obvious?" Addie rolled her eyes as they shook their heads, no. "They want you to be my new best friends."

"Us?" Britt swiped her bangs to the side. "What's so special about *us*?"

"Nothing. That's the point."

They watched Addie nibble on her thumbnail, waiting for a punch line that never came.

M.J. thought of the team-building retreat she and her cowork-ers went on last winter, and how they were asked to describe her in a single word. They used: *witty, inspiring, talented, stylish, emaciated,* and *tone-deaf*. Now, only a few months later, she was *nothing special*? Is that how California saw her? Did unemployment matte her glossy finish or had she been born matte and *City* made her shine? "Explain."

Addie leaned back on her elbows and lifted her face to the chan-delier. "You have a disease called 'settling down,' and Gloria wants me to catch it."

"I haven't settled down!"

"I have," Jules said, "and I couldn't be happier."

"Same," Britt added. "What's wrong with settling down?"

"The husband, the kids, Costco."

"I love Costco," Britt said.

"Yeah, well, while you're pushing your giant cart through their giant aisles, I'll be in Europe having sex with hot foreigners who can't pronounce my name."

"You're leaving the women's clinic?" M.J. asked.

"You know where I work?"

"You told me."

Addie's icy expression softened; melted by the heat of humiliation, or maybe, the warmth that comes from being heard. "I'm giving my notice at the end of the summer and getting as far away from Pearl Beach as American Airlines and its Oneworld Alliance will take me."

"Why?" Jules asked, as if offended. "What's wrong with Pearl Beach?"

"Autopilot, that's what. Everyone over thirty has the exact same life—marriage, babies, rescue dog, spin class, date night, school fund-raisers, girls' weekends in the desert . . . I swear, if I go to one more bridal shower I'm going to shoot myself in the face with a Crate and Barrel registry gun. I need more." Addie stood, moved by the force of her own conviction. "No offense."

"Lots taken," Britt muttered while checking her phone, a watched pot that refused to boil.

"So you think Gloria would create a fake club just to keep you in town."

Addie popped open her clutch and pulled out a tube of red gloss. "You don't know Gloria like I do." She drew the spongy wand across her lips, then kissed the top of her hand to blot. "I grew up without a mother, so she was kind of it," Addie said. "And she was a saint. So were Aunt Liddy and Aunt Dot. But I don't need a mother anymore. I need a scotch." She peered narrowly toward the front of the shop. "Easton!"

"You didn't have a mother?" Jules asked, hand to heart.

"I was born, she died ten minutes later, her best friends took care of me while my dad was at work, the end," Addie said. Not knowing that her words hit M.J. like a punch between the ribs. Because, yes, mothers did die, and it sucked in ways that Addie's glib resignation couldn't begin to describe.

"Do you think they wrote about her in their letters?" Jules asked.

"Maybe she was a member," Britt added. "You know, back in the early days."

"Okay," Jules said, "I have got to read those letters."

M.J. was equally intrigued: the secrets, the books, the history, the possibility of friends. But these girls? They seemed better suited for Oprah's Book Club than Gloria's. And what if she ended up going back to New York? The eighth tenet said, if one quits, everyone quits. It wouldn't be fair.

Outside, a car horn honked.

"There's my date!" Addie announced.

"David?" M.J. asked, remembering Gloria's son and how he had bathroom sex with Addie at Leo's shiva.

"David went back to Colorado," Addie said, closing her clutch with a definitive snap.

"Oh, I thought he was your boyfriend."

"Nope, just a buddy."

Another honk, this one longer than the first.

"I better go."

"Hold on a minute," Jules said. "Are you really dating a horn honker?"

Confused, Addie nodded.

"Oh, shugah, you can't. That man needs to go to cotillion and learn some manners."

"As long as he hits clit-illion first," Addie said, fluffing her cleavage and then turning to leave.

"Wait!" Jules said. "What about the you know what?"

"You mean the fake club?" Addie called over her shoulder. "I told you, I can't do it. I'm leaving in September."

I might be heading back to New York, so I can't do it, either, M.J. wanted to say, mostly to show Addie that she *was* special, that she too was allergic to Costco. But that little girl tugging on her dress wanted to give the club a chance.

"September is back-to-school and back-to-soccer. I won't have time to read a stop sign, let alone an entire book," Britt said. "Maybe we should pass."

"But I've never been in a secret club before," Jules whined. "Well, unless you count my teen pregnancy support group. But after a few months that secret was out." She held her hands in front of her belly. "Way out."

Addie kept walking.

"Oh, please, can we at least try? Y'all can quit when you have to."

"Good point," M.J. said. "Britt?"

"My kids *are* gone."

"Addie?" Jules called. "Pretty please? We can't do it without you."

"It's a trap!"

"I'll give you a free pass for the Majestic spa . . ."

Addie kept walking.

"For the entire summer."

"With a guest?"

"With a guest."

Addie stopped. "I'm not going to read the books."

"The tenets don't say squat about actually reading," Jules pointed out.

"And I'm not going to wear this necklace," M.J. said, lifting it over her head.

"Hold it . . . ," Britt said, looking up from her phone, her eyes wide with concern.

"Fine. I'll hold it, but I'm not wearing it."

"No, I meant hold the conversation. Where did you say Dan was?"

"Java."

"That's near Jakarta, right?"

"Yeah. Why?"

Britt flashed the news alert on her screen.

"Sneezes H. Crust," Jules muttered.

Addie hurried back.

Easton was summoned—asked to bring water, Xanax, a brown paper bag—anything to help calm M.J. down while they searched for more information. She wanted to call Dr. Cohn, but her mouth was too dry. Her hands were shaking. She couldn't breathe; she couldn't stop breathing. It was happening all over again and these three wackos were the closest things she had to friends.

CHAPTER

Ten

"Y OU SHOULDN'T BE alone right now," said Sara Hart. Or was it Marni Wells? It was the first time M.J. had spoken to Dan's mothers and it was hard to tell them apart. Not because they sounded similar—Sara's voice was calm and measured, Marni's croaking with short-*A* sounds that linked her to Boston—but because they were both on the call, talking over each other. Had these been happier times—say a 7.8 magnitude earthquake hadn't rocked Jakarta and Dan hadn't been among the hundreds of people missing—M.J. would have marveled at her sudden discovery: that his surname—Hartwell—was his mothers' last names combined. But these weren't happier times.

"Hop in the Mini Cooper and drive up to San Francisco," Marni said. "Stay with us. Benita, Randy's wife, is here with the kids. It helps. Being together helps. "

"I don't have a Mini Cooper," M.J. answered, though her mode of transportation was hardly the point. But better they think she was an uptight stickler for details than a self-involved neurotic who would steer a conversation about their potentially dead son into one about her fear of driving.

"So, he went with the Range Rover?"

"It wasn't a Range Rover, Marni, it was a Land Rover."

"There's a difference?"

"Yes, honey," Sara said, her clench-toothed smile audible. "Of about sixty thousand dollars." Then to M.J., "So, what did Danny settle on?"

"Settle on?"

"For your birthday."

"Sara!" Marni hissed. "Don't ruin the surprise."

"I thought he did it already," she whispered back. "He was going to hide the key in her—" Sara whispered something to her wife. It sounded like *ache*.

M.J. bicycled the sheets off her stubbly legs and padded to the front window. A white Mini Cooper convertible was parked in front of the cottage. It had been there since Dan left. She had assumed it belonged to a neighbor or was placed there by the city in lieu of an ugly grate. But hers? No way!

After wrenching the black key from the bottom of her purse, M.J. pressed the lock icon with her thumbnail and the headlights flashed—a lady in waiting, found.

"Ohmygod."

Marni gasped. "Is it Dan? Did you hear from him?"

"You were right." M.J. sighed. "He bought me a Mini Cooper."

A ticker tape of bratty thoughts scrolled across her brain: *Why would Dan get me a car? He knows driving gives me panic attacks. He knows I'd never get white. White makes me look washed-out. He knows all of this. . . .*

The part of M.J. that appreciated Dan's thoughtfulness, creativity, and good intentions were in there, too. But all gratitude would have to wait until he was safe.

She turned away from the window, rested her forehead on the cool kitchen counter. An ant scurried across the gray-veined marble. She considered crushing it with her finger, then decided not to bother. The cabinets were empty. It would die of starvation soon enough. Maybe they both would.

"Don't waste time packing," Marni said. "We have four daughters and a garage filled with clothes they've been meaning to collect for ten years. Just get on the road."

M.J. promised she would be there by dinner and then began searching flights to San Francisco. She wanted to thank Dan for having such wonderful mothers. She wanted to strangle him for not being there when she met them.

There was a knock on the door.

M.J. wanted to ignore it, but what if it was Dan? Head wrapped in bandages, delivered to her by a kind Samaritan.

It was Britt, dressed in a frayed denim skirt, silver Birkenstocks, and a white T-shirt. Her *My Other Bag Is a Birkin* tote hung heavily off the crook in her elbow like a punishment, the tray of brownies resting in her palm, a reward. "What took you so long to answer?" she asked, as if waiting for hours. Maybe she was. "I have a broker preview at Gloria's and thought I'd check in."

"Still no word." M.J. considered inviting Britt in for coffee or whatever people in small towns did when unexpected visitors stopped by. But she had a San Francisco flight to book and more crying to do. Entertaining was not an option.

Britt adjusted her grip on the brownie tray. "Last time, I spent two hundred bucks on croissant sandwiches. I had no leftovers and even fewer offers. So I'm going homemade this time. Fuck the free-loaders, you know?" She glimpsed M.J.'s rounded shoulders. "Speaking of food, when's the last time you ate?"

M.J. thought of Dan. Hadn't he asked her the same question the last time they Skyped? She was in a playful mood that afternoon and asked him if toothpaste counted. A response she might have given Britt. But it didn't matter if toothpaste counted. M.J. hadn't used any in days. She started to sob.

Britt put the tray on the kitchen counter, pulled a white T-shirt from her tote, and insisted that M.J. use it to blow her nose.

"On your shirt?"

"I always bring an extra. I tend to spill on myself. But I won't need it because I'm leaving the brownies with you."

"No—"

"My husband, Paul, made them. He loves to bake." Britt lifted the edge of the Saran Wrap, slid out a corner piece, and held it in front of M.J.'s tear-soaked face.

"I can't," she said, her insides too clenched to eat.

But in between gasps, Britt stuffed it in M.J.'s mouth.

Saliva rushed to the bottom of M.J.'s teeth. She swallowed and reached for another.

"They're all yours. If I need a fucking brownie to help me sell a beachfront bungalow in June, I'm in the wrong business." She cut a look to the sealed DBC box by the microwave. "Open it. Our first book is *Fear of Flying* and there are erect nips on page one. It might be a good distraction."

M.J. WAS LYING on her bed, legs stretched before her in a limp V, tray across her chest like a feedbag, sunglasses on. The midday sun seemed amplified, her need for curtains immense. But even if they had curtains, M.J. wasn't sure she could have closed them. Her muscles felt leaden, her limbs a prosthetic sort of numb.

She considered her options: harass the Red Cross for updates (again!); book another emergency session with Dr. Cohn; open the DBC box; reread Gayle's offer, which she exhumed from a pile of black cashmere while packing . . . Her flight to San Francisco wasn't until 7:00 PM. Unfortunately, there was time to do it all. And yet, all M.J. could do was stare up at the ceiling fan through polarized, bronze-tinted lenses.

Then, suddenly, as if she was a balloon being filled by helium, she felt light . . . tingly . . . giddy.

"Giddy," she said aloud, then giggled. What a funny little word. Wobbly as a toddler, it woke her mouth like a pack of Pop Rocks. It grew fingers and tickled her brain.

The sensation quickly spread to her cheeks, her gums, her torso, and all the way down the limp V of her legs to the tips of her chipped pedicure, until laughter claimed her entire body. She hadn't felt this wonderfully untethered in years.

Then her phone rang. Trilling along as if in on the joke and laughing, too. If she picked up, the caller would ask why she was so amused—a question she couldn't answer. If she didn't pick up, no one would want to know why she was so amused. And few things in life were more awkward than cracking up alone.

"Hello?" she managed. There was interference on the other end. A seashell's hollow hiss. "Hello?"

"M.J.?"

The helium feeling stopped; something more grounding was filling her now.

"Are you there?" said the voice. "Can you hear me?"

M.J. sat up so quickly the brownie tray toppled onto the floor. "Dan?"

"Hey!"

"You're alive?" her voice echoed, the connection was terrible.

"Of course I am," he enthused. "How are you? How was your birthday? Did you like the cake?"

"The cake? Who gives a shit about cake? I thought you were dead!" Her voice was shaky and unfamiliar; maybe they were both dead. "What happened? Are you hurt? Why didn't you call?"

"You heard about the earthquake, right?"

"Um, yes, Dan, I heard about the earthquake."

"I was surfing when it happened. You should have seen the swell, babe, it was epic."

"Epic?" Was she glad he was okay? Of course! But his euphoria in the face of her despair felt like being trampled by a conga line.

"Waves five to six feet overhead. By the time we paddled in, the quake had stopped, but man, it was chaos." The connection dropped out. At best she heard every other word. "Broken sewage pipes . . . contaminated water . . . used our filters . . . life savers." While Dan went on about his work with the search-and-rescue teams, M.J. texted his mothers to let them know he was okay.

"How's Randy?"

"Incredible. We cleaned wounds together all night. We've met so many brave people, M.J. The humanitarian effort over here is mind-blowing."

"And not one of those humanitarians had a phone?"

"Most of the cell towers collapsed. The ones left standing were maxed out. This is real front-lines shit. Full-on triage. Thank God you stayed home. What if you had been touring around Jakarta when—" An ambulance siren wailed in the background.

M.J. moved the phone away from her ear. Every part of her gnashed with a premenstrual-type of irritability. Hundreds of Jakartanese (if that's what they were even called) were dead, dying, missing, displaced—and *she* felt irritable? What right did she have? If anything she should be leaking relief because Dan was safe, or gushing pride because he was saving lives. She should have been *giddy!* And yet, that word no longer wobbled or popped or tickled inside her body. It felt flat, drained of its titillating delight much like sex after the orgasm or sushi once full.

"M.J.? Are you still there?"

She curled into a comma and gave in to her heavy eyelids. "Yes," she managed. The sudden exhaustion was bone-deep. She balanced the phone between a pillow and the tip of her nose to relieve her tired hand.

Everything would be better once Dan was back—*she'd* be better. She'd have four days to sort out her ambivalence with Dr. Cohn, get some sleep, and give him the welcome he deserved. "Home Friday night, right?"

"Actually, about that . . ." *Actually about that . . .*

M.J. squinted through the infuriating echo.

"The Red Cross asked me to stick around for a while and help out."

A red cross popped into M.J.'s head. It had Kardashian-sized curves, a nurse's cap, and a sultry Marilyn Monroe whisper: *Hey there, Dr. Dan, I just love how man-shaped you are. What do you say you stick around for a while and help me out?* Then she wrapped her brick-thick arms around his war-torn scrubs and blushed herself redder.

The front door opened with a bang. Then footsteps. Not heels, though, Birkenstocks. "Stop eating!" Britt called as she charged the bedroom, bangs parted like tent flaps. "Don't eat—" She stepped on one of the brownies, slid across the floor, and landed forehead-first on the unopened DBC box.

M.J. wanted to ask if she was okay, but she couldn't speak—she couldn't even breathe—she was laughing too hard. A staccato of guttural clicks was the only sound she could make.

"Baby, are you crying?" Dan asked. "I know you were worried and I—"

Britt cupped M.J.'s face between her hands and looked at her with those whiskey-brown eyes of hers. "How many did you eat?"

"Have your lashes always been that thick?"

"M.J.?" Dan called. "Can you hear me?"

"How many did you eat?"

"Dan is alive!" M.J. told her. "And he's fucking a red cross."

"How many did you eat?"

M.J. raised two fingers. Then three more.

Britt found the phone in a lump of sheets. "Dan, I'm so glad you're alive. Listen, M.J. ate five pot brownies and . . . She didn't know . . . I didn't know, either . . . What should I . . . Okay . . . Bye."

Britt dialed 9-1-1.

"What are you doing?"

"Calling an ambulance!"

"Why? It was just a bump on the head. You look fine."

Britt snickered. "It's for you, dumb-ass."

"Me?" M.J. knocked the phone from Britt's hand. "I don't need an ambulance."

"I know, but you need a hospital and my electric golf cart won't get us there."

"Come." M.J. began crawling toward the kitchen, finding comfort in the low center of gravity.

Britt followed, tracking chocolate all over the floor.

"Take my Mini," she said, pointing up at her purse, which she'd left on the counter.

"It's *yours*?"

"Yeah, but you can have it."

CHAPTER

Eleven

THE FIRST FIFTEEN minutes M.J. spent at the Good Book
had been fine, pleasant even. She sat in the reading lounge,
sipped prosecco and flipped through her notes on *Fear of Flying*. She
couldn't wait to deconstruct Isadora Wing's brazen affair with Adrian.
Couldn't wait to read the forty-two-year-old letter in the dust jacket
of her book. Couldn't wait for some company, having spent twenty
days without Dan. And yet, all she did was wait.

Outside, the full moon was bright and bloated. Instead of casting
an approving glow on the first gathering of the new Dirty Book
Club, it mocked M.J. by shining a light on the three members who
didn't show; on Dan, who missed his connecting flight in Hong
Kong and wouldn't be home for another day; on her voice mail that
hadn't heard an apology from Gayle in over a week.

While Easton scurried about, returning errant books to their
proper shelves, M.J. lifted her eyes to the chandelier and summoned
her father, a shrewd investor who always knew when the market was
about to collapse, when to get out. "I promised I'd give Pearl Beach a

chance and I did," she said. "I decorated the cottage while Dan was gone. I took a stand-up paddleboard lesson. I even joined a book club!"

The ceiling creaked. He was all ears.

"Yeah, well, don't get too excited. I'm at our first meeting right now and no one is here." She twisted the gold wedding bands on her thumb. "Dad, it was a mistake for me to leave *City* the way I did. I wasn't thinking clearly and now I think I should accept Gayle's offer and go back to New York before she changes her mind. I'm bored and lonely and the tap water here tastes like saliva."

A bookmark, one of the hundreds that hung from the rafters, drifted to the floor. It read, *Sorry, yesterday was the deadline for all complaints.* M.J. laughed. Her mother, a pull-yourself-up-by-your-bra-straps kind of gal, must have been eavesdropping.

"I'm not complaining, Mom, I'm confused." M.J. drained half a glass of prosecco in a desperate gulp. "If I go, I'll lose Dan. If I stay, I'll lose my mind. What am I supposed to do?"

The chandelier began to swing.

"Leave?"

The ceiling shook.

"Stay?"

The chandelier swung harder. Bookmarks began raining down from the ceiling. Either they wanted her to leave or this was the start of something biblical.

M.J. crawled under the coffee table and took shelter. If the movie *San Andreas* taught her anything it was that. "It won't be long now," she told her parents—an RSVP to the family reunion she assumed was decades away.

"There you are," Easton said, poking his face under the coffee table.

"Earthquake!"

"Nah, it's just Addie, stomping around her apartment." He offered his hand.

"She's home?"

Seething, M.J. began the climb to Addie's apartment. The flat soles of her gladiator sandals reprimanding the stairs with resentful stamps. If only she had worn her Lanvins, those chunky square heels would have landed like anvils.

Then footsteps came toward her, carrying the satisfied spring of a boy who had just become a man.

"'Sup?" he said, tucking in his Enchanted Florists uniform as he passed.

M.J. stomped harder.

"Back for more?" Addie cooed from the open door at the top of the landing. She wore a gauzy white cover-up that revealed her dark areolas like a botched surprise. "Oh, sorry," she said, disappointed, "I thought you were Marilyn, the delivery guy." She twisted her cinnamon-colored hair and fastened it with a chip clip.

"That guy's name was Marilyn?"

"The tattoo on his back said Marilyn, so I'm going with it."

M.J. swallowed her laughter as punishment. "Why did you blow off the meeting?"

"That's tonight?"

Normally, M.J. would have fired back with something biting, then walked off with a smirk. An underdog who got the last word. But then what? Another night spent rearranging furniture, stalking Liz Evans on social media, and popping an Ambien at sunset? She couldn't tolerate more solitude; how it coiled around her lungs and squeezed.

So, there she was. Plucked, showered, and dressed in a tasteful black jumpsuit. Ready to embrace the Dirty Book Club and its ragtag members. Only now had it occurred to her that they might not embrace her back.

"Yes, Addie, the meeting was tonight. No one showed. Easton locked up the store. We're done."

"Relax," she said, yanking her inside. "This is California. Everyone's late."

Moments after she texted the change of address, Addie, still flitting about in a see-through dress was welcoming Britt and Jules into her cozy one-bedroom apartment; breezily asking them to remove their shoes because the floorboards were old; being praised for offering to host on such short notice.

"Sit wherever," she said, indicating the small but opulent living room. Gold foil wallpaper, black velvet furniture, splays of animal hides, flickering vanilla-scented candles. It was sensual and sexy with an undercurrent of illicit behavior—perfect for a drug lord's paramour or a Rihanna video.

M.J. sat on the curvaceous daybed, behind which was a mosaic of ornately framed oil paintings of Rubenesque women, pale and exposed.

"Y'all are never gonna guess who I just met with," Jules said, as she unbuckled her sandals and placed them neatly by the door.

ISIS? M.J. might have joked had they been better acquainted. Instead, she remained silent while Jules went on about her three-hour caucus with Piper Goddard and her fiancé, Gill—whatever his last name was. It didn't matter. Piper *was* Goddard Cosmetics. And she had just hired Jules to plan her third wedding at the Majestic.

"You don't understand," Jules said. "I worked the Goddard counter at Saks for two years. It's the only thing I use. See?" She closed her lids, showcasing an expertly blended gouache of indigo and violet shadows.

"You're a makeup artist," Britt said, as if that explained everything.

"Self-taught," Jules chirped. "I was accepted into the cosmetology school at Paul Mitchell but"—she sighed—"life. You know?" With a resilient grin she sat on the couch, removed two Goddard pouches from her tote and placed them neatly by the roses that were probably from Marilyn. "Come," she said to Britt, patting the cushion beside her. "Let me cover that 'stache rash for you."

"Is it still red?" Britt fingered her upper lip. "Serves me right for getting waxed at a nail salon."

M.J. cut a look to Britt's glossy reds. "*That's* why you were late?"

"Paul's taking me to Marrow. It's our thirteenth anniversary." She cast a wide-eyed glare at M.J.—a silent reminder to keep the brownie incident under wraps. Even though Britt accidentally fed her the batch Paul was making for a friend with colon cancer—*not* himself—she didn't want the others to know. "Why stir the pot?" she quipped on the drive home from the hospital.

"You're going out for dinner *tonight*?" M.J. asked, more peeved by Britt's early exit than the unintentional overdose.

"Our reservation is in forty-five minutes." She beamed.

"How romantic," Jules squealed. "Wha'daya say we glam you up? It's amazing what a wee bit of I-give-a-*beep* can do, especially around the eyes."

Britt scratched at a crusty splotch on her mouse-gray maxi dress. "I did give a beep."

"I know, shugah. You just need to give a twinge more."

Compulsion shot up the back of M.J.'s throat and straight out her mouth. "Actually, the word is tinge."

"Not where I come from," Jules declared, then to Britt, "Look up so I can get your lashes."

Addie returned from the kitchen with a warm bottle of chardonnay and a tower of red plastic cups. "Isn't it a little soon for a make-over scene?"

Jules turned away from Britt and sneezed. "Sorry." She sniffed, then sneezed again. "It's the—*Ah-poo*—roses. I'm allergic." She popped a Claritin.

"Say no more . . ." Addie opened her window and dumped the roses onto the street.

"You didn't have to do that!"

"Poor Marilyn," M.J. said.

"Marilyn didn't buy the roses, he delivered them." Addie lowered herself onto the zebra hide and leaned back on her elbows. "The flowers were from some hottie I met at the juice bar on Teal Street."

"Did you know the hottie or was it a zipless fuck?"

"What's a zipless fuck?" Addie asked.

"Spontaneous sex with a stranger," Britt told her. "It's from *Fear of Flying.*"

"Really?" Addie asked as she coaxed a floating piece of cork from her cup and flicked it across the room. "What's it about?"

"Didn't you read it?" M.J. asked.

Addie shook her head. "We agreed that I didn't have to, remember?"

With a slight eye roll, M.J. turned to her notes. "Written by Erica Jong and published in 1973, this novel is a mock memoir about Isadora Wing, a New York writer who travels to Vienna with her husband, Bennett, so he can attend a conference. While there, she meets Adrian Goodlove—a scruffy Englishman who becomes her lover after helping himself to a fistful of her ass."

"Sounds good."

"It was," M.J. said, hoping for backup. But Jules was busy contouring Britt's cheekbones, and Britt was busy urging Jules to contour faster because Marrow didn't hold tables. M.J. felt like a substitute teacher on the last day of school.

With that in mind, she pulled Gloria's letter from the inside of the book and began reading it aloud, desperate to cover the material before the bell rang and she lost them forever.

THE DATE: Thursday, January 10, 1974
THE DIRTY: *Fear of Flying* by Erica Jong
THE DETAILS: By Gloria Golden

I was in the checkout line at Safeway, flipping
through one of those women's lib magazines when I
learned about *Fear of Flying*. The review claimed that
Isadora Wing's erotic fantasies—along with her affair—
proved that women love sex just as much as men. And I
thought, *Now this, I have to read.*

My plan was to start tonight's meeting with a poll:
Hands up if you think women love sex as much as men.
I needed to know if anyone else disagreed with this
statement. If they, like me, didn't love sex as much as
men, they loved it more and thought there was something
wrong with them. But Marjorie asked if anyone had had a
real-life zipless fuck (as if she didn't already know),
so we ended up starting with that.

Liddy, Dot, and I had not. Of course, Marjorie had
had several. There were a few at Woodstock, one in
the back row during *The Poseidon Adventure*, and Flight
#645: New York to Heathrow.

Liddy said, *It was Marjorie, in the lavatory, with a
pilot*, like we were playing Clue.

I wondered why anyone would *want* to have spontaneous
sex with strangers. To me, making love without the love

part was the same as preparing meat loaf without meat. What was the point?

Pleasure, Gloria. Pleasure is the point. (Marjorie.)

But Isadora loved Bennett, I said. And they had pleasurable sex. So why did she cheat?

Because Adrian made her underpants wet enough to mop up the streets of Vienna.

So?

So, love has nothing to do with it, Marjorie said, like she was Dr. Joyce Brothers or something. *Lust and love are different. I love lust. Which is why I'm never getting married.*

Liddy, of all people, agreed with her. She said that most people get married because society makes us think it's the hip thing to do. And if magazines and movie stars said being a spinster was cool no one would do it.

Dot said: *Speak for yourself, floozy. I couldn't wait to marry Robert. Society had nothing to do with it.*

Then I said: *Maybe it's genetic, like some people are born wanting more sex than others . . . Like me.*

Marjorie practically choked on her cigarette smoke. *You want more sex than Leo?*

Be grateful you even have a libido (Liddy), *Patrick and I are trying so hard to get pregnant, my Mother Mary is red, raw, and stuffed as a nose in flu season. I think I have a penis allergy.*

Marjorie raised an eyebrow as if to say, *I told you she was a lesbian.*

Robert and I do it four times a week. Five when Jenny spends the night at her grandparents'. (Dot)

What about you, Glo? (Marjorie)

Once.

A day?

A month. Leo's always at work, and by the time he gets home he's too tired.

They looked at one another like they had a secret.

Have an affair, Marjorie suggested as if offering me a second slice of pie. *That's the groovy thing about Isadora, she shows us that it's okay to spread our wings. If men can fly, we can fly, too.*

Isadora isn't groovy, I said. *And she shouldn't be spreading her wings. She's married. And now poor Bennett has to spend the rest of his life wondering why he's not good enough.* I could hear the despair in my voice, taste its vinegar on my tongue. I wasn't sure where it was coming from. Maybe the vodka. *Anyway, why does anyone have to fly?*

Marjorie told me to ask Leo.

This time everyone looked at her, not like she had a secret, but like she spilled one.

What? Marjorie said, all big eyes and innocence. *I assumed it was one of those things we all knew but never talked about. Like how Robert would rather be in Vietnam than work another day at his father's grocery store and that Liddy is gay.*

I am not gay! I'm married to a pastor!

Marjorie opened a new pack of Camels and didn't even offer us one. Then she said: *I thought when you're best friends with someone for twenty years you can speak the skinny, but I guess we're still pretending here; so, Glo, about that Durex wrapper you found in Leo's racquetball bag. You're saying that was yours?*

You know about that?

They nodded.

We also know about the Chantilly on his dress shirt, the crumpled-up receipt from the Biltmore, the mysterious midnight phone calls, and those autograph pictures. (Liddy)

One for every pot roast that went to waste. (Dot)

I became angry and told them to stop; angry because I expected them to pick up these tidbits of information like a fallen Cheerio—dump them in the trash and move on—not come to conclusions behind my back. I was also angry at Leo for making me look like a fool. Angry with myself because I didn't cook like Julia Child or look like Raquel Welch. If I did maybe Leo would think I was enough. But most of all I was angry because they were right. I knew Leo was messing around. I had always known it. I was just too scared to admit it, because once I did, then what?

What am I supposed to do now? I asked while they rubbed my back, lit my cigarettes, refreshed my martini. *We have four kids and three fund-raisers next month. What will I tell my parents? How will I face the neighbors? Who will hold my hand at the movies?*

I bet a romantic vacation will help you two get back on track. Hawaii or maybe even Florida. (Dot)

And let him get away with it?

Yes, let him get away with it. Gloria, you keep things from Leo all the time. (Marjorie)

Like what?

You call his curved penis Captain Hook. You get dolled up for that Little League coach. You prank-call Leo's busty secretary. And what about this club?

What about it?

You say you're at a town hall meeting, Leo says he's working late.

We're talking about affairs, not white lies.

His affairs are like our dirty books—a cheap thrill between covers to fill the void—that's all.

Void? What void could Leo possibly have? I give him everything.

No one gives anyone everything. He'll never understand you the way we do, and you'll never stroke his ego the way those desperate little starlets do. We get different things from different people. It's nothing personal. It's how we survive.

Well, my void is full. (Dot)

Same. (Liddy)

If your voids were so full you wouldn't be reading about Isadora's orgasms, you'd be having your own.

We purred.

As usual, Marjorie made it all sound so neat and logical. Doable, even. I get support and laughter from my friends, romance from my books, love from my sons, security and companionship from Leo. All I had to do was change my perspective. Live off the à la carte menu instead of the prix fixe.

It would take some adjusting. But I could do it. I could greet Leo with a smile on my face and love in my heart, even when he carried a whiff of Chantilly. Because he needed those starlets like I needed this club.

I'm sitting alone now at my kitchen table writing this letter. My brain is soaked in vodka, my body is heavy from crying, and Leo is three hours late.

It's as if I'm at the end of *Fear of Flying*. I am both Isadora in the bathtub and Bennett returning to his hotel room unaware that she is there. I am inside that parenthetical moment. Before they see each other. Before they are faced with each other's pain. Before decisions have to be made and action has to be taken. Like Isadora, I have no idea what will happen next.

—G.G.

———————

"WELL," ADDIE SAID, refilling her red cup with wine. "We all know how that turned out."

"You think Bennett took Isadora back?" M.J. asked, pleased that Addie wanted to explore the novel's ambiguous ending. It wasn't the most logical place to start, but the question was valid nonetheless.

"I'm talking about Gloria and Leo," she said. "Gloria stayed with Leo even though he was cheating on her. It's pathetic," Addie practically spat. "It's weak."

"Maybe she busted Leo and then held it over him for fifty years," Britt said. "Made him kiss her ass and buy her diamonds so she wouldn't leave."

"Hold still," Jules said, her lip liner hovering inches away from Britt's mouth.

"My guess is that Gloria let Leo think he was getting away with it," M.J. said, remembering the "five-minute warning" Leo got from Gloria the day she stopped by. At the time she assumed the phone call was a harmless little ritual, but what if it was an act of preservation—a chance for Leo to extinguish his cigarette or shove his girlfriend out the back door—to keep them from an unwanted run-in with the truth?

"Why would she let him get away with it?" Britt asked.

"To keep her family together," Jules said. "It's the opposite of weak. Putting her marriage before her ego is strong."

Addie yawned. "Sounds like a pussy move to me."

"Isadora was the pussy," M.J. said, with a self-conscious giggle. It was the first time she had referred to a literary character as such and was tickled by its subversiveness. It was liberating. Not only to her but also to Isadora, who suddenly stopped being a character trapped in the 1970s and became another confused woman just like the rest of them. "She was all talk."

"All talk?" Britt asked. "Isadora had an affair."

"Yeah, but she went back to her husband's hotel in the end. And what about her fantasy—where she meets a stranger on a train and has sex just for the sake of sex? No attachments, no ulterior motives? Isadora had an opportunity to do that and when it came down to it she was revolted."

"Y'all wanna know what I found revolting?" Jules asked. "The ending. How are we supposed to know if Bennett and Isadora stayed together?"

"What's the difference?" said Britt. "Marriage is boring. Single is lonely. They're screwed no matter what."

M.J. shuddered. It was all so depressing. "So what's the answer?"

"Maybe the answer is pull a Leo," Britt said. "Tie the knot, but keep it loose."

"A slipknot," Addie suggested, plucking the chip clip from her updo and mussing her hair.

"Exactly."

Jules lowered her gloss wand. "Y'all can't be serious."

"We have two choices: married or single," Addie said. "And they both suck. So why aren't we, as a society, throwing out some new options? Why aren't tastemakers planting seeds of change? Why isn't anyone TED-talking about it?"

"But marriage is so romantic," Jules said.

"And romance isn't real. It's conceptual. Only reality is real," M.J. said. "We all have romantic visions of how our lives are supposed to play out. Then someone dies unexpectedly, or we get passed over for a promotion, or your partner is never around—"

"The skin above our knees starts to sag," Britt added. "Random hairs grow out of our chins, our boobs look like pencils when we're in doggy style."

"Exactly," M.J. said. "Then the romantic vision fades to black and we spend the rest of our lives trying to figure out what went wrong. But what if everything is going exactly the way it should and we're too busy clinging to our bullshit fantasies to roll with it? What if *Fear of Flying* ended where it did because Isadora and Bennett are supposed to let go of their expectations and accept whatever mess they're in today?"

"So, what mess are you in?" Addie asked.

M.J. told them about the car accident, Liz Evans, Dan's extended trip to Java, and the unsigned contract at the bottom of her suitcase. The one Dan knows nothing about. "I gave up my career to be with him. Now he's off doing what he loves and I'm stuck here watching another one of my visions fade to black."

"Oh my gosh!" Jules gasped. She was holding a long thick clump of Britt's hair in her hand. "Do you have—"

"Yes, along with one in eight American women so can we not make a big deal about it?"

"Oh no, shugah." Jules pulled her in for a hug. "You're going to get through this, you'll see. Aunt Barb on my mother's side is a cancer survivor and—"

"Cancer? I don't have cancer."

Confused, Jules examined the clump more closely.

"I have hair extensions."

"Phew," Jules said, "because I was fibbing about Aunt Barb. She passed away last year."

"What about your ass?" Addie asked. "Is that real?"

"Yes," Britt said.

"Lucky Paul."

"You're assuming he's aware of it."

"He's not?"

"Truth?"

They nodded.

"Paul smokes more weed than a wildfire. He only notices my ass when it's blocking the TV."

"So the colon cancer brownies . . . ?" M.J. asked.

"They were his," Britt confessed. "He broke his back on a landscaping job two years ago and is still quote, unquote, *recovering*. Apparently pot helps his pain. Meanwhile, I'm the one suffering because while Paul's on the couch cupping his balls, I'm juggling twins, pet turtles, cooking, cleaning, *and* a career." She paused while Jules dusted her T-zone. "This is not what I signed up for. I wanted to be a stay-at-home mom. I actually love soccer practice and playdates and homemade teacher gifts. And now some nanny named Josephina gets to do all that while I work. Because if I don't work, we won't have a house, and who's going to hire a homeless Realtor?"

"When will Paul be well enough to work?"

"Um, eighteen months ago, but he won't. He's had dozens of offers but none of them are good enough. Nothing is ever good enough and I'm over it. We sleep in separate rooms and communicate on sticky notes. Not even the big ones. The tiny ones. My romantic vision didn't fade to black, it went up in pot smoke." Britt wrapped the hair extension around her finger until the tip turned red. "Sometimes I think it would be better if he just died."

Jules's blush brush froze midstroke.

"Relax. I don't have a weapon or anything. But I've fantasized about it. Like, would my life be easier if Paul magically disappeared— a zipless death, if you will."

"Get a divorce," Addie said.

"I don't want to," Britt said. "I like being married, at least I used to, back when Paul was . . . Paul." Then with a nostalgic smile: "I miss him."

Jules drew back her head, took in Britt's newly made-up face. Her skin was luminescent, her features defined and enriched. "Dang, I'm good."

"Wow, you just might get laid tonight," Addie said.

Britt put down Jules's hand mirror. "Not if I'm late," she said, reaching for her clutch with renewed energy.

"Wait, what about the closing rituals?" M.J. pulled the key necklace from her purse, dangled it for inspiration.

Jules tapped her décolletage; she was already wearing hers.

"Addie? Britt?" M.J. said, hating to be a stickler. But without the rituals and traditions, this was just another book club—one that was bound to lose its magic and fizzle out.

"It's somewhere in my room . . . I'll have it next time."

M.J.'s shoulders slackened. "And the cigarette?"

"I have chewing tobacco," Jules said. "Will that do?"

"Really?"

"Nah, I'm just playing. I stopped chewing when Destiny was born."

Addie stood. "I might have an e-cig." She quickly returned with a shoe box filled with items that her various one-night-stands had left behind: a navy dress sock, skull-and-crossbones cuff links, gold earbuds, a BlackBerry, and thong underwear. "Got it!" She wiped the tip with her gauzy dress and turned it on.

All four women inhaled the clove-flavored vapor, all four of them coughed and tried again.

"The smoke entering our bodies," M.J. finally said, her voice pinched to keep the vapor from escaping, "carries secrets that will stay locked inside us forever." Those who had keys turned them. Then, on an exhale, their beams crossed, blended, and rose as one.

WHILE RIDING HOME in a Lyft, feeling unsatisfied and slightly duped, M.J. wondered if maybe her expectations had been too high. What she had anticipated—a night where everyone arrived on time, thirsting for wine and stimulating conversation, where personal boundaries melted like the clocks in Salvador Dalí's famous painting—was another romantic vision gone awry. Because unlike the original members of the Dirty Book Club, M.J., Jules, Addie, and Britt did not share memories that predated the invention of color TV, seat belts, and the publication of *The Cat in the Hat*. They didn't make secret pacts or communicate in half sentences and inside jokes.

Their relationship was more like an arranged marriage designed to preserve a bloodline and uphold traditions. It lacked history, chemistry, passion. Still. There would be a next time.

Fifty Shades of Grey

CHAPTER

Twelve

IT WAS THE *way* Dan had taken to the new sectional that hurt M.J.: spine erect, legs rigor-mortis stiff, hands clasped tightly over his crotch. A crisp capital *L*, not the yielding *C* she had anticipated.

"Ouch!" he barked as she pressed her pinkie nail into another one of his bug bites. There must have been thirty on his shins alone. "Why do you keep doing that?"

"To help you," she said, pressing again.

It was a trick she had learned at summer camp. A carved *X* in the center of a bite stops the itching. Not that Dan was scratching. He wasn't doing much of anything other than yawning and mumbling, "It's so *sorreal* to be back home."

Had he not survived a deadly earthquake, spent weeks volunteering with the Red Cross, and slept on the floor of a Hong Kong airport, M.J. would have reminded him (again!) that the word was *surreal*. Instead, she said, "Try to relax," then began rubbing his calloused feet. Which wasn't easy, they smelled like Doritos.

After twenty days apart—the most since they'd met—M.J. expected Dan to kick open the front door and carry her into the bedroom. Wake her flesh with stubbly kisses and defibrillate her heart with his love. But he was exhausted—that glazed stare, the gray tinge to his tan, the mealy quality to his voice—she could *see* it. She understood.

What she didn't understand was his blatant disregard for the sectional. As if it had been there since childhood, like some sort of down-filled Giving Tree, existing solely to provide while asking nothing in return. As opposed to what it really was: brand-new and definitely not there before he went to Java.

Neither was the driftwood coffee table, the fluffy white rug, the kitchen appliances, the art, or the basket for his medical magazines. And Dan didn't seem to notice any of it until M.J. lovingly propped a pillow behind his lumbar and the price tag, which she must have forgotten to remove, stuck him in the back.

"Two hundred dollars?" He snapped it off. "For *this*?"

"Yep." M.J. beamed. It was the Kelly Wearstler "Kiss" pillow and had been marked down from $295. A steal!

Dan tossed the tag onto the coffee table. "How much did you pay for all of this?"

"So you did notice." M.J. flicked him on the forearm to keep things light. "Don't worry, I put everything on my card and I'll return what you don't like."

"It's not that I don't *like* it—"

M.J. wrapped her hands around his feet and squeezed relief.

"It's just a bit . . ."

"A bit . . . what?"

"I dunno." Dan squinted as if trying to remember an online banking password. "Excessive?"

"How is a place to sit *excessive*?"

Tears pinched the backs of M.J.'s eyes. All those trips to furniture stores, the money she wasted on rushed deliveries, that surge of joy she felt when she imagined Dan's reaction, it was all for nothing; another failed attempt to fit into his world.

"I'm sorry," he said, then pulled her toward the coffee stain in the middle of his T-shirt. Though hurt, M.J. allowed herself to be pulled. She craved the intimacy and wanted to smell his coconut-scented skin. She also needed somewhere to dry her tears, and the couch hadn't been Scotchgarded yet.

"I should have waited. It's your home. I had no business doing it without you."

"It's *our* home," Dan said, like he used to. "And I'm glad you did it. You know how much I hate shopping. If it were left up to me this place would look like one of those terrorist crash pads—nothing but a bare mattress and a cell phone charger."

She laughed. He was starting to thaw.

"I love everything you did. It's just—"

M.J. lifted her head. "What?"

"Do you know how many filters the Red Cross could have bought for the cost of that pillow? Enough to give four hundred people clean drinking water for a year."

"I'll return it," M.J. said, even though it was a final sale. "We can donate the money to the Red Cross and—"

"I love the pillow." Dan rolled toward her and wrapped her in his arms. "And I love you even more. Just give me a day to acclimate."

M.J. nestled into the relaxed curve of his body and synched her breathing to his. And there they slept, straight into the next morning, like perfect *C*'s.

M.J. WAS SITTING on her new porch swing, when Britt pulled up in the Mini—top down, hair whipping against her sunglasses, Mariah Carey's "Dreamlover" blasting from the stereo.

She turned off the engine. "So, how pissed is he?"

M.J. planned to say that Dan was livid; that she never would have made Britt drop everything on a Friday afternoon if he wasn't. That he has a "thing" about loaning cars and the fact that it had been a birthday gift made it worse. But when it came down to it, she didn't have the heart, especially since Dan hadn't even noticed the damn thing was gone. "Turns out he's fine. Not pissed at all."

"I thought you said he was—"

"I lied."

"Lied? Why?"

M.J. got in the car and shut the door. "I'm bored."

"Why didn't you just say *that*?"

"Would you have come if I did?"

"No." Britt's dimple deepened. "But only because I was getting laid."

M.J. LEANED BACK in her plastic chair, giving the busboy the space he needed to wipe the sticky sheen from their table. The raucous beach bar, with its bikini-clad waitresses, two-dollar test tube shots, and sand-footed clientele was nary the atmosphere M.J. had in mind when she suggested lunch. But Britt feared an unexpected run-in with a client or mom friend who would think nothing of asking to join them—the "small-town sabotage" as she called it—and was certain there would be no such interloper at Poncho and Frieda's.

"So you were getting day-laid? Sounds like your big date went well," M.J. said, once the busboy had gone.

"Date?"

"At Marrow. With your husband."

"Oh, you mean Paul?"

"Yeah, sorry, isn't Paul your husband?"

"He is, but that's not who I met at Marrow."

Fleur, their waitress, chucked two baskets of glistening crab cakes onto their table.

"Paul never showed," Britt said. "He had passed out on the couch with half a salami sandwich stuck to his pregnant stomach. He has no clue he even missed it."

"So who did you meet at Marrow?"

"Long story medium: I couldn't let Jules's makeup go to waste, so when they gave my table away I hit the bar and small-town sabotaged Mandy, this girl I know from high school. She was with her boyfriend and a couple of his work buddies and those work buddies were buying me shots and calling me sexy. So, being the tragic married-mother-of-two cliché that I am, I soaked up the attention like a super sport tampon."

"And then?" M.J. asked, eager to know how drinking with random guys lead to Britt forgiving Paul and having sex with him on a Friday afternoon. She loved when seemingly incongruous threads of a story came together in the end. It was so satisfying.

"Then, one of them had me laughing so hard—something about a wad of toilet paper he found in his Tinder date's V when he was going down on her—that a bit of pee dribbled out. I was tight as a nostril until I had twins. It sucks. Anyway, while I was waiting for the bathroom, the manager kicked them out for being too loud."

"That's it? That's the end?"

"No." Britt grinned. "It's the beginning."

CHAPTER

Thirteen

*T*HEY'RE IN AN *elevator. Before she knows it he grabs her ponytail and yanks down, bringing her face up to meet his. His lips are on hers. She moans into his mouth. She can feel his erection against her belly . . .*

M.J. shut her *Prim*-covered copy of *Fifty Shades of Grey*, pulled the sheets over her naked body. Why did her inner snob insist on making bitchy faces at Anastasia's inner goddess? Why couldn't she fall in love with Christian Grey, like millions of other women had? Why couldn't she let poor Ana fall for a tortured dominant if that's where the day took her? *Whatever tickles your clit*, M.J. would have loved to say, and mean it.

But she couldn't.

Britt's "encounter" at Marrow was so much hotter, not to mention the high-stakes drama surrounding it, and M.J.'s thoughts were consumed by it. If Britt's secret went public she'd suffer more than one of Christian's stinging slaps to the ass. She'd be nursing the kind of pain that lasts a lifetime; the kind that red wine and a warm bath couldn't soothe.

"What do you mean, it's the *beginning*?" M.J. had asked during her lunch with Britt the day before. The vodka in her Bloody Mary was not about to let Britt's comment fart by and evaporate into the salt air. "The beginning of *what*?"

Britt leaned forward and whispered, "Promise you won't tell a soul?"

M.J. did. Still, Britt made her prove it by stuffing a whole crab cake into her mouth. When M.J. dry heaved Britt said, "That's the feeling I want you to have if you even *think* about telling someone what I'm about to say, okay?"

Eyes watering, stomach lurching, M.J. said, "Okay."

"So I'm waiting for the bathroom and checking my messages to see if Paul called—which he didn't—when reality sets in. I'm not a sexy, free-spirited party girl; I'm a drunk mom with a loose bladder who was blown off by her husband on their anniversary." She stirred her Bloody Mary. "I was about to start bawling when a man says, 'You're incredible,' in that throaty Bruce Willis kind of whisper, you know?"

M.J. nodded like someone who didn't think a Bruce Willis reference was decades too late. "Was it Paul?" she asked, still hoping those loose threads would come together and explain how it led to sex on a Friday afternoon. "Did he finally show up?"

"No," Britt hissed. "It was a hot guy leaning against the wall across from me, arms folded across his chest and shirtsleeves rolled to his elbows like he's posing for a Rolex ad."

"He was wearing a Rolex?" M.J. asked. She treasured her father's old Timex but had always wished he'd sprung for the crown.

"No, a Fitbit. Even better, right? And he was bald."

"How bald?"

"Bald. A young bald, though, not an old bald."

"Like Mr. Clean?"

"Yeah, but without the hoop earring. More like a Brazilian wax."

"And he said, 'You're incredible'—out of nowhere like that?"

"Actually, he was on the phone when he said it, but he was looking right at me. And when I say looking, I mean look-*ing*. It was primal. And I swear, M.J., my loins ignited like a gas burner. Which is weird, because I'm usually attracted to guys like Paul—dark hair, dark eyes, atrophied muscles . . . but his body was tight and he was licking his lips and watching me—all while telling whoever he was talking to that he'd had a sudden change of plans and *whoosh*"—Britt indicated a gas explosion over her crotch—"rational thoughts ceased to exist and I—Stanford University graduate, recipient of real estate's prestigious Gold Medallion Award, mother of twins, and three-time winner of the Thanksgiving Turkey Trot marathon—was reduced to a throbbing slab of meat with nerve endings."

M.J. was struck by the brazen confidence of this stranger as much as Britt's ability to be seduced by it. Had some creep who smacked of a Brazilian wax gazed at her in a bar while whisper-speaking like Bruce Willis, she would have ignited *his* crotch.

"So he hangs up the phone and says, 'What are you drinking?' And you know what I said?"

M.J. shook her head.

"I said, 'You.'" Britt smacked the table. "Can you believe? Then I shoved him into the men's room, because the women's was still occupied, and straight up fuck-attacked him."

"So the guy you were with when I called today, that was—"

"The Brazilian." A slow sunrise of a smile brightened Britt's eyes, which she was now lining in black kohl.

"What's his deal? Is he married? What does he do?"

"Dunno. We haven't done much talking. We didn't even exchange names. I'm keeping it zipless. The less I know the less real it is and the less I have to feel guilty about."

"So you feel guilty?"

"Not really." Britt laughed. "Weird, isn't it? If anything I feel like I deserve it. Like I've done everything I possibly can to fix my marriage and Paul's completely checked out. At the same time I love the guy. So what am I supposed to do? Get divorced and break up my family? Drink myself numb? Resign myself to a lifetime of missed anniversaries and forgotten couples therapy sessions? God, I'm bone-tired of feeling like I don't matter and the Brazilian makes me feel like I do, you know?"

M.J. lied and said she could relate. But in truth Dan was a devoted adviser, lover, grief counselor, and friend. If anything she took him for granted and was now starting to wonder if that's why he stayed in Jakarta for so long. To get away from her apathy and surround himself with people who not only needed his help but also appreciated it.

Just as she was about to share her newfound concern with Britt, Addie appeared. She had an hour-long lunch break at the women's clinic and chose to spend it drinking with friends and handing out invitations (condoms with the particulars written in Sharpie) to her thirty-fifth birthday party. Though the intrusion was poorly timed, it filled M.J. with delight. She had been small-town sabotaged *and* invited to a party in the same afternoon. She was starting to be-long.

Now, still in bed and close to noon, M.J. kicked off the covers and followed the sound of CNN into the living room, eager to show Dan how much he mattered before someone else did.

CHAPTER

Fourteen

Pearl Beach, California
Monday, July 4
New Moon

B ELOW THE ROOFTOP bar, which was cleverly named Rooftop, cars sharked the narrow streets looking for parking, kids ran along the beach waving glow sticks at the dusking sky, and a bouncer worked his way through a line of Pearl Beach B-listers hoping to crash Addie's party and get an unobstructed view of the fireworks.

"Was she actually born on Independence Day?" Dan shouted above a thudding remix.

M.J. followed his gaze to the train of blondes, dancing on a low table, gyrating rhythmically; their red, white, and blue bikini tops and high-wasted cutoffs a predictable homage to America's birth. And then there was Addie—the redhead at the center of it all— wearing a flowing gown made of iridescent green and black feathers in a true show of independence.

"She was," M.J. said, with a parent's proud smile. Proud because she was part of Addie's celebration, proud to be holding Dan's hand amid it all, and prouder still because after three years of social celibacy she was back in the game.

Then, a zap of trepidation. She wriggled free from Dan's protective grip.

"You're twisting your rings," he said, the sky's last fiery streaks of the day lighting his eyes. "What's wrong?"

"Was I?"

Dan nodded. "You're allowed to have fun," he said. "No one is going to die if you do."

M.J. looked out at the hilltop homes that shimmered gold in the setting sun. He knew her so well. Better than she knew herself. She gazed up at him with a rom-com actress's lovestruck grin. "How did I get so lucky?"

Dan traced the scar above her eyebrow. "Sunscreen." He smiled. "Now let's go break some hearts." He ushered her past humid bodies, sloshing cocktails, and the predatory glances of men—and M.J. allowed herself to be ushered. It was one of the first times they were both heading directly into the fun instead of steering around it, a silent but mutual desire to escape the relentless haunt of car accidents and earthquake victims and enjoy each other instead.

"Look who it is," Dan said, indicating Britt. She was seated alone at the bar, chin resting on her fist, grinning as if savoring a delicious secret. She turned at the sound of Dan's voice and greeted them both with a chardonnay-scented hug.

Joy swelled inside M.J.'s chest. Not only was she at a party, she knew one of the guests. Granted, said guest had a wet spot on her tank top, but life was about progress, not perfection, as Dr. Cohn liked to say.

"Where's your better half?" Dan called above the DJ's stuttering beats.

"Pressed against this stool," Britt said, pointing to her ass, which was shrink-wrapped in a pair of white skinny jeans. "Oh, did you mean Paul? He's stuck on a job." She cut a look to M.J. urging her to play along.

"He's working on the Fourth?" Dan asked.

"Yep. Looks like you'll have to fetch my chardonnay tonight in his stead." Britt raised her empty wineglass and gave it a *This isn't going to refill itself* jiggle.

"I thought membership to the Downtown Beach Club included manservants," Dan joked.

"Downtown Beach Club?"

M.J. bristled. "The manservants are on backorder until the fall," she said, with a play-along pinch to Britt's sinewy bicep. "Would you mind filling in?"

While Dan was busy flagging down the bartender, M.J. quickly explained that she'd been using the Downtown Beach Club as her alibi for the DBC and asked Britt what she'd been telling Paul.

"Nothing. He never asks." She dabbed the corner of her eye with a cocktail napkin, expunging a mascara booger in one efficient blot. Then she peered past M.J.'s shoulder, threw back her head, and laughed with hearty, borderline psychotic, jubilation. "That is *hilarious!*"

M.J. drew back her head. Was Britt bipolar?

"Laugh," Britt insisted from the side of her mouth.

"Huh?"

"Act like I just said something funny." Britt giggled. "Do it!"

M.J. laughed. She sounded more asthmatic than amused. "What's happening right now?"

"He's here," Britt whisper-smiled.

"Who?" M.J. turned to follow Britt's gaze, when— "Ouch!" She gripped her stinging thigh. "Why did you just flick me?"

"Because I don't want him to know I know he's here."

"*Who?*"

Britt lowered her head. Black hair flanked her face while she swiped her lips with gloss. "The Brazilian!" she said. "He just walked in."

"The Brazilian knows Addie?"

Britt shrugged. "He said he wanted to watch me in my natural habitat, but I have no idea how he found me. He doesn't know my name, let alone my schedule." She swiped her bangs and stole a quick peek. "It's kind of hot, don'cha think?"

Heat prickled the base of M.J.'s neck. A bald voyeur was lurking somewhere behind her. "If by *hot* you mean potentially dangerous and probably deranged, then yes, it's extremely hot."

"What's hot?" Dan asked, returning with their drinks.

"You," M.J. said.

"Me?"

"Yeah," Britt added. "Getting M.J. a car for her birthday and hiding the key in a cake is hot."

"It would be hotter if she actually drove it," Dan said with a teasing smirk to M.J.

"Well, if it makes you feel any better I love it," Britt said, "Though an upgrade on that stereo wouldn't hurt. The bass gets lost when the top is down. Not that I'm complaining," she said with a quick side-eyed glance at the Brazilian. "Anything is better than what I'm driving."

"Seriously?" Dan scoffed. "You have a Land Rover *and* a Prius."

"That's the car version of ordering a Big Mac and a Diet Coke," M.J. said.

Britt threw back her head and laughed uproariously, a reaction so disingenuous that M.J. found herself wishing the Brazilian away.

"The Land Rover is gone. Paul traded it for an electric golf cart to save the quote, unquote, *environment*," she rubbed two fingers against her thumb to show what he was really trying to save. "Meanwhile, we look like the Flintstones in that ridiculous thing."

"Stop," M.J. tried. "Those carts are cute."

"Cute isn't going to get me to work on time."

"What about the Prius?"

"Paul's been taking it. Where to, I have no idea. Probably the dispensary," she grumbled.

"Dispensary?" Dan asked.

Britt lowered her wineglass, punishing it for speaking out of turn. "The plant dispensary, I mean. Because Paul is a landscape architect and— Look, there's Jules!"

M.J. turned to find her emerging from a plume of secondhand vape smoke wearing an enthusiastic A-line dress befitting a PTA luncheon. With outstretched arms she processed toward them with a cellophane-wrapped gift basket and an accomplished grin. Martha Stewart presenting her Christmas roast to the troops.

"I can't take all the credit. It's from Brandon, too," she said, as Britt gushed over her presentation.

"Brandon is Jules's husband," M.J. explained to Dan. "He's in Oceanside but he's moving—"

"Actually," Jules said, "Brandon's here." She wedged her basket between Britt and M.J. and heaved it onto the bar. "The gym is closed for the holiday, so he came up."

Britt scanned the densely packed guests as if searching for Brandon, though it was the Brazilian she was looking for. And it became clear by her waning smile that he was gone.

"He's in the little boys' room," Jules said, off Britt's disappointed expression. "He'll be right back."

M.J. brought Dan's hand to her lips, kissed the smooth arches of his meticulously cut fingernails. Tonight she didn't have to tell anyone Dan would be right back. Tonight Dan was there.

"So, I take it you know M.J. from the Downtown Beach Club," Dan said to Jules.

A round of *pop-pop-pops* interrupted the conversation before Jules could object. And while red, white, and blue tentacles dripped through the star-spangled sky, M.J. explained her alibi.

Jules nodded in solidarity, then tended to her vibrating phone.

"Oh shoot." She pouted as she took in the screen.

"What is it?"

"Brandon has a sour tummy and wants to go."

"I can take a look at him if you want," Dan offered.

Alight with hope, Jules texted their good fortune to Brandon, who immediately shut it down. "He wants me to take care of him," she said. "He's fussy that way."

"Is it me or does Brandon have a bad case of Snuffleupagus syndrome?" Britt asked, once they had left.

"Meaning?"

"Jules is the only one who sees him."

The music stopped and Easton, the bookstore manager, began sound-checking the mic.

Thud . . . thud . . . thud.

"Is this on?"

After a collective groan assured him that it was, he summoned the birthday girl to join him and five other plaid-suit-wearing gentlemen in the center of the gathering crowd.

Addie smoothed her feathers and swished boldly into the circle, ready to receive.

"Ladies and gentlemen . . . ," Easton said, "we, the members of Choral Fixation, would like to sing a very special 'Happy Birthday' to Addie Oliver."

With that, the men surrounded Addie, hummed themselves into pitch, and began. Their arms rose and fell with the song's inflections, their metronomic toe-taps perfectly timed. What could have easily been dismissed as party kitsch turned out to be a spellbinding tribute to a girl who was just as comfortable standing in the spotlight as she was sitting on a zebra rug in a see-through gown.

"Why don't I hate her?" Britt asked.

When the performance ended the guests erupted in applause while Addie thanked each member of Choral Fixation with a breasty hug. Then Easton handed her a black envelope.

Addie flipped it over—front to back, back to front—searching for a clue to its contents. But Easton's proud grin gave nothing away.

With a *What have I got to lose?* shrug, Addie sliced open the flap and read the enclosed card while Easton waited, hands clasped behind his back. His eyebrows seemed to ask if she found the news as exciting as he did; hers seemed to answer no. Then she crumpled the note in her fist, gathered the train of her dress, and left the party.

WHILE DAN WAS getting the car, M.J. peeled back the tissue paper inside her gift bag to find a bottle of sex toy cleaner, two AA batteries, and a vibrator named Fat & Natural. The note inside said:

Thanks for coming . . . and coming . . . and coming.

Love, Addie

"The pleasure will be all mine," M.J. thought as fireworks detonated overhead.

Three miles south at the Majestic Resort and Spa . . .

JULES CLOSED THE gift bag.

What was Addie thinking? What if Brandon had been pulled over and their car was searched? The police would think Jules actually paid good money for something so vulgar. Not to mention she was married and had a husband for that, thank you very much.

Well, she *would* have a husband for that if Brandon hadn't gone back to Oceanside for his medicine; medicine for a stomach condition Jules was totally unaware of.

"Destiny and I will go with you. We can spend the night," she tried. The thought of him suffering alone pained Jules more than every stomach condition combined. But Brandon reminded Jules of the breakfast meeting she had with Piper Goddard and insisted she stay. It was the "responsible" thing to do, he said. And so she did. Jules also set her wake-up call for thirty minutes earlier than usual so she could creep over to the dumpster on the other side of the resort and dispose of the gift bag by the cheap rooms.

———————

DAN ENJOYED A finger in the ass while he was getting a blow job, particularly right as he was about to come. But unlike M.J.'s past lovers, Dan was a quiet climaxer, so the moment often came and went before she could capitalize on it. Sure, the sudden hitch of his breath was a reliable indicator—a call to action for the dutiful girlfriend who aimed to please—but aiming anything in *there* seemed more sinister than sexy. It was so fleshy and damp. A sea anemone's suction with a toothless hooker's grip. And so M.J. blamed all those unfortunate missed opportunities on Dan's muted orgasms and managed to look herself in the mirror just fine.

But thanks to Addie, Fat & Natural could do the dirty work for her.

So M.J. burrowed under the covers and took Dan in her mouth. She played with his balls, worked his shaft, and flicked her tongue expertly against the head of his cock. She did everything and all at once while listening for that sudden hitch. When she heard it, M.J. powered up Fat & Natural, introduced its vibrating tip to Dan's clenched asshole, and—

———————

At the Riley residence . . .

BRITT SLAMMED HER head against her daughter's Hello Kitty pillowcase, as if the jolt could summon the return of happier times: Paul home from work smelling like soil and sweat . . . family dinners in the tree house . . . sex in the garage while the kids were asleep . . .

At the very least, maybe the jolt would shatter her eardrums so she couldn't hear Paul snoring in their bedroom.

How many times did she beg him to wear those Breathe Right nasal strips? See a sleep specialist? Widen the airways in his throat with uvulopalatopharyngoplasty? But the more Britt lobbied for change, the more Paul stayed the same.

She gazed up at the glow-in-the-dark stars on Margot's ceiling and thought of the Brazilian. Though they'd only slept together since Marrow and no one actually slept, she could tell his airwaves were unobstructed. And if they weren't, he was the kind of guy who would do something about it. He didn't get those shoulders from working a TV remote. Those were the shoulders of a man who thrived on heavy lifting. Lifting that included, but was not limited to, hoisting Britt onto the Kahangs' washing machine twenty minutes before she showed their home to a potential buyer. God, it was hot.

Britt sighed with her entire body. She couldn't believe she cheated on Paul with a nameless, hairless stranger. *Her!* At the same time, why hadn't she done it sooner? Paul's indifference was so much easier to tolerate when she was getting attention from someone else. Not to mention the amount of money she had wasted on antidepressants and shrink appointments. The Brazilian's latest text alone was enough to flood Britt with serotonin, maybe even eliminate her need for caffeine.

She read it again:

Watching u tonight made my dick hard. Jerking off now. Thinking of ur ass in those tight white jeans.

Britt opened Addie's gift bag.

———————

M.J. CAME TO with an ice-filled Ziploc on her forehead. Her ears were buzzing. She assumed it was a concussion until she realized that Fat & Natural had been knocked off the bed and was now vibrating against the wood floor.

"What happened?"

"My knee slammed into your frontal lobe," Dan said. "It was a reflex. I wasn't prepared for something that big. I'm sorry."

To prove it, he slid down her naked body and spread her legs, giving M.J. what she would refer to as "the best apology ever."

———————

TO JULES, THE female orgasm was like winning the Publishers Clearing House sweepstakes; something that happened to a blessed few, not her. But what if that *thing* under her bed was the answer? What if it worked?

Jules banished the thought from her perverted mind. It's not that she was opposed to sex toys, per se. She was a live-and-let-live kind of gal. It's just that something about it felt like cheating, only worse, because poor Brandon was sick.

Maybe it would be easier if Fat & Natural didn't look so realistic—not that Jules had much to compare it to. Brandon's penis was her only penis, and it was more fit than fat. Actually, it was thin, but Brandon never liked being called thin. Trim, yes. Athletic, yes. But never thin. Also, his penis had a slight left curve as if it was peering around a corner to see what it was missing. Which, in this case would be his wife, making love to a rubber phallus that was not his. And Jules couldn't betray him like that. She needed to keep her deranged curiosities at bay. She needed to pray for Brandon's stomach. She needed rest so she could be alert for her meeting with Piper Goddard.

Even if Jules wanted to try it, and she wasn't saying she did, she'd be lost. The back of the box mentioned an "easy to control interface" and "three stimulation modes" but where were the instructions? If she was going to try it, and she wasn't saying she would, Jules needed the facts. Was it loud, how far "in" did it go, and was she at risk for electrocution?

"Hello, Siri," Jules whispered into her iPhone. "How do you use a vibrator?"

"Okay, I found this on the Web for *How do you use a vibr—*"

Jules silenced her at once.

BRITT LOADED THE batteries into the base of the balls and conjured an image of the Brazilian in what she hoped was his current state: jeans around his sturdy ankles, stroking his shaft, bucking wildly as if she were on top of him . . . She exhaled the day and then lowered the vibrator past her Soul Cycle T-shirt, over the front of her boyshorts, and—

Fuck you, Selena Gomez!

How was she supposed to lose herself when surrounded by posters of the pouty starlet and a photo collage of Margot's friends? The guest bathroom it was.

Once situated on the bathmat, which desperately needed a vacuum, Britt removed the bottle of lube from inside the gift bag and squeezed the slippery solution onto her fingers. The sound reminded her of ketchup squirting onto a hot dog, which reminded her of family barbecues, which reminded her of the twins, which re-minded her that she had a million things to do before they came home from camp—none of which involved lying on a hair-filled bathmat with a vibrator.

Still. Britt spread her legs. Her hip-flexor popped. She needed to stretch more after spin. She needed to stop thinking about spin. She reached into her boyshorts and applied the lube. She closed her eyes. Her vagina began to burn. And not in the "ignited gas burner" way, in the "someone doused it in gasoline and tossed a match on it" way.

"Ow, ow, ow, ow, ow ow!" She jammed a monogrammed towel between her legs and waddled to the tub. *A burning bush!* she might have joked, if she wasn't seriously considering a call to 9-1-1. But what would she ask for—an ambulance or the nearest hook and ladder?

After hosing down her crotch with cold water, the pain finally began to subside.

"What the hell?" Paul asked, eyelids too swollen to notice the splay of discarded paraphernalia on the bathmat.

Britt emerged from the tub, shivering. "Cramps."

He yawned. "You woke me up."

"Sorry. I know you have a big day watching Netflix tomorrow . . ."

"It's okay," he muttered, returning to bed.

Back in Margot's room, Britt checked the bottle of lube for the name of someone she could sue. Instead, she found a warning: "This product was designed as a sex toy cleaner and should not come in contact with the skin."

She whipped it at Selena Gomez's throat.

———

In the apartment above the Good Book . . .

ADDIE LEANED FORWARD and spit.

"Fuck!" she said, wiping her lips on the back of her hand—her thirty-fifth birthday and the only thing in her mouth was an electric toothbrush. The night was not supposed to end this way. No night was!

It didn't matter how many times she brushed, the taste of resentment was still there—metal and dirt, like prison bars—prison bars disguised as a gift from Gloria, Liddy, Dot, and Marjorie.

What could have possibly made them think she'd want Liddy's bookstore for her *birthday*? The gift was of no use to her, unless of course she could sell it for travel money or burn it for warmth. And so Addie decided she would simply give the Good Book back. Thanks but no thanks. Delete from cart.

CHAPTER

Fifteen

Pearl Beach, California
Tuesday, July 19
Full Moon

T HE FULL MOON called the Dirty Book Club's second meeting to order, and tonight's G-spot, thanks to Jules's pull, was the Majestic's ultra-exclusive Oyster Bar. Located on the beach, the torch-lit cave could seat only thirty people and—after months of reading about the mesmerizing sitar music and vanilla-spice incense imported from Morocco—M.J. would finally be one of them. Management promised them a table for sixty minutes, provided they were out before Solange Knowles arrived, but Jules was convinced they could push it to ninety if they dressed like "hoochie mamas."

Which was why M.J. was miffed when Britt drove past the valet and chose free parking two blocks away. Her hoochie-mama shoes were not made for walking. But Britt allegedly saw Paul drive out of the Majestic and was adamant that they not waste chardonnay money on pricey hotel valets. "Because when a woman sees her unemployed husband pull out of a resort on a Tuesday evening, every dollar in her Coach wallet gets drafted for active duty. Mission: drink to forget," she said. Hands shaking, she released the Mini

166

Cooper key into her clutch. "I'm the one who's supposed to be having an affair, not him!"

"Are you sure it was Paul?" M.J. asked, as she clacked through the lobby trying to keep up with Britt's urgent steps.

"How many wool-beanie-wearing ass-bags drive blue Priuses in this town?"

"If you're including Lyft drivers I'd say hundreds."

Out on the beach, a college-aged staffer wearing a guayabera shirt and an at-your-service smile, was standing in front of the red ropes that blocked access to the cave. Once he found their names on his list he welcomed them to the only five-star barefoot bar in Orange County. "Can I check your shoes?"

M.J. lifted her leg and rolled her ankle, offering him an unobstructed view of her Louboutins.

"No, ma'am, I mean, can I check them for you while you're at the Oyster Bar? Then, you know, give them back when you leave. Like a coat check but for—"

"How much?" Britt asked.

"The service is free, but oftentimes patrons thank me with a tip."

"Yeah, well, unfortunately your tip has its heart set on being a bottle of chardonnay, so I'll handle the shoes myself, thanks." Britt removed her strappy sandals and rolled up her gold lamé genie pants in deference to the rising tide. Her arched spine poked through her black tankini top like a threat: *If you so much as think about calling me MC Hammer I'll cut you.*

"Same," M.J. told him, then kicked her iconic red soles across the sand. Anything to avoid bending down in her leather leggings and Ginsuing her intestines. "There are so many ways to interpret 'hoochie mama,'" she said. "Tragically, all of them are tight."

They continued through the cooling sand toward the torches, walking to the windshield-wiper beat of M.J.'s thigh-scraping leggings. "You don't really think Paul is cheating, do you?"

"No, I really *know* he's cheating on me." The tangerine rays from the setting sun highlighted her certainty. "He sneaks out of the house without saying good-bye, takes showers when he gets home, and"—her chin dimple pulsed—"I found pubes in the bathroom trash can."

The gentle hiss of settling waves filled the silence between them while M.J. considered her response. It was possible to rationalize sneak-outs and showers, but shorn pubes? They were the crumbs of infidelity. But M.J. didn't dare point that out. Nor did she ask why Britt hadn't shared her suspicions with Paul. She was enjoying the role of confidant and didn't want to scare Britt off. Besides, who was she to judge? Maybe Paul had his reasons. Britt certainly believed she had hers.

"What are you going to do?"

"I'm not going to be like Gloria Golden and let him get away with it, that's for sure."

"Meaning?"

"I'm going to down a keg of wine, then I'm going to catch him in the act, then I'm going to down another keg of wine, and then . . . I have no idea."

A frantic wave from Jules, who was seated posture-perfect on a rattan chair got them past the appraising hostess and into the candlelit lounge. Dark and moody with an air of exclusivity, it was the perfect backdrop for their *Fifty Shades of Grey* gathering, unless one was claustrophobic.

Britt claimed the love seat to the left of Jules, lowered her clutch to the sand, and extended her bare feet to rest by a plate of bruschetta. "I smell pot," she said, cutting a smirk to M.J. that said, *See? Paul was here.*

Jules unpenned her Pillsbury Doughboy giggle. "It's not pot, silly. It's silver sage." She popped a Claritin. "Gray foliage is hard to come by in the summer, but I called in a favor." Then she indicated the bottle of Grey Goose by Britt's feet, the pitcher of pink fruit juice beside it. "Would anyone like a Fifty Shades of Greyhound?"

"You *themed*?" M.J. asked, as if accusing her of peeing in the hot tub.

"Of course I did." Jules lifted the striped tie that hung over her gray sweater set. It was an exact replica of the tie on the book cover. Beneath it was the ancient key that both Britt and M.J. had dutifully brought but refused to wear. "I'm the Liaison of Love. Atmosphere is what I do."

A confounding amalgamation of naïveté and moxie, charm and social awkwardness, it was impossible to tell if she was in on the joke or the unsuspecting punch line.

As M.J. sipped what tasted like grapefruit-flavored antibacterial soap, she considered Dan. How he had always wanted to have a drink at the Oyster Bar and how M.J. would never be able to tell him that she finally had. Because Dan thought she was at the Downtown Beach Club planning a fall fund-raiser. Between that lie and her ongoing failure to mention the hidden contract in the bottom of her suitcase, M.J. felt like she was having a tryst of her own.

"I just realized something," she said. "If you replace the *y* in the word *tryst* with a *u* it spells *trust*. Funny, right?"

Jules cocked her head, confused. "Is that Sudoku?"

"Sudoku is numbers," Britt snipped, then, eyes wide with distrust, "M.J., why are you talking about trysts?"

"I wasn't referring to *that*. I was thinking about Dan and how I lied to him about where I was going tonight."

"Referring to *what*?" Jules asked, stirring her grapefruit juice.

Before M.J. could fabricate an answer, Addie appeared. Her cinnamon-colored hair had been plumped and tousled, her eyeliner artfully smudged, and her curves encased in a sleeveless black dress. She looked like a tube of red lipstick. "Which one of you does real estate?"

Britt raised her hand.

Addie handed her a manila folder.

"What's this?"

"A terrible excuse for a birthday present."

Addie started biting her nails while Britt flipped through the pages.

"Liddy is giving you the bookstore?"

"Unfortunately."

"Beats the heck out of my gift basket," Jules muttered.

Britt closed the folder. "Why is this terrible?"

"The store is the last thing I want and they know it." Addie attempted to cross her legs but her dress was too tight, so she shifted her body sideways and crossed her ankles instead. "Will you sell it for me?"

"Do you own it?"

Addie shrugged.

"Did you sign a deed?"

"No, but I can."

"Keep in mind," Britt warned, "once it's signed you're accepting the transfer of ownership."

"Fine. Whatever. Let's do it tomorrow. I want to cash out before September and first-class the shit out of my trip."

"I can't sell it that fast."

"Why not?"

"That old place would never pass a safety inspection, not with that buckling ceiling. The structure has to be updated to the current building codes, which have changed since Liddy bought it. That's going to take time and a lot of money."

"Ugh!" Addie slammed the armrest. A rugged beer-swigging bunch at the bar, each with mud-stained jeans and day laborer's tans, took a sudden interest in the buxom redhead with the high-glossed pout. A pout that suddenly transitioned into a coquettish grin when she saw them. "The one in the middle is a babe," she muttered through a clench-toothed smile.

"I know that guy," Britt whispered. "He's an arborist. He used to work on landscape projects with Paul. They called him Bungee because he has a super-long—"

"Dibs!" Addie announced. "I'm calling dibs on Bungee."

"Why didn't Bungee have to dress like a hoochie mama?" M.J. asked, adjusting the crotch of her pants in a preemptive strike against camel toe.

"Staffers can drink at the Oyster until nine because no one important shows up before then. You should see what he's working on. It's called a living wall. By August the entire front facade of the hotel will be covered in plants."

"What happens if I don't sign the deed?" Addie asked, cleavage aimed at Bungee, the rest of her parts trained on Britt.

"If you don't sign the deed the store stays with Liddy."

Addie laughed at the simplicity of it all. "That's it?"

"That's it."

Addie took a victorious shot of Grey Goose. "So, who had fun at my party?"

Jules's lashes fluttered. "You're not even going to think about it?"

"Nope," Addie stole a side-eyed glance at Bungee, fluffed her hair, and then tipped her chin, offering him a view of her photogenic side. "Can we please talk about my birthday? Did you like the vibrators?" she asked, loud as a mating call.

"What do you say we get started?" Jules said, lifting her *Prim*-covered copy of *Fifty Shades of Grey*.

"Five stars," Britt said, refilling her glass. "Am I right?"

Jules nodded vigorously. "That moment when Ana e-mails Christian and says she doesn't like him anymore because he left after sex and"—she fanned off a rush of tears—"and minutes later he appears at her door and says, 'You said you wanted me to stay, so here I am.' That was the most romantic thing I've ever read."

Britt agreed.

"You *bought* that crap?" M.J. gasped.

"Full price, paid in full."

"The sex scenes were great but you have to admit the prose was a bit unrefined," M.J. said, fingers longing for the feel of her red editing pencil.

"Prose?" Britt sneered. "Honey, reading *Fifty Shades of Grey* for the prose is like drinking wine to be heart smart. That is not why we're here. We're here because everyone wants to be Ana. Including me."

"You're into . . ." Jules glanced over her shoulder, then whispered, "*that?*"

"If by *that* you mean getting my tits smacked around by a gorgeous, fit, well-endowed billionaire pilot who speaks French, plays the piano, books my wax and gyno appointments, and wants me to eat even more than I normally do, then, yes, Jules, yes I am."

"Doesn't that make you a prostitute?"

"No, it makes me a goddamn genius."

M.J. sat back and folded her arms across her blouse. "I don't know what's more shocking. That you gave *Fifty Shades* five stars or that Addie isn't keeping the bookstore."

Addie looked at her like, *Really, we're still doing this?* "Those women are trying to handcuff me to Pearl Beach and I'm not going to let them. So can we drop it?" She liberated the wing necklace from her cleavage and gripped it like a security blanket. "Is it me or are my boobs getting bigger?"

Jules respectfully looked away. "Speaking of handcuffs . . ." She jangled the key around her neck like a dinner bell. "It's time."

With that she unfolded Dot Crawford's letter and began reading.

THE DATE: Wednesday, May 2, 2012
THE DIRTY: *Fifty Shades of Grey* by E. L. James
THE DETAILS: By Dot Crawford

When I told the girls that *Fifty Shades of Grey*,
with all its whipping and flogging, was the novel
I identified with more than any of the others we've
read, they nearly pooped their pantsuits. Because Dot
Crawford doesn't choose pain—not anymore.

I've always believed that those who do must have an
abundance of pleasure in their lives. Why else would
they doff their caps to suffering if not for the thrill
of an irregular experience? And I've suffered enough.

So it wasn't all that Red Room nonsense that grabbed
me, it was the question Anastasia had to ask herself
each time she entered it—How much torture will I endure
in the name of love? It was a question I asked myself
for almost fifteen years, and the answer was always the
same: "As much as I deserve." But unlike Anastasia, my
tormentor wasn't a Renaissance man with a sex fetish.
It was my husband, Rob.

We met the summer after I graduated high school. I
got a job as a checkout girl at Crawford & Sons Grocery
and spent my shifts checking out the twenty-year-old
"Son."

He was Paul Newman handsome, drove a Ford Fairlane

convertible, and was the heir apparent to Frank Crawford, owner of thirteen stores statewide. It didn't discourage me when the other checkout girls told me Rob got kicked out of his father's country club for stealing a golf cart or that he named his surfboard Johnnie Walker—it inspired me. I was Dotty Snip after all—head cheerleader, valedictorian, and best friends with Marjorie Shannon (the biggest troublemaker at Pearl Beach High!). And I still graduated with honors. I welcomed a challenge like a neighbor with a swimming pool.

Rob and I fell in love that summer. We spent our days off at the beach, going to drive-ins, and necking in the back of his Fairlane. In the fall, I started teachers' college, Rob was promoted to produce manager at the store, and we saw each other on the weekends. I was happy. And he was, too. But as time went on he complained more and more about his job. He was bored. Uninspired. Obligated. Trapped. Doomed to decades of answering to his father and smelling like vegetables. "Thank God for Dotty Snip and Johnnie Walker," he'd say. "The two things that keep me going."

I assumed he was talking about me and his surfboard. He wasn't. Though I didn't realize it until after we were married.

"Alcohol helps me relax," Rob used to say. So I'd make sure he had plenty of it when he got home from the store. It was the least I could do, especially since I left my teaching job to raise Jenny. He worked so hard for us. But the odd thing was, he seemed more relaxed before he drank. After, he'd become angry, impatient, critical, mean.

I'd tell myself that that wasn't Rob. It was the

alcohol. If it was Rob he would have woken up the next morning and known why I was covered in bruises. He would have known why the trash can was filled with broken china. He would have known why my lip was swollen or why our daughter was scared to be in the room with him. He would have known. And he didn't.

So I blamed Johnnie Walker for those things and Johnnie Walker blamed me. "If you could make Jenny stop crying I wouldn't be so angry," Johnnie would say. "If I didn't have to work all day to support you I wouldn't be stressed." And when he got that speeding ticket, which led to a Breathalyzer test and a DWI, somehowit was my fault again. . . .

I apologized because Rob was my husband. I placed him on a pedestal and wanted him to stay there. Because if he fell off, who would I look up to?

I apologized because if it was my fault I could work hard, just like I always did, and make things right. But if Rob was the one who needed changing, then everything would stay the same. And I couldn't live with that.

I apologized because I was afraid of what would happen to me and Jenny if I didn't.

After every "incident" the girls would ask how much more I would put up with. I never had an answer. I didn't know. I didn't think I had a choice. Rob was addicted to alcohol, and I was addicted to Rob's potential. I believed he would return to being the sweet boy I met in 1961, just as soon as I stopped making him so angry.

I clung to my belief the same way that Anastasia clung to hers. The idea that love and patience were enough to rid Christian of his vices and turn him into

the man that he wasn't—the man she wanted him to be—was
just as naive.

August 14, 1982, was the day I stopped being
naive.

I was home in bed with a terrible stomach flu and
needed Rob to get Jenny and her friend from their tap
lesson. He said he would and I was relieved—maybe he
wasn't so terrible, I thought, and I drifted off to
sleep. Thirty minutes later I was woken up by a phone
call from Gloria. She had been at the grocery store and
saw Rob stumbling to his car. He looked blitzed and she
wanted to make sure he arrived home safely.

I thought of Candy Lightner, the founder of Mothers
Against Drunk Driving and how her thirteen-year-old
daughter was killed by a drunk driver. Jenny was also
thirteen. In a swirl of nausea and panic I gave the
police an anonymous tip.

Rob had driven three blocks with the girls before he
was arrested and charged with blowing five times over
the legal limit and two counts of child endangerment.
He was sent to jail for thirty days.

When Rob returned home he found a Tupperware full
of my tears and a note that said Jenny and I would not
move back into the house until he was sober. The choice
was his: Dotty or Johnnie?

Five days later, Jenny and I were back home, but
not because Rob stopped drinking. He drove through
the window of Crawford & Sons, split his head open
on the steering wheel, and died instantly. Rob chose
Johnnie.

Once again, I blamed myself: It was my fault for
moving out. My fault for not being good enough to fix
him. My fault Jenny would grow up without a father. It

was years before I realized that there wasn't anything
I could have done. That there were things in this world
that Dotty Snip couldn't control. And Rob Crawford had
been one of them.

I, like Ana, was seduced by the soft licks of hope
into believing that I could change the man I loved.
Then flogged by whip-sharp reminders that I couldn't.
So, like Anastasia, I turned myself over to grief and
eventually came to accept that the only person I *can*
change is myself. At which point, I got the help I
needed, learned how to cut the ties that bound me to
guilt, and set myself free.

Shit happens is life's dominant; *wishful thinkers*,
its submissive. And happy endings? Well, they don't
come until we accept the sad ones. And so, Anastasia,
with the help of this club, I did.

—Dotty Snip Crawford

"GOD." ADDIE SIGHED. "I knew Uncle Rob liked his whiskey, but I
had no idea he was an Abe."

"Abe?" M.J. asked.

"Abe User," she said. "It's what we, at the old women's clinic, call
a wife beater."

Jules blew her nose. The solemn peal, like reveille from a bugle,
drew M.J.'s thoughts away from Dotty and placed her back in the
Oyster Bar.

"Poor Dotty." Jules sniffled. Tears stumbled drunkenly down her
cheeks. "She really loved him."

"That wasn't love," Addie stated, as if a parquetry of Harvard degrees decorated the walls behind her. "How could she love a man who popped her in the lip every time the baby cried? It's not possible."

"Then why did she stay?" Jules pressed.

"Pity, fear, denial, maybe a bit of Stockholm syndrome. You know, he breaks up the abuse with bits of kindness to give her hope that he'll change. But hoping that someone will change is a red, heart-shaped herring, there to distract romantics from the truth. It's what we in the biz call 'trauma bonding.' Trust me. I see it all the time." She punctuated her statement with a swift shot of vodka.

Britt and Jules watched Addie slam down her glass with wide-eyed fascination. Like M.J., they were probably struck by the unexpected reach of her knowledge. How many men, if any, saw this side of her? How many knew that front, back, and doggy style weren't the only points of view Addie Oliver had to offer?

"And for the record, Anastasia doesn't love Christian, either. She was seduced by his power."

"Too far!" Britt announced.

Jules nodded in agreement.

Addie poured herself another shot. "Do you honestly think she'll be melting over Christian's 'gray gaze' when he's sixty-five, bald, and chasing her around the apartment with a riding crop and a leaky colostomy bag? No! She'll shackle him to the radiator and Facebook the nice guy . . . oh, what was his name . . . ?" She rolled her wrist as if invoking a sneeze. "José!"

"You read the book!" Jules cried.

"More like skimmed."

"That's so depressing," Britt said.

"Well, it shouldn't be. I told you I'm not much of a reader."

"No, the visual of Christian chasing Ana around with a leaky colostomy bag and a whip."

"Only because it's true," Addie said. "Love is accepting someone for who they are, not who they'll be once you change them. Because guys won't change unless they want to, and most of them don't want to. If you think otherwise, you're in for a shit-storm of disappointment."

M.J. thought of her struggle with Dan. How she admires his white knight complex, benefits from it even, and at the same time resents it and, at times, wishes it away. Did that mean she didn't accept him? Because she did. She loved Dan whether it suited her or not. She couldn't help it. Love was impervious to logic, uncontrollable as the weather. "Feelings don't make sense, Addie. We can't decide who to love."

"And people do change," Britt insisted. "We grow up and do all kinds of things we never thought we'd do when we were younger. Take those twenty-year-olds at my gym who say they'll never get boob jobs. They can't picture themselves with ape tits any more than I could picture myself cheating on Paul, and then next thing you know—"

Jules's breath hitched. "You cheated on Paul?"

Britt froze, stunned by her accidental admission.

With a toss of her hair, Addie leaned forward. "Tell us everything, don't leave one thing out. Start with ten minutes before it happened. Back when you were still innocent."

Britt evaluated the three women staring expectantly at her. After a moment of grave consideration she reached for the plate of bruschetta. "I'm not going to tell you anything until you jam an entire piece of this toast in your mouth."

They exchanged glances and then did what they were asked. As M.J. suspected, Britt waited for them to gag, then said, "That's the feeling I want you to have every time you even *think* about repeating what I'm going to say."

Chewing, they agreed.

"Do you love him?" Jules asked when Britt finished her story.

"Who, the Brazilian?" Britt answered.

"He's Brazilian?" Addie asked, impressed.

"No," Britt said. "Just bald."

"Do you love him?" Jules asked again, now gripping the arms of the rattan chair bracing herself for what was sure to be a disappointing response: If Britt said yes, Jules's heart would break for Paul. If no, it would bleed for the premature death of a fairy tale—a romance that never made it to term.

"I love my husband," Britt said. "And I want to stay married, but I think he's—"

"Not what you *hoped* for?" Addie asked smugly.

Britt cut a look to M.J., a plea for guidance. *Do I tell them about Paul's affair or not?* To which M.J. mouthed back, "Wait." There was no sense in riling everyone up until they were sure.

"How's the sex?" Addie asked.

"With Paul?"

"No, the Brazilian."

Britt grinned. "Toe-curling."

Jules giggled. "Toe-curling?"

"You know." Britt hugged her knees to her chest. "The way it probably was when you started dating Brandon."

Jules's Tweety Bird–blue eyes blink-blinked. M.J. could almost hear a cartoon's high-pitched piano notes.

"You *have* had sex before, right?" Britt teased.

"Um, I have a daughter, remember?"

Addie snorted. "So you've only done it once?"

"Of course not, silly, but I—" She leaned forward and whispered, "I have a shy vagina. So it's never been like . . . you know, the way it is with Anastasia and Christian. I mean, is that whole thing even realistic?"

"What whole *thing*?" Addie laughed.

"The orgasm thing. It's so easy for her. That doesn't happen to real people, does it?"

"Definitely not in the bath," M.J. said.

"Yeah, I'm calling bullshit on the bath orgasms," Britt agreed. "All that sloshing and jabbing makes me feel like a plunged toilet."

"Then you're doing something wrong," Addie said.

"You can come in the water?" Britt asked.

"How hard can it be?" Addie said. Then, with another toss of her hair, "David used to say I could come from a hiccup."

"What ever happened with you two?" M.J. asked. He was the only guy Addie ever seemed to reference. The only one who seemed to last longer than a holiday weekend.

"Gloria happened. She thought we were a bad influence on each other and did whatever she could to keep us apart. But I didn't care. I wasn't out to change David, and he wasn't out to change me. We liked each other exactly as we were—genital warts and all. The only reason we're apart now is because he got a job coaching a high school snowboarding team in Colorado and I don't do puffy outerwear or long-distance relationships. But if he lived here . . ."

"Well, then, you must be excited about the news," Britt said.

Addie pinched a lone tomato chunk off the bruschetta plate and dropped it in her mouth. "News?"

"About David. He didn't tell you?"

"Tell me what?"

"Gloria took her house off the market. David is moving in on Friday."

Addie checked her phone as if expecting to find a flurry of missed messages and plausible explanations as to why she was just finding this out now. After a moment she looked up, her face lit frostbite-blue from the screen and said, "That little fucker! He's going to surprise me." Then, with a one-two slap of her palms, "Are we done here?"

"What's the rush?" Britt asked.

She aimed her cleavage at Bungee who was signing his tab. "He's leaving," Addie said as if it should have been obvious. "He looks a little dirty, don'cha think?" She stood and smoothed her dress. "I think we could both use a bath."

"What about the closing ritual?" M.J. asked, once again.

"And our next book," Britt added. "It's *Henry and June*, right? I have the letter. It's from Liddy. Not that I read it. It slipped out of the sleeve when I was unpacking the box and I might have seen a few sentences, something about her getting kicked out of the DBC. But that's it." She raised her right hand. "Swear."

The music suddenly became louder and the hostess flashed Jules a terse nod. She held up her hand—*Five minutes*. Long enough for them to charm four cigarettes off the bartender and complete the closing ritual before they were told to snub them out.

"Now what?" M.J. practically whined after Addie took off. She didn't want to trade this warm, giddy feeling for the sound of CNN on the TV or the soft whistle of Dan's nose as he slept. "Should we hit the restaurant for a nightcap?"

"It's packed on a Friday night." Jules pouted. "But I'm pretty sure my villa has a minibar."

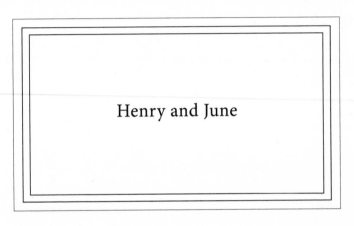

Henry and June

CHAPTER

Sixteen

FIRST A SWIFT metallic *swoosh*, then daylight. Aggressive, aggressive daylight. M.J. splayed her palms into the mattress—whose mattress was another matter entirely—and pushed herself upright; a cascade of miniature liquor bottles rolled toward her thigh and settled with a collective clink. It was too soon for upright. The nausea was so unbelievably disorienting. Through a squint that was framed by a headache, M.J. saw a backlit figure of what appeared to be a sickly, possibly mentally ill woman: fuzzy socks, robe limply tied, and hair in cornrows. Behind her, the parted curtains swayed to a stop.

"Jules?"

A whimper.

"God, you look as bad as I feel."

"How many Claritin did I take last night?"

M.J. leg-swept the miniature bottles onto the floor. "I don't think it was the Claritin."

"Shoot," Jules said, in a whisper. "I'm not supposed to take antihistamines with a cocktail."

"You didn't take it with a cocktail." M.J. flipped her pillow to the cold side. "You took it with an entire minibar."

Jules's breath hitched. "Did you hear that?" She cocked her head and froze. A deer after the *chik-chik* of a hunter's rifle. "It's Destiny! She can't see me like this." She hurried for the bathroom. "Can you let her in?"

"I'm not sure," M.J. said to the room service cart that was lodged in the bedroom doorway. Silver trays were stacked high but unevenly. It was a carpet-cleaning fee waiting to happen. M.J. summoned her strength, which was none, and shoved.

The cart didn't budge, but the tray tower collapsed and toppled. A dirty bomb of syrup-soaked pancakes, french fries, bacon bits, and shrimp tails spilled onto the cream-colored rug. Over was the only way out.

Shielding her eyes from the brain-biting sun, M.J. opened the door to find not Destiny, but Addie, in an ivory dress and pigtails, radiating youth and innocence. The whites of her eyes were actually white and her forehead dewy with hydration.

"Did you ride that here?" M.J. asked, glimpsing the skateboard pinned beneath Addie's high-top sneaker.

"I'm low on gas." She handed a grocery bag to M.J.

"What's this?"

"Hangover helpers."

M.J. peeked inside and found a glorious assortment of bagels and artisan cream cheeses. "Carbs! How did you know?"

"There were messages."

"Oh no."

"Oh yes. You wanted to know if Bungee was in my bathtub, if

we were having sex in my bathtub, and if I came in my bathtub. Then you all sang 'Aqua-*come*' to the tune of 'Aqualung' and laughed for, like, fifteen minutes. Alcohol was obvious, the hangover implied."

"Are you sure it was me?" M.J. asked. Not because she was incapable of blowing up someone's phone with drunk messages and goofy bastardized songs. She had done it hundreds of times in college. But that was college. And this was now.

Nodding a mighty yes, Addie flashed her phone log. There were eight missed voice mails from NYC Ninja.

"NYC Ninja? That's what you call me?"

"Only behind your back. Skinny New York Chick Who Dresses Like She Works at the Morgue was too wordy. God, it smells like a beer burp in here." Addie eyed M.J.'s lavender nightie upon which was one very coy looking Minnie Mouse sniffing a bouquet of tulips. "What's that about?"

M.J. glanced down. "I have no idea."

"Hey, Sweet Child," Jules chirped. She dislodged the room service cart and breezed past the spilled food, coral caftan billowing around her calves, floppy hat shading her face.

"Stand down," M.J. said. "It's just Addie."

"Oh." Jules removed the hat. "Make yourself at home," she said, then shuffled back into the bedroom.

"What's up with your hair? Are those cornrows?" Addie asked as she followed Jules with the self-righteous prance of someone who hadn't pickled her kidneys. "Who did that to you?"

"M.J."

"Well, can she undo it?"

Jules starfished onto the bed. "Decapitate me. It's easier."

Addie cast a sweeping glance around the room. "Where's Britt?"

"Probably at home," M.J. said. "Why?"

"She has the deed to the bookstore. Will you call her for me? The speaker on my phone is waterlogged. It got wet during the bathtub challenge." Addie's lips curled into a wicked smile. "So did I."

Jules lifted her head. "Does that mean you . . . ?"

"It means if Easton calls me 'boss' one more time my nipples will invert. I need to send that deed back to France and be done with this nightmare. Then we can talk about the bath."

M.J. found her phone under the bed along with four missed calls from Dan and a chain of texts, none of which she remembered.

DAN: Hospital fire in Boston. If ur near a TV turn it on. Might be terrorism.

DAN: Not terrorism. It was electrical. Oxygen from tanks and incubators made it worse.

DAN: Evacuating. Terrible.

DAN: Answer ur phone.

DAN: U still at the beach club?

DAN: Are u getting these?

DAN: Why aren't u picking up? Should I be worried?

DAN: OFFICIALLY WORRIED.

M.J.: Hey, s'me. Ha, my font just slurred.

DAN: Where are u?

M.J.: Majestic. In Jules' room with bro.

M.J.: I mean bro.

M.J.: I mean Britt.

M.J.: Duck I hate auto-correct.

M.J.: DUCK!

M.J.: I mean fuck! This phone keeps iJacking my texts.

M.J.: iJacking instead of hijacking cuz it's an iPhone. Get it?

DAN: When will u be home? I have to talk to u about something.

M.J.: Minnie mouse is a lesbian.

DAN: U wasted?

M.J.: Wayyyy-stud!

M.J.: Ha! Way-stud. You're a way-stud. Get it?

DAN: What are u drinking?

M.J.: More.

"Shit," M.J. said. "I have to go."

"Not yet!" Addie snatched the phone and called Britt, anxiously twirling a finger around one of her pigtails while she waited for the call to connect. Once it did, they heard the soft strum of a harp. It was coming from under the sheets.

It strummed again.

Then again.

Jules pulled back the duvet to find Britt with half a head of cornrows, a brown M&M stuck to her collarbone, and the phone resting on her cheekbone.

"You're *here*?"

"No." Britt pulled the duvet back over her head just as Destiny appeared in the bedroom doorway. She was dressed in denim cutoffs, a black mesh tank, and devil-red sneakers that maintained a safe distance from the scattered food. "What's going on, Mom? Why do you look like Stevie Wonder?" She cut a look to M.J. and Addie. "Who are *they*?"

"I left a window open last night and the raccoons got in. My friends offered to help me tidy up. Destiny, I'd like you to meet—"

"You have friends?"

Jules giggled. "'Course I do, silly. Now tell me, how was Oceanside? How's Daddy?"

Destiny's upturned nose crinkled. "You don't know how your own husband is?"

"Of course *I* know. What I meant was how was he with *you*? Did you have fun?"

"Yeah, Mom, we raged." Her gaze lifted toward the three pairs of underwear hanging from the blades of the ceiling fan. "Not as much as those raccoons, though."

Jules managed a tight-lipped smile. "Are you working the reservation desk today or the Kids Club?"

"I gave my shift to Krista."

"Why?"

"Chest has the day off so we're gonna hang."

"*Chest?* Who's Chest?"

"My boyfriend."

"I thought you were seeing Alex from back home." She brought a hand to her heart. "Did you two break up?"

"No, we just call him Chest because he never wears shirts."

Addie snickered.

Jules lowered onto the edge of the bed. "So where will you and Alex be *hanging*?"

"Around."

"And what will you be wearing?"

"This."

"You're just pickin', right?"

"No."

"Destiny, honey, you're going to get old *and* new monia dressed like that. How about a pair of jeans and that cute white top from Brandy Melville?"

In a glyph of teenage impatience, Destiny rolled her heavily lined eyes toward the heavens, as if God was the only one who could possibly understand the extent of her intolerable existence. "I have to go."

"Keep your phone on and please be home by five." Jules stood and pulled her daughter in for a hug. "Actually, home by three would be better, you know, before it starts getting dark." Destiny stiffened, arms hanging limply by her side. "And make good choices."

"I'm not going to an orgy, Mom."

"That's unfortunate," Addie mumbled.

"Addie!" Jules snapped.

"You're *Addie*?" Destiny stepped into the room. "Addie Oliver?"

"Guilty."

"You *know* her?"

Destiny ignored her mother's question and introduced herself. "Some girls at the beach were talking about you the other day."

"All bad stuff, I hope," Addie said.

"They said you showed them how to—" Destiny widened her eyes, goading Addie to read her mind.

"Surf?" Addie guessed.

Destiny shook her head.

"Skateboard?"

Another shake.

"Make Botox?"

"No! How to use a—" She lifted her index finger and made a buzzing sound.

"Vibrator!" Addie called, a charades player with the winning answer.

"Yes."

"*What?*" Jules yelped.

"It must have been Laura and Amy," said Addie.

"No."

"Mary-Elizabeth and Stephanie?"

"It was Jenn and Camille."

"Right, I remember them. They stopped by the women's clinic last week for—" Addie stopped herself. "Actually, I can't tell you why they were there, that would be unethical. But, yes, I did teach them how to use a vibrator."

Jules's nostrils flared. "And that's *not* unethical?"

"I didn't demonstrate! I hooked them up with a gift bag and a couple of Duracells. It was nothing. Know your own body before you share it with someone else, I always say."

"Why?" Jules asked.

"Why, what?"

"Why do you always say that?"

"Because young girls need to take control of their sexuality. Especially, when they're coming into the clinic asking for birth control." Addie slapped a hand over her mouth. "Shit! You didn't hear that." Then to Destiny, "I can put a package together for you if you want."

Jules wedged herself in the narrow space between them. "My daughter does not need a *package*."

"She's right," Destiny said. "Mom's the one who needs the package. At least until Dad moves up here, which will probably be never." With that she turned on the heel of her red sneaker, leaving Jules to vomit on the Majestic's fine linens—a mortifying embarrassment that she would later tell Housekeeping was the unfortunate result of the stomach flu. Destiny's, of course.

———————

"HUNDREDS OF SCENARIOS went through my head last night when I was trying to get in touch with you," Dan said, when M.J. staggered into the cottage. "And Disneyland was none of them."

It took a moment for M.J. to realize that he was referring to Jules's Minnie Mouse nightgown, which she was still wearing. She would have explained that putting on leather leggings while hungover was like forcing a twin sheet on a California king. On a boat. During a category four hurricane. But that required speaking, and her headache demanded silence. So M.J. didn't ask about the khaki duffel bag by the front door. Instead, she would spoon the couch pillows and wait for Dan to shed some light (dim, please!) on what appeared to be some sort of exit strategy, minus the strategy.

"I wanted to talk to you about it first, but . . . ," he said, lifting himself to sit on the kitchen counter.

She needed him beside her so she could sniff his coconut-scented skin like smelling salts, enmesh herself in the ropy muscles of his arms, let him do the breathing for them both. But Dan's heels, which were knocking against one of the cabinets, were too restless to spoon.

"I have to go to Boston for six days. Seven, max."

Shock propelled M.J. upright. "Boston? Why?" There was a high-pitched quiver to her voice. She needed water. She needed central air-conditioning. She needed this to not be happening. Not again. "Are you leaving because I didn't come home last night?"

"No. I'm leaving because of the hospital fire. Makeshift wards are being built all over Boston and the Red Cross needs experienced volunteers to set them up."

"Like hospital pop-up shops?" M.J. peeped, though she wasn't sure why. Neither of them seemed amenable to cutesy comments, least of all her.

"A guy from the team I worked with in Jakarta asked if I could help."

"Of course he did."

Dan slid off the countertop, opened the fridge. "What's that supposed to mean?"

"It means you say yes to everyone." M.J. bit the insides of her cheeks. "Except me."

"Are you implying that I'm not here for you?"

"No, Dan, I'm stating it quite directly," she wanted to say but didn't dare. Not while Dan was glaring at her with such narrow-eyed contempt, a glare so chilling it literally made her shiver. Not a single ember of amusement warmed his face. This time, for the first time, M.J. had gone too far.

She should have apologized, blamed her snark on the hangover, erased his memory with a mind-numbing blow job. But the four chambers in her heart were pumping pistons, loosening the dormant feelings that had been calcifying inside her for months. "You tricked me."

"*Tricked* you?"

"You sold me on a life that doesn't exist." She watched him twist the top off a beer and toss the cap in the sink even though he knew caps went in the trash. "I moved here so we could be together and you've been gone ever since." She was crying now. Leaking tears and snot and all the selfish sentiments she wished she didn't have. "I want to be supportive, I really do. I know these people need you, and I admire you for wanting to help, but I gave up my career for you and—"

Dan slammed the bottle on the countertop. "Seriously?"

Unable to meet his eyes, M.J. watched the wedding bands on her thumb blur and distort through her pooling tears.

"You gave up your career for *me*? That's not what happened, M.J., not even close." He was pacing now, traversing the kitchen floor like an animal trapped. "I was your rebound, remember? The one you ran to after Gayle broke your heart. I wasn't your first choice. *City* was. But I never let that bother me. Why? Because you're *my* first choice and I'm happy to be with you any way I can."

"Said the guy who keeps bailing on me," she mumbled, still to her blurring rings.

"I'm not bailing on you, M.J., I'm doing my job."

"You don't work for the Red Cross, Dan."

"And you don't *work*, period! It's like you're purposely trying to not make a life for yourself here. Like you're . . ." He ran a hand through his damp hair, spiking it into dark brown hackles. "Most of your things are still in New York and you've made no effort to get them. Are you having second thoughts? Is that it?"

A fly landed on M.J.'s knee. She banished it with a spiteful swipe. "Dan, you're the one who keeps leaving, not me."

He hung his head and exhaled. Then, calmer, said, "You were fine with all my *leaving* when you lived in New York."

M.J. searched for a suitable response. But Dan was right. She was fine with it. Or rather, she had been too busy to notice.

"You used to love how we gave each other space to pursue our goals. That we weren't needy or possessive. And now . . ." He stopped when he saw her fresh spill of tears and sat beside her. His expression was softer, his touch warm and sincere. "M.J., if you think I'm doing this because I'm not committed to you, you're wrong."

"Well, you seem to be chomping at the bit to get away," M.J. muttered.

"Champing."

"What?"

"It's *champing* at the bit, not chomping."

"No, it's not."

"Yes, it is."

"It is not."

M.J. dried her cheeks on Minnie Mouse, then rested a hand on Dan's wrist. Come sunset that wrist will be gone. "Wanna bet?"

"Sure," Dan said, embers and sparks returning to his face. "What are the stakes?"

"If you're right, you have my blessing to go to Boston."

"And if I'm not?"

"You stay."

They agreed with a firm handshake, drew their phones, and woke their search engines.

Dan's lips moved as he read the results. "Shit."

"Yes!" M.J. trumpeted, hangover be dammed. Of course she felt guilty taking Dan away from the displaced patients of Massachusetts General. She wasn't a monster. But the Red Cross could replace Dan, M.J. could not. "Unpack your rucksack, Dr. Hartwell. Because Bost-on is Bost-off."

He lowered his phone. "Are you sure you want to do this?"

"Of course I'm sure." She beamed. "They'll find another volunteer."

"No, are you sure you want to do *that*," he pointed at her bicycling legs.

"You mean celebrate?"

"I mean gloat." Dan practically pressed his screen against M.J.'s nose.

She scanned four pages of search results before conceding. And when she did she felt as if her bones had liquefied and her soul had been swept away by the current. Not only because she was forced to say good-bye to Dan—again. But because she had said good-bye to her former self at the same time. The self that knew its way around the English language better than most, definitely better than Dan.

In the weeks that she had been in Pearl Beach M.J. had lost her confidence, her sense of purpose, and now this bet. Though she hadn't gotten her period in months, she was bleeding out. And only one thing could stop it.

After Dan left, she yanked the restaurant delivery list from their junk drawer, ordered a buffet amount of Chinese food, and hate-ate her way into a decision: she would sign the contract and overnight it to Gayle. Because if home is where the heart is, and that heart is gone most of the time, the mind was all M.J. had left. And that would be gone by Thanksgiving if she didn't get back to work.

THE FIRST FEW times her phone beeped, M.J. was able to ignore it. Because when one combines a tearful good-bye and a generous intake of MSG, to an already existing hangover, the nap is death-deep. But the beeping continued and it was relentless.

Groggy, M.J. sat up on the couch and checked her text messages.

ADDIE: 911 @ the bookstore. Pls come.

BRITT: Did u see Addie's txt? Heading to the bookstore now. Need a ride? I still have the Mini, remember?

ADDIE: Where r u?

BRITT: Last chance for a ride.
BRITT: Leaving now. Maybe ur not going. J isn't. She's still pissed at Addie for offering D a vibrator.
BRITT: Maybe you're already there. K. Bye.

M.J. shouldered her way through the wall of gawkers to find a blue-collar ballet of first responders: police officers cordoning off the storefront with caution tape, a fireman climbing toward Addie's bedroom window, the man in the Doyle Plumbing shirt at the foot of his ladder with the low ponytail, hand-over-fisting him a giant blue hose.

Addie, as if posing for an album cover, was leaning against the building—sole of her sneaker pressed against the black brick facade, arms folded and hair coaxed into a come-hither tousle. And Britt was dutifully by her side cupping a venti whatever it was.

"You're still wearing that nightgown?" Britt said as M.J. hurried toward them, the heels of her Gucci clogs clunking against the sidewalk.

"I thought it was an emergency."

Addie pushed herself away from the wall. "It is," she said, lifting the caution tape and waving Britt and M.J. under.

"Ma'am, it's not safe in there," called one of Pearl Beach's finest.

"We'll only be a minute, officer."

"Hold up!" Jules called as she scuttled toward them, her key necklace knocking against her chest.

The afternoon sun revealed no sign of the previous night's damage. Her cheeks had been blushed to a rosy rebirth, the merlot-colored puffs under her eyes drained and concealed. Even her hair, now cornrow-free and curling-iron-kissed had been restored to its original factory settings. "Just because I'm here doesn't mean I forgive you for being vulgar in front of my daughter."

Addie reached under the caution tape and yanked Jules toward her. "I'm fine with that."

"Ma'am!"

"We're just grabbing our purses, officer, we'll be right back."

He cut a look to the tote hanging from the crook of Britt's elbow, the cross-body bag at M.J.'s hip, the clutch tucked under Jules's arm. "I'm sorry, ladies, but I was told not to—"

"Thanks." Addie beamed as she shoved the girls inside and locked the door behind her.

"Where are the lights?" M.J. asked.

"Um, electricity might not be the best idea right now," Britt said, pointing at the buckling ceiling, where water leaked in incontinent dribbles and the bookmarks, once stiff and robust, now coiled in shame. And that smell—wet dog and chemicals—it was as if the walls were sweating out the toxins.

"What in the ham sandwich happened?" Jules asked.

"The bathtub challenge, that's what," Addie said. "I never would have brought Bungee back to my apartment if you hadn't—"

"Bullshit," Britt rasped.

"Fine, but we wouldn't have taken a bath together."

"Bullshit again."

"Okay, but I wouldn't have tried to aqua-come. I would've moved to dry land for that." Addie lifted her sundress and revealed her bruised kneecaps. "Bone meet porcelain, porcelain meet bone. I had to down half a bottle of Macallan to dull the pain."

"Ah-ha! So you admit it, then."

"Admit what, Jules?"

"That it's impossible to, you know, in the bath."

"Not when you run the warm water and spread your legs under the faucet."

Jules examined the tips of her hair as if checking for dead ends. "Is that a thing?"

Everyone nodded.

"Did it work?"

"No," Addie said. "But only because I passed out."

"And Bungee?"

"No clue. When I came to he was gone and my bathroom was flooded, so I went to buy bagels."

"You just left it like that?" M.J. asked, realizing that Addie must have known about the deluge when she had stopped by Jules's earlier that morning.

"No, I didn't leave it like that. I opened the windows so it would evaporate." Above them a water pump began to rattle. Bookmarks fell from the ceiling like soggy autumn leaves.

Britt, Jules, and M.J. exchanged a worried glance.

"Will you help me tarp the shelves before the books get ruined?" She held her hands together in prayer. "Please?"

"If you promise to quit having irresponsible conversations with my daughter."

"Masturbation is not irresponsible, Jules."

"Oh, really?" She stabbed her index finger toward the sagging ceiling. "Then how do you explain that?"

Addie managed a clench-toothed smile. "Fine, I'm sorry, okay? I was only trying to help."

"Help?"

"These girls need someone to talk to. Someone they can trust. And I can be that person."

"Why? Because you have a daughter?"

"No, Jules, because I don't. Not to mention I work in a women's clinic. And every day our waiting room is full of daughters. Daughters hiding under the hoods of high school sweatshirts begging our receptionist to get them in to see a pregnancy counselor before their lunch period is over so they're not late for class."

"Well, please leave my Destiny out of it, okay?" Jules released a cleansing sigh and then twisted her hair into a low chignon. "Now let's get to work, shall we? I didn't cancel a meeting so I could stand around and look pretty did I?" She giggled. "I'm just playing. I mean, I did cancel a meeting, but I don't think I look very pretty." She glanced toward the door marked HOLY WATER. "Hey, is Easton around? I'm sure he'd be a big help."

"I told him to take the week off because the building was being sprayed for termites. If that busybody finds out this was my fault, Liddy will find out. And if Liddy finds out she'll make me pay for the damage, and if I have to pay for the damage I won't be able to go on my trip, and if I don't get out of this town I'll die and haunt you for—"

The rattling water pump stopped.

Then, a new sound, like the crack of a tree branch before it breaks.

"Look!" Jules indicated the bulge overhead. "The ceiling is pregnant."

"More like crowning," Britt said.

There was a distant rumble, like thunder, and then—

"Run!" Britt shouted as Addie's bathtub—a five-foot, claw-footed mass—fell from her apartment and crushed the Pride aisle to dust.

CHAPTER

Seventeen

"TWENTY-EIGHT," M.J. COUNTED. She had checked her in-box twenty-eight times that morning and, still, no word from Gayle. The contract arrived in New York yesterday and, according to the shameless call she made to the mailroom, Gayle had signed for it herself. So where was the celebratory phone call, the welcome-back fruit basket, the company-wide announcement that their beloved M.J. would be returning to *City* magazine in September as editor in chief? Fine, coeditor in chief, but still, a little acknowledgment, please. Unless Gayle had sent the e-mail to M.J.'s old work account and not her Gmail address. "Twenty-nine. . . ."

The doorbell rang.

M.J. answered to find Addie—hair big and makeup bold—wearing a tight white lab coat and pink Crocs. She looked more like a porn star pedaling nurse fantasies than a pregnancy consultant on her way to work.

"I need some advice."

"Is it about those shoes?" M.J. teased.

"Shoes?" Addie said as she peered at the Goldens' house.

"Oh, I see what's happening here," M.J. said, suddenly realizing, "You don't want advice. You're here to stalk Da—"

Addie slapped a hand over M.J.'s mouth. "Shhh!"

"Relax. He hasn't moved in yet."

Addie lowered her hand. "I thought Britt said Friday."

"She did. But it's only eight thirty," M.J. said, tempted to lecture her on "playing it real," but she was hardly qualified. So she invited her in for tap water instead.

"I'd prefer a frittata if you have one," Addie said. "My anorexic friend Loo's apartment is a bad place to wake up if you don't like mustard for breakfast."

"I have five beers, half a bottle of prosecco, a burnt bagel, and some leftover Chinese food."

"Don't you eat?"

"Not when I'm stressed, which is most of the time."

"So . . . the Chinese food?"

"All yours."

M.J. led her into the kitchen, where Addie helped herself to the take-out box, sniffed the corpse-colored dumplings, and then re-turned it to the empty rack. "Wear a hazmat suit when you toss those."

"So do you really need advice or was that the stalk talking?"

"Mostly the stalk," Addie admitted. "I mean, I am asking my boss, Lara, for an advance today so I can fix the ceiling before Liddy finds out. But I don't really need advice. That woman will do any-thing to get me into bed."

"She's gay?"

"No." Addie reached for the burnt bagel, took a bite. "But she is human."

HUMAN.

The word, though not particularly lyrical, sang in M.J.'s mind long after Addie left for work. It split into syllables—*hu-man, hu-man, hu-man*—that scored her footsteps as she walked to the coffee shop and claimed the corner table. It remained through two refills and an hour of reading her *Prim*-covered copy of *Henry and June*. But it wasn't until she came upon the phrase *white-heat living*, that M.J. understood why.

Though written by Anaïs Nin to describe the kind of intensity one finds in lovers and mistresses, M.J. got that charge from Addie's visit. The unexpected break in routine stirred her senses, woke her to her surroundings, and made her feel human again. It reminded her that she could be a friend's destination. And that she, like the French author, used to journal about those feelings, too.

M.J. took a note card out of her purse and wrote, "Of Anaïs's many relationships, the most intimate was with her journals. Privy to the full extent of her struggles, passions, and longings, they were her most trusted confidants. They were white-hot truth, unaffected by the opinions of lovers, purely her."

Then she considered the Moleskine journal Dan had given her. The pencil. The thoughts that circled her head like airplanes in a holding pattern, waiting for a place to land. Unlike M.J.'s more creative days, those airplanes weren't transporting story ideas, compelling characters, quippy one-liners, or middle-of-the-night revelations. They were carrying fear. Fear of being alone, fear of the unknown, fear of disappointment, fear that at thirty-four years old, her best days were behind her, and now fear that her journals will never measure up to Anaïs's, so why bother?

"They're not supposed to measure up," Dr. Cohn told her on the phone during her walk back to the cottage. Though he didn't dare say it, M.J. could tell by the vim in his voice that he found delight in the unexpected topic of this week's long-distance session. *At least she's thinking about writing*, she imagined him noting. "Journals are dumping grounds for embarrassing thoughts and first-grade grammar. They're not supposed to be art. They're supposed to help you sort through the sludge so you can get to the good stuff. Don't let Anaïs take a crap on that."

With a smile, M.J. promised to get started the moment she got home—Anaïs and her white-hot writing be damned!

But Addie was there when she returned; lying on the porch swing, pink Crocs kicked to the curb.

"What are you doing back here?"

Addie sat up. Her eyes were swollen and red. "Do you still have those beers?"

"I do," M.J. said. "Want one?"

"No. I want three."

M.J. reappeared with the beer, some flat prosecco, and her Moleskine. Not that she had any intention of writing while Addie was there; she simply wanted the journal nearby so they could bond.

"Are we celebrating?" M.J. asked, sitting. The swing dropped like a hot testicle.

"I knew I put on weight."

"It always happens with two people," M.J. lied, because though she had sat on it many times, it had always been alone. "Did you ask for the advance from your boss?"

"Yep."

"And did she bite?"

"Oh, she bit all right. Sank her adult braces right into my head and ripped it off."

"She got mad at you?"

"Yep."

"Why?"

Addie peeled the label off the bottle, rolled the foil paper between her fingers. "Because I was doing my job."

"Meaning?"

"Knocked up, Samantha?" Addie said, earnest as a 1950s public service announcement. "Abortion is a very serious decision. Would you ever consider keeping the baby? No? Well, there are thousands of loving couples in this country looking to adopt. These pamphlets will help you understand the process. Is there a grown-up you trust? Someone to support you during this process? No? Well, you can trust me. I'll be your grown-up. I'll support you." She took a sip of beer. "That was my job. Lara gave me a script and I delivered it."

"So what was the problem?"

"After I delivered Lara's script, I'd deliver my own."

"Which was?"

"Sexual urges are perfectly natural, Samantha, and masturbation is the safest way to explore them. You can't get an STD, you won't get pregnant, and you'll never feel pressured or used. And the best part? You'll have an orgasm. Then, I'd give her a vibrator and make her promise not to let another guy in her pants until it was the right guy. Someone who made her feel *better* than the vibrator. . . ."

While Addie talked, M.J. took in the high pitch of her cheek-bones, the full lips that looked puckered but weren't, and those curves. Her sex appeal was undeniable. It was the skeleton key to every locked door that stood in her way. But to understand Addie was to know that she'd rather open those doors with an impassioned kick than a key; that she only used the key when a kick didn't work.

"Anyway, some of the moms found out about my little giveaways and threatened to picket the clinic if I wasn't let go, and Lara did what any spineless script follower would do and fired me." Addie shrugged like it was no big deal. Then gave way to her tears because it was.

"Why didn't Lara defend you? It's her clinic. She obviously knew about the vibrators," M.J. said, suddenly outraged. Mostly for Addie, but for herself, too, because where the hell was Gayle? It was five o'clock on the east coast, why hadn't she acknowledged the signed contract? "Screw these bosses with their team-building retreats and trust-fall exercises. They're supposed to have their employees' backs and catch us when we're going down. Instead, they just get out of the way and let us crash."

"Lara didn't exactly know," Addie said, in the tiniest of voices. "The vibrators were mine. I bought three hundred during a fire sale because I thought they would help. I never made a dime off them. I swear." She wiped her nose on the sleeve of her lab coat.

"It's not fair."

"It is now," Addie said. "I snagged a bunch of condoms, birth control pills, HPTs, and a model of the uterus on my way out. I also took Lara's Weight Watchers lunch from the staff room. Zucchini lasagna. Want some?"

"I'm not a zucchini person."

"Good." Addie sighed. "Because I'm starving." She padded barefoot across the grass, and popped the trunk of her Mazda Miata. It was overflowing with contraband. "What do you need, and don't be shy, there's enough here to last us until menopause."

"Malnutrition is my method of choice," M.J. said, then realized how glib that must sound to a women's health advocate.

"Seriously, I'm not going to charge you."

"I am serious," M.J. admitted. "I don't get regular periods because I tend to be underweight so—"

"So *what*?" Addie folded her arms. A disappointed school marm. "NYC Ninjas can't get knocked up, is that what you're saying?"

"Kind of."

"Maybe you're not getting your period because you're already pregnant."

M.J. leaned against the Miata, her legs heavy from the prosecco, or maybe the realization that she and Dan had unsafe sex because she was skinny and he was a doctor so what could possibly go wrong?

Addie removed a cardboard box and Lara's lasagna from the trunk, then closed it with a self-righteous slam.

"It's a little late for birth control."

"It's not birth control, they're home pregnancy tests." Addie stomped up the porch steps and opened the front door. "To the latrine."

"What? No! Forget it."

"It's okay," Addie said. "I'll be your grown-up."

Inside the bathroom, which still carried a trace of cherry-almond shampoo from her earlier shower, Addie bit through the silver foil wrapper and handed the stick to M.J. "Pee."

"I can't."

"Why not?"

M.J. closed the lid on the toilet seat and sat. "I don't know," she said, because how could she tell someone whose life just fell apart that she can't handle her life falling apart. Not yet, anyway. It was too soon for another round of punishing what-ifs. Too soon to search for silver linings. Too soon for heavy-lidded debates about the meaning of life and podcasts about accepting what is. It was just too soon.

With an exhausted savior's sigh, Addie switched places with M.J., pulled up her lab coat, and took the test herself. "See? It's easy." She tossed the stick on the shower floor. It landed with a nothing-to-it *plink*.

"I'm not scared of the *test*," M.J. said. "I'm scared of the results."

"There are always options." Addie offered a fresh stick. "Now pee!"

"Options?" M.J. thought as she pulled down her shorts. She couldn't imagine having an abortion any more than she could imagine having a baby, so how comforting were these options? The only positive here would be a negative.

When she was done, M.J. tossed the dripping stick onto the shower floor, hung her head between her legs, and hoped that her sister, April, had enough sense to distract her parents and keep them from looking down.

"Holy shit," Addie said, turning on the faucet. "Look."

Ears ringing, M.J. said she couldn't.

"There's one negative and one positive."

A sudden chill woke the back of M.J.'s neck. "What the—"

"It's a cold compress. Try to breathe."

"Breathe?"

"Some of these sticks have expired and could give a false positive. Let's try a few different ones just to be sure."

Legs quaking, M.J. saturated five more. "Tell me when it's over," she said, praying to the God she'd stopped believing in.

"No way," Addie said.

"What?"

"Anorexic Loo is guest DJing at the Blackbird tonight."

"Who gives a—"

"Shit," Addie said, as if completing M.J.'s thought.

"Exactly. Who gives a—"

"Shit."

"Exactly."

"No," Addie insisted, her wide-eyed disbelief no longer trained on her cell phone but on the shower floor.

Stomach churning, M.J. peeked through splayed fingers. Then no fingers. "Six negatives and one positive? It doesn't make sense."

Then it did. And the realization shocked them into silence.

"How poetic," Addie finally said, as she lowered to sit on the Turkish towel bathmat, hands resting limply by her splayed thighs. "The pregnancy counselor gets pregnant." She covered her face with her hands. "I hate when characters in TV shows get pregnant, don't you? It's my least favorite plotline ever."

"Dan's a doctor; he can help," M.J. tried, though she failed to find comfort in that fact moments earlier, when the baby was thought to be hers.

"This is all Leo's fault!"

"Leo Golden's the father?"

"Ew, no! But if Leo didn't die, David wouldn't have come back from Colorado, and I wouldn't have funeral-fucked him in the bathroom without a condom. I would have funeral-fucked him *with* a condom. Yes, I still would have been fired, but I wouldn't have to use my savings to fix the bookstore because it never would have been mine in the first place. I'd be halfway to a yacht in Italy filled with guys named Fabian and Fabrizio, who wear loafers without socks and lick sweat from my cleavage while I drink Negronis and teach them how to swear in English." She looked up at M.J., green eyes pooling regret. "I *knew* my boobs were bigger."

With a roll of two-ply toilet paper in hand, M.J. set Addie up on the couch, drew the blinds, and ordered a meat-lovers pizza. She massaged her feet with extra-virgin olive oil, then switched to hair conditioner because virgins of any kind were not welcome. She ordered three seasons of *Project Runway* and paid a Lyft driver to bring them gelato. She did everything except search for silver linings, mention David's name, or ask Addie how she wanted to handle the "situation." It was too soon for platitudes, coping strategies, and solutions. Fortune had spun her wheel, and Addie came up short. As someone who understood what that felt like, M.J. insisted they ignore their phones, lie around, and not try to solve a fucking thing.

Eighteen

"**D**O YOU HEAR that?" Addie mumbled into her pillow.

"You mean the knocking?" M.J. asked, eyes closed.

"Yeah."

"No."

"Good."

They settled back into sleep, which was easier now that M.J. had curtains on her bedroom windows. Easier still because their respective bellies were so stuffed with meat-lovers pizza and popcorn from yesterday, that digestion by way of hibernation was the only option.

But the knocking didn't stop.

"You should probably get that," Addie said.

"Why?"

"Don't you want to know who it is?"

"No."

"Well, I do."

"Then you should get it."

"I would," Addie said, "but I'm pregnant."

"Sorry I'm late," Destiny said when M.J. opened the door. "Chest was gonna give me a ride, but his stepdad got all bent because we kept the car out all night so—" She hitched a thumb at the beach cruiser on the lawn, back wheel still spinning.

"Late?" M.J. asked, while she considered Destiny's outfit: labia-grazing cutoffs, a string-bikini top, and a high-glossed smirk that suggested Jules had no idea her daughter was there. "Late for what?"

"Addie's taking me surfing." She removed her blue-mirrored lenses and peered into the charcoal-colored darkness. "No way. Is she still sleeping?"

"Yes," Addie called from the bedroom.

Destiny smiled.

"How did you know she was here?" M.J. asked.

"Find My Friends."

"You and Addie are friends?"

Destiny flashed the app on her phone. "Obviously." Then, she called, "Ready?"

"I don't have my boards."

"There are a bunch out here by the garage," Destiny offered.

"Those belong to my boyfriend," M.J. said, suddenly protective.

"Do you think he would mind if we borrowed them?"

"The problem is Addie's not feeling so well."

Destiny pulled six minibar bottles of Dewar's from her backpack, then entered the cottage with a purposeful stride. "Thirsty?" she asked the cocoon of blankets on the bed.

M.J. turned away to open the blinds. If the proverbial line of appropriateness did exist, she did not want to be there when the rebellious teenager and pregnant woman drank their way across it.

"Wake up," Destiny cooed, bottles clinking.

Addie pushed herself up to sit. "You brought Dewar's?"

"Three for each of us."

Addie took the bottles.

"Wanna shoot them?" Destiny asked, ribs jutting out from under her bikini top.

"No, I wanna dump them."

Destiny laughed. "Yeah, right." But she quickly sobered when Addie strode toward the kitchen sink.

"What are you doing?"

"You're fifteen."

"So? Like you never had a drink in high school?"

"Of course I did, with other high schoolers, not my mom's friends." Addie shot a *Help me out* glance at M.J. "Where is Jules, anyway?"

"Who cares?" Destiny leaned against the fridge and crossed her arms with an indignant harrumph. Then, sensing disapproval from the motherless women standing before her, added, "What? My dad can't stand her, either. Why do you think he never visits?"

"He's wrapping things up with his clients," M.J. tried. "He'll be here soon."

"Please. He's training rich housewives, not Navy SEALs. If he wanted to be here he would." She yanked a denim thread from her shorts. "He hooked Mom up with this stupid job to get rid of her, to get rid of *us*! I mean, *Liaison of Love*? Really? What is *that*?"

"She sweats romance. It's perfect for her."

"Makeup artist was perfect for her. Not weddings. She's allergic to flowers! But I guess that's what happens when you don't wear a condom. Your whole life turns to shit."

Addie bristled. "We should probably paddle out before the tide comes in."

"Yeah," M.J. agreed. "Help yourself to Dan's surfy stuff."

From the deck, M.J. watched them fearlessly charge the ocean. Then, with bellies flat against their boards, they duck-dived through the crashing white water until they reached the school of surfers on the endless stretch of corduroy beyond the break. There, with faces trained on the horizon, they bobbed on the undulating ocean and waited for Fortune to spin her wheel. Would they be lifted up and taken for a ride? Slammed against the rocks? Thrown off course by the current? No one knew.

In that moment, surfing had transcended sport. It became a philosophy or a metaphor for the unpredictable nature of life. To live with grace was to remain fluid, let things roll through us, not get attached. Expect-the-unexpected sort of thing, ride whatever comes along and see where you end up.

This could be something, M.J. thought. A poem, an article, a revelation for Dr. Cohn or something to share with Dan next time they Skyped. Pencil at the ready, she opened her journal and tried to block out the shore pound, the squealing children, the lifeguard's whistle, and listened for more deep thoughts.

"She hasn't changed a bit," said a male voice. Not at all what M.J. expected to hear.

It was David Golden. Elbows resting on the railing of his deck, hands clasped, like Gloria's had been the day they met. He removed his T-shirt and hung it over the railing, revealing a torso that vouched for his active lifestyle. While his faded jeans, which fell an inch below his butt-crack vouched for his lack of underwear.

"We used to sit out there for hours," he mused. Then a nostalgic chuckle. "Addie would do this thing . . . right as a good swell was coming, she'd distract us by lifting up her top and then drop in on the best wave."

Sunshine reflected off the ocean, casting a warm glow on the right side of his face. The left was shadowed and dark. He was attractive, but in a different way than Dan. Less textbook handsome and more black-book dangerous: wry half smile, sexy gap tooth, and eyebrows thick enough to hide secrets.

"You still care about her?" M.J. asked.

"Of course, Addie Oliver was my first . . . everything."

"But not your last?"

He straightened up, stuffed his hands in his pockets. "Like I said, she hasn't changed a bit. And I love that about her. But I—" He lowered his voice. "I want to grow up." Then, with a deprecating snicker aimed at his childhood home, the one that his mom just gave him because he couldn't afford his own, he said, "Trying to, at least."

"Actually, Addie has changed a lot. You'd be surprised."

David turned away from the ocean, found M.J.'s eyes and held them with his own. "You're right, I would be surprised if she changed. But she won't. She can't. She's still playing the kid card and it's bullshit. It's just Addie needing attention and she's too old for that."

"She told you?" M.J. asked, feeling somewhat betrayed. She and Addie had an agreement: they said no cell phones. Then again, this wasn't about her. It was about Addie and David and their unborn child. If Addie sent David a text or snuck out in the middle of the night to tell him the news, it was her business. M.J.'s job was to support Addie, not judge her. But David? David she could judge. So she knocked his shirt off the railing and onto the beach.

"What'd you do that for?"

"I'd have pushed you if you weren't so . . . thick."

His jaw hovered somewhere between outrage and amusement. "Why push at all?"

"Because you're painting Addie to be some shrew who traps men into thinking she's pregnant and that's not what's happening here. She's telling the truth. She took six tests and they were all positive and you're the fa—"

"There you are, Davey," said a Bambi-eyed twentysomething with a bath towel twisted over her wet hair, a second wrapped around her body, and a Star of David necklace adorning her oiled décolletage. "That sunroom would make a great office, am I right or am I super right?"

"Super right." Then, "M.J., this is my girlfriend, Hannah," David said, clear as a warning.

"Are you a snowboard instructor, too?" M.J. asked.

"Me? God, no. I'm a graphic designer."

"Cool. What kind of stuff?"

"You know . . . ," she said, with a surreptitious side-eyed glance at David. "Graphic stuff."

"It's niche," he stated.

A descant of high-pitched shrieks brought their attention to the beach, where Addie and Destiny had collided and were now tumbling ashore.

"Show me what you're thinking for the sunroom," David said, placing his arm around Hannah's shoulder and steering her into the house.

Now what? M.J. wondered as she watched Addie and Destiny giggling their way toward the deck. Was she supposed to forget that she saw David? Forget that he has a girlfriend? Forget that he implied Addie was faking her pregnancy?

Absolutely. At least until her next phone session with Dr. Cohn, maybe he'd know what to do.

M.J. went inside and started cleaning the tissues, pizza boxes, popcorn kernels, and tabloid magazines. The busy work would keep her occupied, give her a place to divert her lying eyes should Addie ask what M.J. did while they were surfing.

But Addie never asked. Her curiosity was directed at Destiny, who was scrolling frantically through a chain of text messages, and repeating, "Oh no."

"It's Chest isn't it," Addie said, as if bored by the male species' never-ending ability to disappoint.

"No," Destiny lowered her phone. "It's Mom. She's in the hospital."

CHAPTER

Nineteen

Pearl Beach, California
Saturday, July 23
Waning Gibbous Moon

"IMMEDIATE FAMILY ONLY," Easton said, while pacing the waiting room. "So, of course, Brandon's in there."

"My dad?" Destiny asked. "He came?"

"All the way from Oceanside. Room 204."

Brows arched with *I'll believe it when I see it* skepticism, Destiny pushed through the double doors and took to the linoleum with sneaker-squeaking determination, leaving them with a mountain biker (branch sticking out of his calf), a toddler (vomiting), and a teenaged girl shivering sweat and scratching herself bloody (withdrawal).

M.J.'s legs began to tingle. She tasted pennies. How did Dan do it? The fetid smells, the bodily fluids, the possibility of death at every wrong turn? "I need to sit."

Addie glowered at the vomiting toddler. "I'll stand."

"I have a lot of sympathy for the Beatles," Easton said, unclipping his bowtie. "Choral Fixation made one girl faint and I'm a mess. Imagine taking down thousands."

"Choral Fixation?" Addie asked.

"My men's chorus. We performed at your birthday, remember?" Addie shrugged.

"One minute Jules is singing along to 'Saturday in the Park,' and the next she's down," he marked her landing with a *clap*. "Luckily, our gig was in the children's ward, so we were already here, but still . . ." He shuddered.

"Do they know what caused it?" Addie asked.

"Is she okay?"

Before Easton could respond the automatic doors yawned open and gave way to Britt, hurriedly unclipping her pink helmet, oblivious to the hair extension swinging from the strap.

"You biked here?" M.J. asked.

"Scootered." Britt fanned her beading forehead. "How's Jules?"

"You leave that to me." Easton approached the receptionist's plexiglass wall, wedged his face into the conversation hole, and on behalf of men's choruses everywhere, threatened to ban all hospital performances if he didn't get some answers, stat.

"Did you really scooter here?" M.J. asked, thinking of all the money she'd spent on Lyft. "Are they hard to ride?"

"Harder than a Mini Cooper," Britt teased. "Anyway, it's not like I wanted to. I didn't have a choice."

"Why?"

Britt opened her mouth to answer and then paused. "Over here," she said, summoning them to the water cooler, the dried-up potted plant. Deciding that the corner wasn't private enough, she began to jostle the leaves, and in a whisper said, "I was showing the Brazilian a condo with a very *open* floor plan when—"

"You still don't know his name?" Addie asked, somewhat impressed.

"I don't know anything. No name, no occupation, no idea if there are dependents on his tax returns, no nothing. He's as zipless as the day I met him. I was going to check his wallet, but I never got a chance. He got an emergency call and took off mid-blow."

"You're obviously not opening your mouth wide enough," Addie said. "If your lips are too tight it feels like he's sticking his dick in a pencil sharpener, in which case, I could see why he answered the phone."

Britt opened wide and closed her mouth around her entire fist proving her wrong. "So, I'm thinking it's a sign," she continued. "Like, go be with your husband, Britt. You're not a cheater. This isn't you. Go home. When I got there Paul was waiting for me in the driveway, all anxious and hand-wringy like he knew. But the only thing he said was, 'I'm late for a meeting. I need the Prius.'" Britt paused so they could absorb the audacity. "Translation? I need to get to my mistress, now, before my pubes grow back."

"And the scooter?" M.J. asked, always the editor, tracking the point.

"Paul took the Prius, so when I got the call about Jules I went for the golf cart, but Mr. Wonderful forgot to charge it, so . . ." Britt lifted the helmet above her head like a winning trophy. The hair extension fell from the strap and landed on her shoulder. She slung it over a branch like tinsel just as Easton announced his victory with a thumbs up.

JULES RODE THE adjustable mattress from flat to forty-five degrees, an angle more suitable for entertaining. "Nothing like extra-strength Claritin and chardonnay to remind a girl she's human," she said, with the satisfied snap of her compact mirror. Her makeup was prom-queen perfect. She did not look like a woman who fainted from mixing antihistamines with alcohol. Not that M.J. knew what that woman looked like. Jules had to be the first.

"She was at a flower expo all morning," Destiny added, as if that explained everything.

"It wasn't the flowers," Jules insisted. "It was that second shot of wine."

Britt winced. "You shot *wine*?"

"It's an old Choral Fixation tradition," Easton said. "We do it before every show. You know—wet whistles, calm jitters . . ." He placed a hand on Jules's shoulder. "Anyway, I'm sorry. I shouldn't have pressured you." Easton handed her a cup of ice chips.

Jules smiled her appreciation.

"As you wish," he said.

Jules's breath hitched at the sound of those words. And while her mouth was open, Easton gently fed her an ice chip. "I guess Brandon had to take off, huh?" he said, while she sucked.

Jules pointed her lavender toenails toward the bathroom by the foot of her bed. "He's in the little boys' room." Then, with an adoring sigh, "I don't know how he got here from Oceanside so quickly. My prince's steed must have grown wings."

The toilet flushed.

M.J. listened for the squeaking faucet, a pumping soap dispenser, the stiff rip of paper towel. But none of the conventional indicators of handwashing were there. All she heard was the pop of the lock, a swiftly twisted handle, and Britt's audible gasp.

———

THE MARKER WAS a watering hole for people whose troubles had troubles. Dimly lit and a stent's throw from the hospital, it had become what locals referred to as the devil's conference room. A urinal cake-scented, red-bulbed hideaway where beer bottles clanged like old bones and the ice machine hummed a zombie's dirge. It's where puffy-eyed family members made funeral arrangements, defeated surgeons recovered after imparting bad news, and sinners on scooters baptized their souls in cheap house white.

"At least you know his name," Addie said.

Britt released her forehead to the sticky bar, pinched the stem of her wineglass, and dragged it toward her ear. "Did you see the color of his face?"

"From hardboiled egg to eggplant," M.J. said.

"Do you think Jules picked up on it?"

"No way," M.J. said. "Her heart-shaped pupils were too focused on Brandon to notice anything. Including that he doesn't wash his hands after he uses the bathroom."

Britt knocked her head against the bar. "I can't believe the Brazilian is married . . . to Jules!" Another knock. "As soon as the wine shots wear off she'll realize that he was already up here. I mean, not even a magic steed could get from Oceanside to Pearl Beach on a Saturday in under two hours. Then she'll start digging around and—" Britt's gaze wandered to the lineup of dusty liquor bottles behind the bar. "Jules's husband's hands were on my naked ass."

Addie finger-stirred her Virgin Mary. "His *unwashed* hands."

"What a piece of shit!" Britt said.

"Why was he at Marrow that night?" M.J. asked. "Did Jules even know he was in town?"

"No idea," Britt said, then she smacked herself on the forehead. "Oh my God, *Rooftop*! I thought he was there to watch me, like I was the hottest thing ever. But he was with Jules."

"The Brazilian was at my party?"

"He was," Britt said. "Until he realized I knew Jules."

"Hence the stomachache," M.J. said.

Britt covered her face with her hands. "I can't believe I had sex with Jules's husband."

"And Destiny's father," Addie added.

"It's not funny! What if Jules finds out? What if they get divorced because of me? What if she tells Paul?"

"Paul?" Addie said. "I thought you two were done."

"*Done?* He's my husband."

"But you're fucking Jules's husband."

"Don't say it like that!"

"Sorry," Addie said. "I meant to say Destiny's dad."

"This isn't funny," Britt said. "It's like when I found out fat-free cookies were loaded with sugar. I had one thing that made me feel good, one thing to look forward to, and that thing turned out to be—"

"Destiny's dad."

Britt finally laughed. "I know what I did was awful and there's no excuse but—"

"Here comes the excuse," Addie said.

"But Paul treats me like an underdeveloped Polaroid—like I'm not fully there, you know? Then the Brazilian came along and suddenly I felt all colorful and seen. And as long as I had that, Paul could ignore me and get stoned as much as he wanted. I wouldn't die from neglect, and our family would stay together. But now my fat-free cookies belong to Jules, Paul's hairless balls are slapping against someone else's ass, and I've got nothing."

"You could keep seeing him," M.J. said, because that's what Dr.

Cohn would have done. Offer up the unthinkable so it could be rejected. Then they could move on.

"Never!" Britt said, much to M.J.'s relief. "I have to tell her. I mean, I can't not say anything." She took a swig of wine. "Can I?"

"Sometimes people are better off not knowing." Addie rested a hand on her belly. "Does anyone else smell that?"

"Don't worry," M.J. assured her. "It happens when you're pregnant. My coworker's farts were so toxic we moved her desk to the stairwell."

"No, it's those nachos," Addie pointed at a passing waiter's tray.

"Wait, you're pregnant?" Britt asked.

"And unemployed and homeless and—" Addie lurched forward, cupped a hand over her mouth, and bolted for the bathroom.

"Is she serious?"

"Found out yesterday," M.J. told her. "After she got fired for handing out vibrators."

"And the baby?"

"David Golden's."

"And the bookstore?"

"Still trashed."

Had it not been for a recent Botox injection, Britt's eyebrows would have shot straight past her scalp. "Does David know?"

"He said something today that made me think she told him. Anyway, she doesn't know what she's going to do, or maybe she does and she doesn't want to talk about it. I don't know."

Addie returned—lips freshly glossed—and downed some water that may or may not have been hers. She lowered the glass like a guillotine. "Get this baby out of me," she said. Then to M.J., "You're annoying."

"What did I do?"

"Nothing," Addie told her. "You're a decent person and right now I find that annoying."

Britt nodded in agreement. "It's true. You would never have an affair or get—" She tilted her head in the general direction of Addie's uterus. "You're just solid."

The way they said it made it sound like an insult. As if a criminal record was required to ride with their girl gang.

"I may be good from afar, but I am far from good," M.J. said, because she had just as many reasons to be annoyed by good people as they did. But to air Dan's pesky little obsession with saving lives and expect the kind of sympathy one might get from, say, an unwanted pregnancy or a doomed marriage, was a fool's game. No one liked the skinny girl with the hot doctor boyfriend whose biggest fault is "he cares too much." But she did sign Gayle's contract behind Dan's back and there was nothing "good" about that.

"Want to know how indecent I am?"

They absolutely did.

"I took my old job back in New York and didn't tell Dan."

Addie cocked her head. "You're going back to New York?"

Britt's dimple pulsed. "When?"

"September," M.J. said.

"Why didn't you say anything?"

"I'm scared he'll never talk to me again."

"No," Britt said. "Why didn't you say anything to us?"

"I didn't think you'd care."

Silence pulled up a stool and sat between them until Britt smacked the bar.

"Damn it," she said. "I was supposed to be an age-defying stay-at-home mom with overachieving kids, a house that smelled like organic cleaning products, and a successful husband who found my aging body sexy. And what did I get? Destiny's dad, a living room that reeks of skunk, twins who won't kiss me in public, a career pimping houses, and a trash can full of pubes. This is it, folks. This is my life." She pointed at the three women seated directly across from them. "See those sad hags over there? That's going to be us in ten years, and then what?"

M.J. placed her hand on Britt's shoulder. "That's a mirror."

"Huh?"

"That *is* us," Addie said.

Britt leaned forward and squinted. "Fuck."

CHAPTER

Twenty

"GO AHEAD, JUDGE," M.J. said, imagining her parents glaring down at her, *tsk-tsking* what she considered to be a legitimate form of cardio. Because every time she clicked on an article about her ex-boss or trolled social media for answers, her heart would speed.

Would she find pictures of Gayle at one of those corporate retreats? Read about a terrible accident or maybe a scandal that forced her to resign? Each tap of the mouse was a step closer to closure—anything that might explain why it had been four days and she still hadn't acknowledged M.J.'s signed contract.

Sometime around her third cup of coffee, the Web connection had become dial-up slow. "How passive-aggressive," M.J. told her meddling parents. "If you really want me to stop, have Gayle give me a call." She shut off her modem and began counting to thirty.

Instead, the call, which was more of a yell, came from the Goldens' house.

"Are you okay?" M.J. asked David's girlfriend, Hannah, when she opened the door. She was dressed this time: white jeans, a navy tee, leather sandals. There was an Upper East Side of Manhattan look about her now: flat-ironed hair, J.Crew pretty, never going to swallow. In a game of "Kill, Fuck, Marry," she'd be altar-bound every time.

"I *was* okay until the Wi-Fi went down," she said. "Do you think you could reboot?"

M.J. didn't understand.

"The cable guy doesn't come until tomorrow, so I've been using yours," Hannah explained with a neighborly smile. "Sorry, I have a deadline and you don't have a password, so . . ."

"You're a graphic designer, right?"

Hannah nodded, maybe even blushed.

"What kind of stuff do you do?"

"Children's books."

"Really?"

"No." Hannah snickered. "You're not religious are you?"

"Atheist, why?"

Hannah invited her inside.

The white tufted furniture and dated accents remained exactly as Gloria had had them, though they were now catch-alls for the gutted suitcases and Xbox games.

"Moving sucks, am I right or am I super right?" Hannah asked.

"Super right."

"Anyway, this is my office," she announced, as she opened the door to the sunroom, which looked nothing like it had the day of Leo's shiva. The table that had once been filled with lasagna, casseroles, and M.J.'s plagiarized garlic bread, had been replaced by ergonomic office equipment and a panic-room style display of computer monitors. The natural light that once bled through the glass panes was now clotted by cartoon renderings of naked Asian women with jagged Crayola-colored haircuts, colossal breasts, tiny waists, and impossibly round asses. Many of them were being vigorously man-handled, some held a lover's face between their legs, and others enjoyed the company of two men at once, men with oozing penises and pendulous balls.

"Wow, when you said graphic—"

"Yeah, I meant graphic," Hannah said. "It's Japanese anime porn. Best. Gig. Ever." She indicated the kitchen. "Tea?"

They sat at the kitchen island the way M.J. and Gloria had weeks earlier, swapping particulars while the kettle boiled. Hannah talked about growing up in San Diego, meeting David at Comic-Con, staying in touch while he was in Colorado, and how she quit her job as a graphic designer for the *San Diego Union-Tribune* to move in with him. "Live in the same zip code, you know?"

"Do you ever worry that you made a mistake? I mean, you had such a stable job and—"

The kettle whistled. Hannah removed it from the burner with the effortless swoop of someone who stayed calm in a crisis. "Now, where are my tea bags?" She began shifting canisters of protein powders and vitamin jars until she found them. "Peppermint okay?"

M.J. nodded, even though it wasn't. The smell conjured her father's futile attempts to conceal his pipe breath with Altoids; how she hated it then, and missed it now. "What if things with David don't work out?"

"I'll leave." She made an O with her lips, blew steam off her mug. "I'd rather regret something I did than something I didn't do, you know? And I'd regret not trying this commitment thing with Davey."

"Trying?"

"We had an open relationship because of the distance, but now that I'm here we're exclusive. Effective the day I moved in."

Relief warmed M.J. in ways that Hannah's peppermint tea could not—David Golden wasn't a cheat. While it didn't change the fact that Addie was pregnant, or that Hannah's boyfriend might be a father, it did mean that David wasn't a self-serving asshole. And that maybe he'd do the right thing, whatever that was.

"What about you?" Hannah asked. "What's your deal?"

"Mine?" M.J. took a thin sip of tea. Then, a window in one of the bedrooms slid open. Footsteps followed, soft and scuttling. A bedspring creaked. "Is he home?"

"No," Hannah whispered. "I think someone's breaking in."

M.J. grabbed an egg-yolk crusted spatula from the sink, while Hannah searched for her phone.

"I'm calling the police," she shouted.

"Who the hell are *you*?" the intruder called, her voice disturbingly familiar.

"Stand down," M.J. told Hannah. "I know her."

M.J. followed the sounds to David's bedroom, where sports trophies lined the cherrywood shelves, a collage of newspaper articles and photographs featuring the star athlete papered the walls. And a dress, too red to be Hannah's, had been draped over the lampshade.

"Addie, it's me," M.J. said to the lump under David's blue comforter.

"That's Addie?" Hannah mouthed. Then with a playful poke, "You're Davey's wild sister, am I right or am I super right? He told me all about you."

The lump stirred and then gave way to Addie, who had the sour expression of a woman who drank spoiled milk. "*Davey?*" She snapped a look to M.J., as if this was her fault.

Oblivious, Hannah offered her right hand and introduced herself. "I moved in on Friday."

"Oh, sorry about sneaking in then," Addie said, her features softening with relief. "I thought David lived here."

"He does," Hannah said. "He gets off work at four."

Addie scooted up on her elbows, the blue comforter now a sagging bridge that hung off her bent knees and sloped toward her black bra straps. "David got a job? Already?"

"He's the new coach of the high school water polo team." Then to M.J., "Apparently it's a big deal. They're talking Olympics."

"Are you his roommate?"

Hannah smiled. "I mean, we live together, so yeah, I guess you could say that."

Addie's eyes narrowed, as if trying to place a distant sound. "David has a girlfriend?" Then to M.J., "And you know her?"

M.J. wanted to say that it all happened so fast. That she wasn't trying to hide anything from Addie, and would have told her as soon as she knew the full story, which she just got, by the way. But Addie kicked off the blankets in a huff.

"Sick curves!" Hannah blurted. "Sexy, voluptuous, and perfectly proportioned. Shit, I'd love to sketch you."

"Sketch this!" Addie spread her legs to reveal the words WELCOME HOME, DAVID written on her inner thighs in fuchsia lipstick. An arrow pointing north indicated "home" should there be any confusion.

"You're not Davey's sister, are you?"

"*Davey* doesn't have any sisters . . ." Addie scooped up her belongings. "And I just lost a friend." With an angry toss, she whipped her dress through the open window and crawled out, leaving a fuchsia smear behind on the ledge.

———

THE SEARCH FOR Addie began immediately and ended minutes later with the sound of Dan honking his horn and yelling, "Surprise!" He didn't bother pulling all the way up to the garage or parking as he usually did, with equal amounts of driveway on either side. He abandoned his car, left his luggage and the bag of See's butterscotch lollypops for another time, and kissed M.J. with the kind of unbridled desire that melts teeth.

Their passion was primal and inspired. A movable feast that stumbled hungrily around the cottage, colliding with surfaces both hard and soft. Consuming enough to keep M.J. from asking why Dan came home from Boston a day early, and yet, incapable of keeping her concern for Addie at bay. A concern so distracting, she lost her orgasm.

It was more than Addie's heartbreaking discovery or the guilt M.J. felt for not mentioning Hannah sooner. It was that Addie called M.J. a friend; that their relationship mattered enough to hurt.

Dan, breathless and sweaty, collapsed onto M.J.'s chest. Her spine was grinding against the living room floor. She rolled him off her. A rush of air filled her lungs. "What's our safe word?"

"We don't have a safe word," he mumbled while kissing her neck. "Why?"

"You came back early. How do I know this is really you?"

Dan lifted his face to meet hers, and M.J. found those gold bursts in his sleepy hazel eyes.

"The real question is, why did I *leave*?"

M.J. giggled. It was the kind of answer one would expect from a character in a romance novel, expertly engineered to make lonely housewives swoon. And yet, she swooned, surrendered her cheek to his chest, and urged him to go on.

"Boston was a grind. The hectic pace, lack of sleep, shitty food, cramped living quarters, all those patients we had to stabilize during the relocation . . . It was more grueling than Jakarta, and still—" He folded his hands behind his head and gazed up at the ceiling. A small boy with big dreams. "I loved it." His heart thumped a tiny bit harder. "But, May-June Stark, I love you more, and I don't want to mess things up between us any more than I already have, so I came back early, and I'm not going anywhere again unless you're with me."

M.J. sat up. Put on his T-shirt. Inhaled his sincerity. Dan was a complete-package kind of a man: batteries included, no assembly required. Most women would spend a lifetime looking for a Dan and never find one. And yet M.J. had been willing to cast him aside because she was lonely. Not willing, mind you, she had actually done it. Signed the contract and FedEx'ed it to Gayle, priority. And for what? A job? A job that didn't save people; it bogged her down with meetings, e-mails, and soul-sucking office politics.

"You haven't messed things up, Dan, I promise," M.J. said. "Fine, it's been an adjustment. But I don't want you to give it all up for me."

"I'm not." Dan turned to face her, touching the tip of his nose to hers. "I'm giving it up for us." His sentiment settled over her like a beautiful but itchy sweater; it flattered but didn't feel right. She didn't deserve his loyalty. Not lately, anyway, with all her omissions and lies.

M.J. traced her finger around the smooth knot of his outie belly button and wondered if Gayle's silence had been more of a blessing than a curse, like a divine nudge. As though it was Mom and Dad's way of keeping her in Pearl Beach so she could fight for the best relationship she'll ever have.

"Are you hungry?" Dan asked as he slid on his jeans.

She watched him walk stiffly to the kitchen, admired the muscles in his back that fired when his arms swung. He opened the fridge, realized it was empty, and then released the door. "What are you feeling?"

Guilty. Confused. Pathetic.

"Italian or Thai?"

"Oh." M.J. giggled. "Doesn't matter."

Dan opened the junk drawer, shifted papers, batted around pens and loose change in search of his restaurant delivery list. Then the shifting and batting stopped. "What's this?" he asked, flipping through a document. He lingered on the final page.

M.J. felt a sting of recognition as she glimpsed the pages in his shaky grip. As if the curtains of amnesia blew open, offering a quick peek of something familiar, but not yet identifiable. Those steely gray letters centered at the top of the cover letter. The numbered paragraphs that followed. Her signature, signed, dated, and not at all in Gayle's office.

The curtains parted again. This time shedding light on why Gayle hadn't responded. The woman was sent a list of local restaurants, why would she?

Dan's gold bursts in his eyes turned dark. "When were you going to tell me about this?" he asked flatly.

She tried for his hand.

He pulled it away.

"I wanted to talk to you about it, but you were in Boston," she lied. Again.

"The cover letter was dated May nineteenth, M.J. You've known about this for over two months and never mentioned it."

She opened her mouth, ready to hose him down with more excuses, then stopped. Nothing could wash the disappointment off his face.

"I was going to give up everything for you, and you were just going to give up."

"If I wanted to give up I would have sent it, Dan, but I didn't. It's right here. And so am I."

He was looking at her like he wanted to believe her, and M.J. was looking back like she needed him to.

"I'm going for a surf."

"Now?"

"What's wrong with now?"

"We're kind of in the middle of something here."

"I know. And I think better in the water."

"I bet sitting on your board staring out at the horizon is a great way to solve your problems."

His upper lip curled. "Wow, M.J.'s being facetious, how refreshing." He wiggled out of his jeans, purposely left them on the kitchen floor as he walked off naked to get his trunks.

"For one, what you said was just as facetious, and for two, I was being sincere!"

"Sincere?"

"Yes, sincere," M.J. said, following him into the bedroom. "I was on the deck thinking about it the other day. When you're surfing you have to be present. If you're not you're going to get crushed. It's humbling and probably puts everything into perspective." She went on to share her thoughts on waves and how they're a perfect metaphor for the ups and downs of life. She showed him the pages in her journal as proof.

"You're insane."

M.J. bowed her head, turned to face the wall.

"Do you actually listen to the things you say? The way you connect ideas and express yourself? It's inspiring, M.J., and you're insane if you waste another day editing that magazine when you should be writing for it."

"Oh," M.J. said, relieved. She turned back to face him. "I thought you meant—"

"Stop thinking, M.J., and just go for it already. Gayle obviously wants you back so you have the upper hand."

"Meaning?"

"Meaning, you've been given a chance to start over. If you want to work for that magazine fine, but do it on your own terms."

The little girl inside her began to tug. Dan had a point. She could work for *City* but as a writer who lived in Pearl Beach with her handsome boyfriend, a doctor who was opening his own practice and staying put. And she would start just as soon as she called Gayle, apologized for sending her a list of restaurants, and humbly asked for it back. Because for the first time in a long time, M.J. was starving.

IT WAS TWO days before Gayle returned her calls.

"It was an accident," M.J. assured her as she settled into the porch swing, journal in hand. "I meant to send the contract. The restaurant list must have been right beside it and—"

"So what's next? Your microwave manual? The local *Penny Saver*?" Gayle teased.

M.J. smiled with her entire body. After several apologetic e-mails and multiple voice messages, she was finally absolved.

"So am I getting that signed contract or not?"

"I'll give you something even better," M.J. told her.

A sharp exhale.

"Trust me. I'm going back to New York in September to check on my apartment, can we grab lunch?"

"How about you give me the pitch now and we'll still grab lunch in September."

"I have to prepare," M.J. said, working that upper hand.

"Not even a hint?" Gayle pressed. "Come on, I'm chomping at the bit here. Give me something."

"It's champing at the bit, not chomping."

"What?"

"*Champ* means to bite down, which is what anxious horses do to their bits, whereas *chomp* means to chew, which implies eating, something they don't do to their bits."

Gayle laughed. "God, I've missed you."

"Does that mean you'll wait for me?"

"Do I have a choice?"

"No."

"Then yes, I'll see you in September." Gayle made a clicking sound with her teeth. "Hear that? It's me, champing."

CHAPTER

Twenty-One

Pearl Beach, California
Thursday, August 18
Full Moon

I T WAS A text message that, had M.J. still been working at *City*, chased by deadlines, choked by unanswered e-mails, she would have celebrated. Canceled plans that did not originate from her iPhone had once been her guilty pleasure. But that night, while the silver moon reflected off the ocean's bloated belly and Dan lay on the couch clipping fingernails to the sound of CNN, M.J. refused to take "rain check" for an answer.

So what if Britt's kids were home from camp and made a mess of her house? That was no reason to reschedule book club. There were traditions and rituals and three weeks' worth of catching up to do. So M.J. made a bid for the unimaginable and offered to host.

"How cozy are you right now?" she asked Dan during a Geico ad.

He looked up at her, nail clippers held above his big toe. "Why?"

"Some girls from the Downtown Beach Club want to get together. They asked me to host, but I could always tell them no . . ."

"Do it. I'll go play Xbox at David's," Dan said, as she'd hoped he would. He had been thrilled by M.J.'s recent return to writing, her newfound acceptance of Pearl Beach, the loving nature of their relationship now that he was home to stay. But he wouldn't rest until she had friends. And anything Dan could do to facilitate that, he did, including driving her to the liquor store before they parted ways.

Though she hadn't gone so far as to brand the night with a *Henry and June* theme (sorry, Jules!) candles flickered, appetizers beckoned, the Global Chill station played on Pandora, and her *Prim*-covered book, complete with highlighted passages, sat stiffly on the kitchen counter. A nervous hostess anxious for her guests to arrive. And once they did there would be hugs and laughter and braided conversations where one line of thought crossed with another and another and another. Because it had been too long since they'd spoken and there was that much to say.

—————

"ARE THOSE FROGS or crickets?" M.J. asked, painfully aware of the distant deep-throated chirps that seemed to be chanting, *awk-ward*, *awk-ward*, as their stilted small talk dragged on.

"Frogs," Jules answered at the same time Britt said, "Crickets."

M.J. checked her phone. "Still no word from Addie, huh?"

They shook their heads.

"We should eat."

Kneeling above the coffee table, M.J. began lifting foil off serving dishes and handing out plates.

"I see you made your famous garlic bread," Britt teased. Then with a nostalgic laugh, "God, I thought you were such a snob when I met you. All that talk about New York and how no one wears active-wear . . ."

"No activewear in New York?" Jules asked.

"There's activewear but people only wear it to the gym, not—" she stopped, noticing Britt's black Lululemon pants and sweatshirt. Her cheeks warmed. "I mean, that's what I thought, but I was wrong."

"No, you were probably right." Britt pinched a cherry tomato from the salad and popped it into her mouth. "I've never actually been to New York."

"I thought you grew up in Brooklyn."

"Huntington Beach." Then with a laugh, "I lied."

"Same!" M.J. said. "I told you I was turning thirty-two, but I'm really thirty-four."

"I fibbed, too," Jules said, happy to participate. "My last name isn't Valentine, but I say it is for professional reasons. I mean no dis-respect to Brandon, but Babcock is plain old bad for business, don'cha think?"

"It's plain old bad for everything," Britt said.

Jules responded with an all-in-good-fun giggle and pressed for more. "So what else have y'all lied about?"

Britt's jaw clenched. "Why do you ask?"

"No reason." With that, Jules hooked her purse over her shoul-der and excused herself for the bathroom.

When the door clicked shut Britt swiveled on the couch to face M.J. and whispered, "Do you think she knows about you-know-who?"

You mean the Brazilian Babcock? M.J. wanted to say, as she imagined a rare exotic bird with a penis-shaped beak. But Britt's eyes were darting: this was serious.

"How would she know?" M.J. asked. "You don't think Brandon told her, do you?"

"What are you two whispering about?" Jules asked, lashes thickened by a fresh coat of mascara.

"Easton," M.J. said. "You never told us why you were hanging out with him the day you fainted."

Jules swiped her hand dismissively. "I'm a softie for a good men's chorus, so he invited me to watch them perform." A flush crept across her cheeks as she settled into the club chair. "What? Why are y'all looking at me like that?"

"Like what?" M.J. asked.

"Like I've got eyes for someone other than my husband, because I don't. Easton's a friend. That's all. I'd never stray from my marriage. I'm not the type."

"And what type is that?" Britt asked.

"So, any updates on Addie?" M.J. said, eager to change the subject. "Did she decide to keep it?"

"I can't exactly imagine her being a mother," Britt said. "Can you?"

"Addie's pregnant?" Jules asked.

"I was asking about the bookstore, not the baby."

"Oh, sorry, yeah, the bookstore is on the market. Liddy found out about the quote, unquote *accident*. She was up for the repairs, but doesn't have the money to get the building up to code. So, she's selling. Addie's off the hook."

"Addie's pregnant?" Jules asked again. "Why didn't anyone tell me?"

M.J. stared back at her blankly, wondering if it was the same reason they failed to mention the bookstore to her; because they had a flash-fry friendship—brief and at a very high temperature—and now it was starting to cool.

Jules fingered the key around her neck.

Britt topped off her wine.

M.J. twirled the gold bands on her thumb.

"Yep." Britt sighed. "Those are definitely crickets."

———————

ADDIE FINALLY ARRIVED. She was forty minutes late and unsurprisingly unapologetic about it. But if anyone took issue with it, they didn't say. The distraction was *that* welcomed.

"Beer or wine?" M.J. asked her with an innocent lilt.

"Scotch."

Glances were exchanged. The baby had obviously left the building.

"Congratulations on your newfound freedom," M.J. said, handing her a beer.

"Meaning?" Addie popped open the button on her jeans, then sat on the short end of the L couch, beside Britt.

"The bookstore. It's not your problem anymore."

"Jeez." She rolled her eyes, which shined absinthe green against all that black kohl. "News travels fast around here."

"Not fast enough," M.J. said. "I hear you've known for a while. I had no idea."

Addie reached for a plate, then the julienne salad.

"I'm really going to miss that place," M.J. said.

"Why? You're going back to New York in September, aren't you?"

Jules's forehead furrowed with fresh hurt. "You're leaving?"

"Actually, I'm not." M.J. leaned forward, excited to share her news. "Remember I told you about that contract I signed?"

Britt and Addie nodded.

Jules said, "No."

"Okay, well, actually, it's a funny story. It started when Dan came home early from Boston and said he wasn't going to travel anymore because he missed me—"

"Do you mind if we skip right to the letter?" Addie checked her phone. "I have to be out of here in, like, thirty minutes," she said, her *Deal with it* smirk aimed straight for M.J.

"Works for me," Jules said coolly.

With a resigned shrug, Britt pulled Liddy's letter from the dust jacket fold of her book and began to read.

THE DATE: October 1988
THE DIRTY: *Henry and June* by Anaïs Nin
THE DETAILS: By Liddy Henderson

I had five miscarriages in eight years.

Patrick wanted to name the babies, acknowledge their individuality, pray that Jesus would welcome them into the Kingdom of Heaven (Mathew 19:14). So I did.

But Christopher, Thomas, Edward, Tina, and Kim never made it to heaven. They went from my womb straight to my heart and stayed, packing on pounds and adding inches the way living children do.

By 1975, the weight was too much to bear. My soul was so heavy I could hardly raise a smile. I was thirty-three years old and desperate to know why the Lord was punishing me. I was a devout Christian, a United Way Community Volunteer, and the goddamn pastor's wife! Where was my fucking baby?

I figured it out in 1976 when we met at Gloria's to discuss *Peyton Place*. Abortion, suicide, rape, incest, murder, illegitimate children . . . the novel was an encyclopedia of sins. It had even been denounced by the Church. And I, Liddy Marie Henderson, was sneaking around behind my husband's back reading it, and so many others. No wonder I was being punished.

And so I quit.

Right there in the sunroom.

Before Gloria served her lemon meringue pie.

And I love that pie.

You girls were devastated. If I quit, you'd all have to quit. I felt the weight of my decision, believe me, but for the first time in years, I had hope. Sixteen weeks later I was pregnant.

Thirty weeks after that we buried Ritchie.

As always, the three of you were by my side. Forcing me to bathe, eat, and laugh.

Jesus wasn't my savior after all.

The Dirty Book Club was.

I stopped wearing my crucifix.

I started wearing our key, and my religious ambivalence, the way Marjorie wears gold sequin.

Around that time, Mrs. Craig, the owner of our holy bookstore, was diagnosed with cancer, and Patrick asked me to step in while they looked for a replacement. So I did.

Angela Kelly worked in the back room. She balanced budgets, placed orders, and took inventory. She listened to Fleetwood Mac and quoted Betty Friedan. She wore clogs and blowsy tops that slid off her shoulders. She smelled like strawberry shampoo and incense. And we had sex for the first time on her thirty-fifth birthday.

(Yes, Marjorie, you were right.)

We were hungry for each other all the time and fed our cravings as often as we could. Reason said I was betraying Patrick, but passion wasn't convinced. The sensations were so different—so explosive and liberating they couldn't possibly be compared. With Patrick, sex was a means to an end. A botched recipe

for making babies. One of the many items on our holy
to-do list. With Angela it was pleasure for the sake of
pleasure, nothing else.

I kept our secret for many years. The only thing I
shared was my newfound joy.

Patrick assumed his unwavering devotion had turned
me around. You girls chalked it up to laughter, our
club, and martinis. Angela said, "Eros."

You were all right.

I needed Patrick, the three of you, and Angela to
feel complete. Unable to find fulfillment in one place,
I siphoned it from three different sources.

I was ashamed by my capacity for betrayal. And yet,
I was enjoying it too much to stop.

In 1986 we read *Henry and June*, and everything
changed again.

Dotty, you called Anaïs Nin "bogus." You didn't
believe she could love Hugo, Henry, June, Eduardo, and
Richard all at the same time.

And Gloria said, *Women don't pile lovers onto their
plates like we're at some all-you-can-eat buffet. We
select them carefully, one dish at a time, and dine.*

So I was counting on you, Marjorie, to speak up and
say everything I had been thinking and feeling. All
those affairs you had with pilots. My God, your cockpit
had runneth over. How could you possibly judge Anaïs?

But you did.

I agree with Gloria, you said. *Sex is a buffet,
but not love. Love is a sit-down dinner for two, not
two vaginas, though, that's not how I like to eat.
No offense, but Anaïs lost me with that whole June
obsession of hers.*

You've never been curious? I asked, desperate for

you, Marjorie, to pave my way. But all you said was:
It's not natural.

Madonna thinks it is, I tried.

The Virgin Mary? Dot laughed. *She said no such
thing!*

No, Madonna the singer.

That's when Marjorie asked who I was fucking.

Patrick.

Who else?

No one!

You're lying, Liddy. What's her name?

Her?

Lighters flicked. Martinis were gulped. Chairs
scraped along the flagstone as you slid in closer to
catch my tears while I confessed everything.

When I was done I expected sympathy. I got contempt.
Not because I cheated on Patrick or had sex with a
woman, but because I didn't tell you about it sooner.

We're the Dirty Book Club, Dotty said. *We keep
secrets from the world, not each other.*

To you, what I had done was cheating of the worst
kind, and you were right. Because we were nothing
without trust and I killed it. I killed us. It was
another death on my long list of many.

The Dirty Book Club 1963-1987.

With this loss, I turned to Angela instead of God.
Sex instead of scriptures. Vodka instead of holy water.
The green futon in the coffee break room became my
pew. It was there that I did all of my kneeling and
worshipping. Taking Angela's body into my mouth instead
of Christ's. Until that spring afternoon in 1988, when
Patrick poked his head in the coffee break room and
witnessed it all.

Angela was fired immediately, and I watched her go without a fight, thinking that with enough repenting and prayer Patrick and I could rebuild what we once had.

But he couldn't get past it.

The betrayal against him was one thing, and the betrayal against God and our congregation? Well, that was two more.

Three sins, you're out.

Doors slammed in my face, my parents' being the first among them.

Angela refused to take my calls. And I was too proud to contact Gloria and Dot, because we hadn't spoken in months. So I checked into the Holiday Inn with the money I made at the Good Book. While I was there I made an overseas call to you, Marjorie, asking if I could join you in Paris and start over.

I got your answering machine.

I left a message.

You never called back.

My savings dried out.

On my last night at the hotel the concierge delivered an envelope. Inside was the deed to the Good Book (in my name!), a set of keys, and a note written on our Dirty Book Club stationery. It read:

> Liddy,
>
> Please consider stocking the shelves with DBC-approved literature, turning the coffee break room into our private meeting place, and hiring four topless bartenders. Three guys for us and a lesbo for you.

Sixteen days until the next full moon. Better
get cracking.

XXX The Dirty Book Club.

P.S. You owe us a letter from that old *Henry and
June* meeting. Don't forget.

And so my dear friends, this is that letter. Thank
you for resurrecting me from the dead and saving *us*.
You have renewed my faith in all that is holy. See you
in sixteen days!

—L.M.H.

Born again

M.J. GLANCED AT Addie, expecting to find her ashamed; after so brazenly rejecting the three things that defined Liddy's life—a child, the bookstore, and this club—how could she not be? But all she said was, "Who knew that old lezzer wanted kids? I always assumed she didn't want any." Then she plucked a chunk of deli meat out of her julienne salad and dropped it on her napkin.

"Sure makes you appreciate the miracle of conception," Jules said.

"Contraception is the real miracle," Addie told her.

Jules blinked. "So does that mean you're not—"

"I can't believe the Dirty Book Club broke up," M.J. interjected. "Twice!"

"The second time didn't surprise me at all," Jules said. "Trust is everything. And when that's gone . . ."

"That's your takeaway?" Britt said, judging. "Wow, I always pegged you for an optimist but . . ."

"But what?"

"To me that letter was about how they were there for each other in the end," Britt said. "You know, a real forgive-and-forget kind of thing."

"Hands up if you googled Anaïs's girl crush to see if she was hot?" M.J. said, raising her hand. Was it a weak transition? Yes, but this conversation had become a minefield of explosive topics and if she didn't lighten the mood it would blow up in her face. "Really? I'm the only one who image-searched June Miller? Well, for the record, she wouldn't sway me gay. And what about the book itself? Personally, I think it lacked drama. Like a sense of what was at stake for Anaïs and Henry if they got caught."

"A bunch of lawless sex addicts if you ask me," Jules practically spat.

"Sex by its very nature is lawless," Addie said.

"And marriage, by its very nature, is not," Jules countered. "There are rules in marriage, and they were married." She sighed. "At least they didn't have children."

"I'm confused. Who are we talking about here?" M.J. asked, "Anaïs and Hugo, or Patrick and Liddy?"

"Both."

"Maybe it's a good thing Liddy couldn't conceive," M.J. said. "If she had kids she probably would have stayed married to Patrick. She would have forced herself to live a lie."

"But she would have had *kids*," Jules said.

"Kids but no sex."

"True," Britt said. "Kids are to sex what coffee is to alcohol—a total buzzkill."

"That is not true," Jules insisted. "I have tons of sex in my life."

"Courtesy of Fat and Natural," Addie said. "Not Brandon."

Jules stomped her foot. "You don't know the first thing about—" She inhaled deeply. Then a blustering exhale, "Brandon was right. You girls are not very wholesome."

"Why would he say a thing like that?" Britt asked with a nervous grin.

"He didn't think you could be trusted. He said it the moment you left the hospital."

"He was right about that," Addie said.

"Meaning?" Britt and M.J. said at the same time.

"Cut the innocent act, M.J. You went behind my back and told David I was pregnant."

A rush of heat needled M.J.'s skin. "No, you went behind my back and told him yourself, after we said no cell phones."

"No, I didn't!"

"You must have because he's the one that brought it up."

"That's impossible. What did he say?"

"We ran into each other on our decks while you were surfing with Destiny and he said you were playing the kid card. Basically implying that you trap men with fake pregnancies, so I defended you by saying it was real. That's all."

"'Scuse me?" Jules said. "When did you go surfing with—"

"He wasn't talking about fake pregnancies, M.J., he was dissing on me for hanging out with a fifteen-year-old. He thinks I befriend girls who look up to me so I can feel important. It's bullshit. But either way, I never told him about—"

"Shit. I'm so sorry. I thought—"

"When did you go surfing with Destiny?" Jules asked again, eyes wide and marble-hard. "Why didn't you say anything? Why would you cuckold me like that?"

"*Babcock*old," M.J. said, desperate to lighten the mood.

No one laughed.

"You were in the hospital," Addie explained.

"And when I got out?"

"It's no big deal, Jules. Destiny needed someone to talk to, that's all."

"About what, abortion?"

"Reality."

Jules uncrossed her legs and stood. "You know Brandon wanted me to quit the 'Downtown Beach Club.' And I was sick over it. I couldn't imagine being responsible for breaking us up. But if we're keeping things from one another, then maybe it's for the best."

"Forgive me, Jules, but you're not the first person on my list of People to Turn to When Contemplating Abortion," Addie said.

"Maybe if I was, you'd have a daughter of your own someday and you wouldn't need mine!"

"Am I on your list?" Britt asked.

With a swift, hair-swinging turn, Jules scooped up her purse. "I'm not like you girls. I get pregnant; I have a baby. I get married; I stay faithful. I stand by my obligations no matter how hard they get."

"What about your obligation to this club?" M.J. asked, her voice urgent and thin.

Jules removed her key necklace and placed it on the coffee table.

"So that's it?"

"Maybe she's right," Britt said. "My kids are back from camp, so I'm not doing much reading these days." She laid down her key.

"You can't do this!" M.J. said.

"You're leaving anyway," Britt told her. "We couldn't continue even if we wanted to."

"That's what I've been trying to tell you. I'm staying in Pearl Beach. I'm going to start writing again."

"Well, I'm leaving." Addie removed a clump of necklaces, bracelets, and hair elastics from her purse. She attempted to separate her key from the tangle, but quickly gave up and tucked it in the pocket of her blazer. She relinquished her napkin of deli meats instead.

And just like that the Dirty Book Club was over; a potential social life that never made it to term.

How to Make Love
Like a
Porn Star:
A Cautionary Tale

CHAPTER

Twenty-Two

Pearl Beach, California
Monday, August 29
Waning Gibbous Moon

CALI WAS A charming cliffside restaurant. Lit by paper lanterns, furnished in shabby-chic flea-market finds, and stocked with farm-to-table ingredients, it was a Pinterest poster's no-brainer. And the conversation was surprisingly entertaining. Dan was right. His Red Cross buddies did have friend potential.

"Tampons, huh?" M.J. asked. "I guess it makes sense."

"It does when you're low on QuikClot and the Syrian girl in your arms is bleeding out," said Marco. He was jockey-short and San Tropez–tanned. "O.B.'s are the Ziplocs of field medicine," said his wife, Catherine, who was taller, Nordic blond, and missing her two middle fingers so it looked like she was calling "bullshit" on everything. "We use them constantly."

"For what?" Winsome asked. She was a fund-raiser for the organization with the ability to make a shapeless caftan look sexy, as proven by Aaron, member of the Disaster Action Team (and her fiancé) who couldn't keep his capable hands off her.

"We use O.B.'s for nosebleeds and gunshot wounds," he told her.

"They even make great replacements for air filters in diesel engines."

"And curlers," Catherine enthused.

Marco reached for his beer and shook his head; he knew what was coming.

Catherine directed her "bullshit" hand at him and said, "Mr. Carry-on here, doesn't let me bring products on missions and my hair gets super limp without mousse. Like, itchy limp, you know?"

M.J. nodded. She really did.

"So when we were in Mosul, I took a few wet strands and rolled—"

Marco gripped the sides of his head. "A few?"

"Fine, nineteen, but I swear my waves gave hope to those poor women in Khazer camp. Like even in Mosul, miracles can happen."

"Speaking of," Winsome said, "my sister just got that endometrial ablation procedure. Can you imagine? No more periods?"

Aaron waved his organic cotton napkin. "Waiter, I'd like to order a new subject."

Everyone laughed, even M.J., who always found joy in playful banter between friends. When the Dirty Book Club imploded she thought she'd never hear it again.

"Are you sure you can't join us in Haiti?" Marco asked Dan as their smiles settled. "It's a short one. A few days of hurricane relief and we're out."

M.J. began stabbing the bush berries in her seasonal green salad. Anything to avoid the longing in Dan's his eyes while he contemplated the offer or the dopey grin she'd have to flash to hide the fact that this was an uncomfortable topic. But uncomfortable it was. Enough to make her palms sweat and her stomach clench. *Dan wanted to leave the Red Cross*, she told herself. *His idea, his choice. His idea, his choice. His idea, his choice.* It didn't matter how many times M.J. thought those words. She still felt guilty for holding him back.

"I am starting my own practice, remember?" Dan told Marco. Then, with a light squeeze to M.J.'s thigh—"Besides, I've spent too much time away from this wonderful woman. I need to stand still for a while."

Need or want? M.J. was tempted to ask, but did she really want to know?

"He must love you to bits," Catherine said, raising her white sangria in honor of Dan's devotion. "Sacrificing a trip like this is major."

"I sacrificed a lot, too," M.J. blurted. Her cheeks instantly burned with the shame that comes from sounding desperate. But why should Dan get all the credit. Or rather, why should she take all the blame?

"It's true," Dan said, his hand on her shoulder this time. "M.J. was promoted to editor in chief of *City* magazine and turned it down to be with me."

M.J. smiled weakly at him, apologizing on behalf of her ego, and at the same time, thanking him for leaving that shitty little "co" word out of it.

"Wow, what an opportunity that would have been," Winsome said, while her furrowed brow seemed to ask, "Why the hell aren't you taking it?"

"M.J.'s really much more of a writer," Dan explained. "And she has the capacity to do great things—"

"It's capability," M.J. said. "Not capacity."

It was Dan's turn to stab bush berries.

"We could always use a journalist in the mix," Aaron said.

"That would certainly raise awareness," Winsome added.

Dan leaned back against his chair. "Interesting idea."

M.J. nodded, though she couldn't fathom anything worse.

"It would take your mind off the Downtown Beach Club," he said. Then to the others, "She's been a little mopey since it closed last week."

"The Downtown Beach Club closed?" Catherine looked at Winsome as if she held the missing piece. "What happened?"

"Actually," M.J. announced, "writing about your missions sounds like a great idea. So how would it work?"

DAN POKED HIS head out of the bathroom, his mouth foaming with toothpaste. "Remember that old lady in New York?" It was the first thing he had said since they left Cali.

M.J. closed her journal, laid it down beside her on the bed. "What old lady?"

"The one who walked into her friend's umbrella and tore her eyelid?"

Her knees weakened at the memory: Dan insisting they escort her to the emergency room, blood spurting from the wound, the taxi driver swerving through traffic. "I fainted the minute we got out of that cab."

Dan returned to the bathroom, spat. "Exactly."

"Exactly, *what*?"

"You don't do wounds. I don't do words. So stop correcting my grammar in public and I won't ask you to scrub in next time I suture an eyelid."

"So that's what the silent treatment was about?"

"Yes, and it's not over yet."

"When will it be over?"

"When I have the *capability* to forgive you," he said, peeing.

"Actually, you should say, 'When I am capable of forgiving you.'"

"And you should say, "I'm sorry, Dan.""

"I can't."

He flushed. "Why not?"

"Because I'm a writer now, and one of the first rules in writing is 'show, don't tell.'"

"Then show me how sorry you are."

"Now, that I can do." M.J. pushed Dan onto the bed, crawled on top of him and thought, *End scene.*

———

THE DAYS THAT followed were uneventful and wonderfully routine. Filled with the "married people moments" M.J. had longed for when they lived on opposite coasts. A good-bye peck from Dan as he dashed off to a meeting. A hello peck when he returned. His day was always great, and hers could only be summed up with a *You wouldn't understand* sigh. Because Dan Hartwell could never sit alone in a beach cottage searching for the perfect way to describe the differences between New York and California. He'd never make a list called Ten Ways to Describe Sunlight on the Ocean, and if he did, "raining diamonds" would not be on it. Dan would not waste time on thoughts because thoughts don't save lives. People do. But M.J. was fresh out of those.

She had tried contacting the DBC girls several times, but they were too busy for lunch and not interested in dinner. Hannah found out about the pregnancy and left David. And Catherine and Winsome were in Haiti. Dan sensed the return of M.J.'s loneliness and urged her to give it more time. But time was the problem, not the solution. M.J. was drowning in it. Free time. Spare time. Downtime. Quiet time. Alone time. Me time . . . And drowning women don't want more water. They need someone to stop the flow; something Dan thought he was doing when he came home from work one night with a bottle of Bordeaux, an army-green backpack, and the need to open both on the deck.

"What is all this?" M.J. asked, glimpsing the legal pads, pens, energy bars, sunscreen, and O.B. tampons. "I don't get it."

Dan handed her an envelope. Inside were two tickets to Bangui M'Poko International Airport.

"Hawaii?"

"Central Africa." He beamed as he filled their glasses. "Destination: about 186 miles west of Bangui in a village called—"

"What?" M.J. laughed, though she found none of this funny. Even if he was joking, still, not funny. "Why?"

"Measles outbreak. There's a team there now, but they'll need relief. Marco, Catherine, Winsome, and Aaron will get there a few days ahead of us."

"Us?"

"Yes, us." Dan chuckled. "We take the red-eye September sixteenth."

M.J. gazed out at the last traces of Catalina Island before the navy-blue darkness swallowed it for the night. "I thought you were done with that."

"I was until my incredible girlfriend told everyone at dinner that she wanted to be a field reporter."

"I never said—" M.J. paused to admire the way hope could

light someone's face. "I was trying to be nice, Dan. I didn't mean it."

The light faded. "Well, you sounded pretty darn convincing."

"Maybe you were hearing what you wanted to hear."

"What's that supposed to mean?"

"It means you want to go. You want to go so badly you're willing to believe that I'd go with you."

"But you said—"

"It doesn't matter what I *said*, you know me. I don't have the constitution to work in a refugee camp. I wish I did, Dan, but I don't."

"You don't even know what it's like." He was looking at Catalina, too.

"How about we drink that nice bottle of wine and you can tell me all about it."

"And then?"

"And then . . . I'll know what a refugee camp is like."

"Is there a chance you'll consider it?"

"There's always a chance."

"How big?"

"Invisible to the naked eye."

"But there is a chance?"

"Yes." M.J. laughed. "On one condition . . ."

Dan took her hand. "Anything."

"If I decide to go—and that's a big, huge *if*—I get to pack my own bag."

"Done."

Twenty-Three

New York City, New York
Monday, September 12
Waxing Gibbous Moon

GAYLE SNAPPED A breadstick and released both halves to her plate. "You look relaxed, too relaxed. Are you even wearing a bra?" She waved an arm, thin as six o'clock, at M.J.'s yellow maxi dress, then peeked under the tablecloth to assess her braided sandals. "What are those made of? Hippie hair? God, did I look this bohemian back when I was getting laid?"

It was then that M.J. realized how out of place she looked among the tucked and belted power lunchers at Del Frisco's. "Bicast leather," she said in defense of the ethically friendly footwear she bought from a local surf shop. "No animals were harmed."

"Then why bother?" Gayle unfolded her napkin, laid it across her black Herve Leger dress. "If you were a goalie I'd be able to get one past you without even trying."

"Did you just make a sports analogy?"

"I oversee seven magazines now. Unfortunately, *Ballers* is one of them."

"I'm sorry to hear that."

"No one is sorrier than I." Gayle raised her pinot grigio. "Anyway, welcome home."

They grinned over the rims of their wineglasses, casting off months of resentment into the clamor of clinking forks and background chatter.

"And now for your belated birthday present." Gayle lifted a maroon crocodile embossed satchel out from under her chair, held it proudly by her side. "Many animals were harmed."

"Alexander McQueen?"

"Thank God," Gayle said, hand to chest. "It's really you."

"I found a leather alternative," M.J. said, "not Jesus."

"In that case, it's yours."

M.J. sniffed the bag; it smelled like new car and compliments. "Are you serious?"

Without waiting for an answer, M.J. transferred her things into Gayle's $1,800 apology.

"What are those?" Gayle asked, as M.J. moved a handful of turquoise envelopes into their new silk-lined home.

"Offers to buy my apartment. The doorman gave them to me on my way out. His name is Hamlet," she added because she finally could.

"You're not going to sell it, are you?"

"Dan wants me to. He thinks it will prove I'm committed. But I can't. Not yet. I bought it with the money I got after my parents—" She lifted her eyes to the stained-glass ceiling, and drank. "Hopefully, packing up my stuff and shipping it across the country will be proof enough. At the very least it will prove we need bigger closets."

Gayle's eyebrows leveled. Her smile sank. The good-time glint in her dark eyes turned matte. Small-talk time was over. "You're going back to that beach town?"

"That's the plan."

"And how, exactly, is that going to work with *City*?"

"You got the article I sent, right?"

"I did."

"That's how."

Gayle flicked her wrist at a passing waitress, signaling for another round. "What you sent was a woo-woo piece comparing life to waves. I assumed it was another accident."

"No." M.J. laughed, though she knew Gayle wasn't joking. "It's my solution."

"Staring at the ocean and contemplating life? I don't understand."

"I want to live in Pearl Beach and write for *City*."

Gayle reached for M.J.'s glass of wine and drained it. "You can't be serious."

"I am."

"That's your big proposal?"

"It is."

"My God, M.J., what have those bohemians done to you?" She leaned forward, hands clasped on her empty plate. "Forgive me, darling, but are you saying that the cute little musing about your summer vacation was actually—"

"My submission? Yes," M.J. said, trying to remain upbeat. "The first of many."

"I'm not a magazine editor anymore, I'm the CEO of Pique Publishing Group. But allow me to spare you the humiliation of a rejection letter. *City* won't run that. It's too—"

M.J.'s phone buzzed. It was Dan. She sent him to voice mail. "Then, I'll submit something else. I've been working on a piece about the differences between the coasts. Like, have you ever noticed that New York looks like film and Los Angeles more like video?"

"M.J.—"

"Seriously. It has something to do with the position of the sun and light saturation. And then there's the psychological differences: work ethics for example. New Yorkers are fiercely driven, and Californians are laid-back. Why? Because everything you see in Manhattan was built by humans, whereas Californians are surrounded by nature: the ocean, the desert, mountains . . . Everywhere they look, they're reminded of a power greater than themselves. So they're more, to use your term, woo-woo."

"M.J.—"

"It sounds out-there, but I'll write it in a way that works for *City*. I know the tone of that magazine better than anyone else and—"

"M.J.!" Gayle's palm came down on the table. "You can't pitch these California-stoner stories to a magazine about New York."

"*City* has a global section."

"And Pearl Beach isn't global, it's in Orange County, which by the way, is the only nod to color in that entire region. Colleges hand out affirmative-action scholarships to tanned people because they can't find anyone darker."

"So it's a race thing?"

"Show me one black person who isn't there because of a wrong turn and we'll talk."

M.J.'s phone started to buzz: Dan, again. She let it ring. "What about Central Africa? Is that black enough for you?"

Gayle, reaching for her breadstick, paused.

"Picture me in a refugee camp 186 miles west of the capital Bangui with a team of rescue workers from the Red Cross."

"This conversation is over."

M.J. pushed back her chair. "Why?"

"Because I no longer believe this is you."

"It's me. And I'm going to be *me* on this trip, that's the point. It will be a real fish-out-of-water story. I'll roll tampons in my hair instead of curlers and sleep in my Louis Vuitton steamer trunk," she enthused, grateful that Dan wasn't there to witness the salacious tabloid-sized crap she was about to take on his benevolent mission. "Imagine the opportunities for product placement. Energy bars, Evian water, fitness apparel. Advertisers could sponsor food drops, and if I photograph it all with my iPhone, maybe we can get Apple on board."

Gayle tapped her cheek imagining the possibilities. Had she always worn this much foundation? "I still don't see it for *City*, maybe *Travel Bug*, but that said, I really don't understand why you'd want to do this."

"Dan really cares about these missions and he wants me to go," she said, like a dedicated girlfriend and not the determined writer who would say anything to get herself published. "I guess it's what you married people call compromise."

"Darling, a compromise is, 'I'll do Indian tonight if you'll do Japanese tomorrow.' Not, 'Give up your career, follow me to a refugee camp.'"

M.J. realized it did sound ridiculous when put that way. "My therapist thinks it's good for the relationship and it will help me fill a void."

"What do *you* think?"

"I think . . ." She paused while the waiter topped off their wine. "I think I'm not giving up my career, because I don't have a career. You took my career and you gave it to Liz, remember?"

"And now . . ." Gayle placed the contract on the table, slid it toward her. "I'm giving it back."

"I can't work with her."

"What if I let her go?"

Something like an elastic band snapped behind M.J.'s chest. "You would do that?"

Gayle flicked her chin at the pages lying between them, inviting M.J. to see for herself.

Dan was calling. Still, M.J. pulled the contract closer and flipped to the final signature page. The only name at the bottom was hers.

Shock waves, warm and tingly, rippled throughout her body. There was too much to consider, too much at stake, too much sludge churning inside of her. What was she supposed to say? What did she *want* to say? She had to stop drinking wine and think. She had to pee.

Her phone *dinged*. It was Dan again, only this time he sent a text:

ADDIE IS IN THE HOSPITAL.

He used words like *blood, hemorrhaging,* and *head wound*. Though weak in the knees, M.J. stood. "I'm sorry, Gayle, I have to go. It's an emergency."

"So now what?"

"Give me a chance to write the Africa piece. Let me prove I can do this."

"And if it doesn't fly?"

"It will," M.J. said.

Then she stuffed the contract inside her crocodile purse, on the off chance that she was wrong.

———

ADDIE DRAGGED A hand sluggishly across her face. "You're judging me," she muttered. "I can feel your condescending glare widening my pores."

"I'm not judging," M.J. said, over her pinot grigio headache made worse by six hours in a middle seat, an in-flight chicken wrap, and a long crawl home from the Los Angeles airport in a Lyft that smelled like cumin. And now beeping machines and whiffs of steamed asparagus. She tried to open the window. It was sealed shut.

"If you're not judging, why do I feel all hot and melty?"

"It's the pain meds," M.J. said. She needed a hot shower, a toothbrush, and an explanation as to why Addie had a baby-carrot-sized lump on her forehead and tubes in her arms. She sat in the nubby chair by Addie's bed and refused to faint.

"What happened?"

"Cramps," Addie said, her complexion beige as the curtain that divided the room. "One minute I'm helping Easton pack up the bookstore and the next, I'm on all fours."

"Why?"

"Verizon is buying it, can you believe? Ew, right?"

"No, why all fours?"

"Worst. Pain. Ever. Like a cat inside my stomach clawing its way out. And the blood? It wasn't a super-plus tampon amount, it was a shove-two-mattresses-up-there amount. The Wrath section looked like a crime scene."

M.J. gripped her tingling knees.

"I don't have insurance, so I called Dan. After that I'm not really sure what happened. I passed out at some point"—she indicated the lump—"and I woke up in here after a transfusion, CT scan, and surgery."

M.J. hung her head between her knees while the nurse checked Addie's vitals, changed her bags, updated her charts, and adjusted her tubes.

"Who knew miscarriages were so grizzly?" Addie said after she left.

M.J. lifted her head. "Miscarriage? You said you had an abortion."

"Did I?"

M.J. helped herself to Addie's ice chips. "Okay, now I'm judging. Why would you lie about that?"

"I didn't want David to know I was keeping the baby, and you were like, the last person I trusted."

"I'm lost."

Addie rolled onto her side and faced the window. "When he found out I was pregnant he broke up with that little girlfriend of his and proposed." The beeps on the heart machine quickened, the wavy lines became jagged spikes. "How messed up is that?"

"It's not messed up, Addie, it's sweet," M.J. said. "He loves you. And I know you love him."

"I do." Addie breathed, her throat too dry for sound. "But I don't want kids."

"So you told him you had an abortion?"

Addie nodded, loosening her tears. "I'm going to Europe," she said. "He never would have known, everything would have been fine."

"Except for the part about you being pregnant and not wanting kids."

"I was going to have the baby there and then put it up for adoption. Think of all those women like Liddy who wanted . . . and couldn't—" Addie turned back and looked at M.J. for the first time. Her gaze was hollow and unsteady, her electric-green eyes dim. "It felt like the right thing to do." The beeps on the machine slowed. "Did you come back from New York to tell me what an idiot I am?"

"No." M.J. grinned. "I came back from New York to hold your hand."

Addie thanked her with a weak squeeze and a grateful smile—a smile that returned one hour later when she woke up and saw that M.J. was still there.

CHAPTER

Twenty-Four

NOTHING SAYS REFUGEE camp like a hot paraffin wax treatment and two coats of Pink Flamenco," M.J. said when she returned home from her mani-pedi, hands splayed to avoid smudging. "Wait," she said to Addie, who was jamming the last of her satin robes—of which there were many—into her suitcase. "You're leaving?"

"I'm not the one leaving, you are," she said. "Unless you're finally over this whole Africa thing."

"Nope. We're going tonight. But I thought you were staying here while we're gone."

"I was, until David said I could have Michael's old room until I leave for London, which, according to Dr. Dan should be in about two weeks, and I'd rather not be alone." Addie stood carefully, hand on belly as she scored her pain with an old person's grunt. At least she could stand. It was progress. Color had returned to her face, which was thinner now, her cheekbones sharper, and yet her edge had softened.

Hands still splayed, M.J. began folding the sheets and blankets that Addie had used during her stay. "So why Michael's room? Why not David's?"

"Hannah's back, and I'm not sure she'd like it," Addie said. "Though I'm not opposed."

"So, what—you're, like, platonic now? How long will that last?"

"At least until my stitches come out, but hopefully forever."

M.J. cut a look to the yellowing bruise on Addie's head. Had that fall somehow loosened the part of her brain that was stuck in high school and hurtled it into adulthood?

"We want different things," she continued, as she gathered her hair into a ponytail. "David really wants kids and I really, really don't."

"What *do* you want?" M.J. asked, playing the role of Dr. Cohn.

"I want him to be happy, and I want him in my life. So platonic it is."

"How healthy of you."

"I know, right?"

Addie barefooted into the kitchen, where her prescription bottles were lined up like chess pieces. Antibiotics, anti-inflammatories, painkillers; she took one of each, then one more painkiller. "Nap time."

And then it wasn't. Destiny called in hysterics.

"I have to go," Addie said.

"Where?"

"The Majestic. Destiny's in trouble."

"Where's Jules?"

"Working. It's Piper Goddard's wedding." Addie found the key to the Mini Cooper in the mail basket. "Later, Salivator." Then with a giggle: "I have no idea why I said that."

"You're not driving."

"Why not?"

"You just took two Percocet."

Addie tossed her the key.

"Thank you," M.J. said, appreciating her compliance. "I'll call a Lyft."

Addie was standing in the open doorway, still barefoot. "Lyft? There's no time for Lyft. One of us is driving and if it's not me . . ."

"Dan is on his way home from some medical supply store and then we're going to Africa. I can't just drop everything."

"I'm not asking you to drop *everything*, just this bullshit driving phobia of yours."

"I don't understand," M.J. said, bicast leather sandals planted firmly on the shag. "What's the urgency?"

"Chest is dead."

"Dead? Well, why doesn't Destiny call the police?"

"She thinks she killed him."

———————

"MY NAME IS May-June Stark and I am fastening my seat belt," she said, probably out loud, but who knows? It was impossible to hear above the anxiety orchestra crescendoing inside her: heart on percussion, ears on strings, thoughts on brass. "I am adjusting my rearview mirror. My nails are painted Pink Flamenco. The neighbor's goldendoodle is barking."

Addie turned on the radio.

M.J. shut it off.

"I am putting the key in the ignition. I can't breathe. Yes, I can. I can breathe. I am breathing. I couldn't be talking if I wasn't breathing."

"Are you going to do this the whole way?"

"It's one of my tools. It's how I stay calm." M.J. swallowed. "I'm going to turn on the car."

"Please do."

M.J. pressed the start/stop button. The engine giggled its way to a steady hum. "It's on. I'm sweating."

"You're glowing."

"I'm terrified."

"You're a Powerpuff Girl."

"Why a Powerpuff Girl?"

"It's fun to say."

"True." M.J. white-knuckled the steering wheel, hands at six and three. "What if we get in an accident?"

"I'll give you a painkiller," Addie said. "Now drive."

DESTINY POKED HER pierced nose through the crack in the door of room 729, before opening it all the way. Smeared makeup marred her face as if she had just collided with an oil painting. And her hair—dyed rebellion black—spilled from her professional bun. Her Majestic Resort uniform, however, remained perfectly intact: crisp white shirt and burgundy blazer with a pleat down her slacks sharp enough to slit a wrist. Or a boyfriend's neck, as the case might be.

"What took you so long?" she asked with the urgency of a girl whose afternoon took a turn for the worse.

"We got pulled over for going five miles an hour in a thirty-mile zone," Addie explained. "Are you okay?"

Destiny nodded, though her rasping breaths told another story. "Is she?"

M.J., who was fanning her face with a Do Not Disturb sign, lied and said she was.

Inside the room, the cream-colored duvets were fluffed to a five-star standard. The plein air paintings were meticulously centered on the sand-colored wallpaper. Central air sang a pleasant tune called seventy-two degrees. And a shirtless, listless sixteen-year-old boy was lying faceup on the carpet between the queen beds.

Addie lifted her ear off his shaved chest. "He's not dead, but he is one burp and a flame away from blowing the place up."

"What?" Destiny asked, wringing her hands.

"He's filled to the gills with cheap booze." Addie fired off a quick text. A doctor alerting her nurse to send in the next patient. "Nothing a bottle of Advil and a burger can't fix."

Destiny collapsed onto the bed and cried relief.

"So what actually happened?" M.J. asked. Someone had to.

Destiny sniffled. "I was working my shift at the front desk and he just showed up, super wasted. So I got a key for a vacant room and snuck him in so he wouldn't make a scene, but of course, he thought I was bringing him here so we could do it, and when I said, 'I broke up with you, so why would we do it?' he called me a tease and pushed me on the bed, so I pushed him onto the floor and then his eyes closed and he didn't get up, so . . ."

Addie stretched out on the couch and yawned. "When did you break up with him?"

"Last night."

"Why?"

"Sex."

"It wasn't good?"

"No," Destiny said, padding off to the bathroom. "It wasn't . . . *anything*. That was the problem."

"Chest is impotent?"

"No." Destiny blew her nose. "It's me."

"*You?*"

"I know it's lame but"—she returned to the bed—"I'm not ready, and Chest was."

"Does your mom know?"

"Why would I tell *her*?"

"Because she thinks you're a slut."

"I know." Destiny smiled wryly.

"Why do you want your mom to think you're a slut?" M.J. asked, deciding in that moment that she'd rather give rise to a cancerous mole than a teenaged daughter.

"It makes her mad, and I like when she gets mad."

"Because . . . ?"

"Because I'm over her whole 'let's whistle a happy tune and pretend everything is perfect' bullshit. Because it's not perfect. It's pathetic. I'm a bitch; Dad's an asshole; she's literally allergic to her job, and sometimes I wish she'd just get off the friggin' cross and act like it."

"Is this how you talk when I'm not around?" Jules asked from the open doorway, holding a key card and her composure with equal amounts of grace. "Meet me at the bar."

"No," Destiny said. "I'm going back to work."

"Not you," Jules hissed. "Them. We're staying right here."

She closed the door with a reverberating slam that seemed to chase M.J. and Addie down the hall and straight into the elevator.

THE LOBBY WAS their only option since the rest of the resort had been commandeered by the Goddard wedding. Though it lacked the intimacy of the Oyster Bar and the classic dark wooded elegance of the steak house, there were couches and salted nuts and enough alcohol to quiet M.J.'s nerves and flood her blood with an indisputable reason to ditch the car and take a Lyft home.

"I think my Percocets could use a scotch after that, don't you?" Addie said, ordering a round. Then: "Look who it is . . ." Her unsteady gaze led to a woman sitting next to the piano, peering above a copy of *West Coast Living* magazine, foot shaking restlessly inside a neon-green Nike Air Zoom.

"Britt?"

Addie limply whipped a cashew at her and laughed, as if they had just ended a pub crawl, not broken up a book club that spanned two generations.

"Stop!" Britt set down the magazine and heel-toed toward them in a huff. "I'm trying to be discreet."

"Then you should have worn different shoes," Addie said with a self-amused snort.

"My Spouse Spotter app is saying that Paul is here," Britt said, ignoring the dig but not the waitress. "Double chardonnay, please."

"I'm sorry, miss, do you mean two glasses?"

"I mean, hurry."

The pianist claimed his bench and began his set with the creeping notes of Beethoven's Für Elise.

"So what are you ladies doing here?" Britt asked. "Have you been"—she removed her tennis visor and revived her flattened bangs—"hanging out?"

"Not at all," M.J. downplayed. "Destiny needed Addie, and Addie needed a ride, so—"

"You *drove*?"

Addie rolled her eyes so hard she lost her balance and timbered into M.J.'s shoulder. "I wouldn't exactly call it *driving*."

"Is she okay?" Britt mouthed to M.J.

"Probably not."

Britt smiled a deep dimple, and just like that, any tension M.J. felt between them was gone.

And then it was back.

This time in the form of a petite blond in a cream-colored suit, a voluminous blowout, and a huge bone to pick with Addie.

"I cannot believe what you did." Jules sneered.

"She was trying to help," M.J. said.

"Oh, I know exactly what she was trying to do."

"You don't," M.J. said to Jules's flared nostrils. "She was genuinely worried, and you were at the wedding and—"

"S'okay," Addie slurred, and then tried to stand.

Before M.J. could stop her, Jules helped her up with a friendly yank. Then she pulled Addie into her arms and said, "Thank you," into her ponytail.

"Thank you?" Britt asked, just as surprised. "What did *she* do?"

"She texted me and told me Destiny was in trouble, that's what she did."

Jules gripped Addie's shoulders and grinned.

"Don't look at me like that," Addie said, turning away from her high-beaming admiration. "Shouldn't you be at the wedding?"

Jules removed her blazer, folded it over her arm, sat. "I was relieved of my duties."

"Fired?" Addie gasped. "For leaving?"

"No. Because the beautician I booked was a no-show."

M.J. gave Jules her martini. "I'm sorry."

"Don't be," she said, popping an olive in her mouth. "While Piper was working herself into a lather, yours truly was turning bridesmaids into beauties. Which was no easy feat, let me tell you. And now you're looking at the lead makeup artist for the new Goddard Cosmetics boutique, opening right here in the resort."

Amid squealing congratulations, Britt ordered a celebratory round.

"What are you doing here?" Jules asked, as if seeing her for the first time.

"Waiting to catch Paul in the act."

"The act of what?"

"Cheating," she said, as if it should have been obvious.

"What do your other friends think about all this?" M.J. asked.

"I haven't told them. Everyone thinks Paul and I are perfect."

"Maybe you are," M.J. said.

"Never doubt a wife's instinct," Jules said, her eyes icy blue and sure. "For example, I found *this* on the passenger seat of Brandon's car when he drove me home from the hospital." She pulled out a Ziploc snack bag out of her purse. A dark brown hair extension was sealed between its plastic gums. "I'm like Prince Charming with Cinderella's slipper. I'll carry it with me until I find its rightful owner."

Britt quickly put on her visor and looked out the window, suddenly taken with the sunset.

"He told me it was a color sample he brought for Destiny, you know, so he could coax her into dying her hair back to a more approachable shade of brown. I believed him until he told me to quit the club and"—she snapped her fingers—"just like that, my green flags turned red."

"Jules, I—"

She silenced Britt with a flash of her palm. "I mean he didn't wear a wedding ring. So, really, I can't blame the women, now could I?"

"There were *others*?" M.J. asked on behalf of Britt, whose shaking hand was covering her mouth.

"Oh, shugah, that boy sowed more oats than Quaker. Not to say that Brandon is a bad man, he's not. I got pregnant in high school and was trying to do the honorable thing—we both were, but it backfired and Destiny sees right through it. She lost respect for him because he cheats, and for me because I let him get away with it. But that's about to change." She shook the bowl of nuts the way a miner sifts gold through a strainer. "I filed for a divorce."

"No," Britt cried. "You can't. It's my fault. *I* fuck-attacked *him*. I'm the bad one. Granted, I did stop the second I found out who he was, but still, I started this and I'm going to make it right."

"There's no making this right, Britt. Not between me and Brandon, anyway, but you can make it right between you and Paul."

"I agree. I'm going to tell him everything tonight."

"Like hell you are," Jules said, plucking a pistachio from the bowl.

"'Scuse me?"

"Telling Paul will tear you two apart. And what kind of Liaison of Love would I be if I let you do that? No, what you're going to do is promise me you'll never cheat on him again and that you'll do whatever you can to make your marriage work while you still have a chance."

"I promise," Britt said, crossing her heart. "But what about you? How can I make things right with us?"

"Agree to be my plus one at work parties, you know, if I can't find a suitable date."

"Of course I will," Britt said, hugging her. "I'm so, so sorry," she cried.

Jules *pat-patted* her on the back. "I can imagine," she said. "Brandon never was very good in the sack." Then in a whisper, "Easton is much better."

"Easton?" Addie squealed. "Easton is gay!"

"No, he's just a liberal Republican." She cracked down on a pistachio nut. "A liberal Republican who's got my shy vagina talking a mile a minute."

Laughing, M.J. checked the time: Ninety minutes until her airport shuttle arrived. Ninety minutes until the four of them moved on.

The pianist started playing Norah Jones.

"Now what's this Paul of yours like?" Jules asked. "Is he one of those slick nightclub types?"

Britt laughed at how off-base she was—not just about Paul's perceived slickness, but the relevance of nightclubs in general. She scrolled through her phone in search of a photo that depicted her husband before he became a ball-powdering pube-plucker.

"Here he is at the dog-a-thon with our old pug, Maple." She handed Jules the screen.

"That's Paul."

"Yep."

"No," Jules said, "that's *Paul*. I see him around here all the time. Come"—she scribbled her account number on their check—"let's catch this critter in the act."

OUTSIDE, ON THE great lawn, a white tent gave cover to an assemblage of middle-aged wedding guests who, by lubricating their replaced hips and pinned knees with Veuve Clicquot, came to believe that dancing to a cover of "I Feel Good" was in no way painful.

M.J. wondered why they needed a tent at all. It hadn't rained in months. And the bride and groom, who undoubtedly paid a premium for the cliffside location, couldn't even see the sunset, which was now painting the sky with gashes, as if a tiger had run its claws across a mass of blue flesh and drew blood, orange blood that was deepening to red.

"Why are we standing out here on the grass?" Britt asked Jules. "And where are Addie's shoes?"

Jules answered the first question with a switchblade's flick of her finger, which was aimed back at the resort, where thousands of plants covered the building's exterior like a patchwork quilt. Some waxy and thick-leafed, others feathery, swordlike, or lily-pad round. And the colors? Chartreuse, aubergine, cucumber green, yellow striped . . .

"It's called a living wall," Jules told them.

"Trippy," Addie mused.

M.J. snapped a picture.

"What does this have to do with Paul?" Britt asked.

As if on cue, a small white truck rolled up to the wall, extended its hydra-ladder, and raised the man inside the bucket toward the center of the installation. Once stopped, he turned on his misting hose and began figure-eighting it over the plants.

"He's been working on it for months."

Britt's wide eyes darted from Jules to Paul and back to Jules. "What about his back?"

"He designed it and his team installed it."

"Bungee!" Addie swatted Jules on the arm. "He was working on this. He must be part of Paul's team."

"Paul has a *team*?"

Jules nodded. "His crew did the installation, and then Paul comes by at night to water it."

Britt watched Paul ascend and descend in his bucket, misting his leafy canvas. "No bush in the bush," she snickered. "That was his motto. Pubes, pit-hair, even eyebrows, he trims it all when he works outside, something about feeling the breeze."

"Why didn't he tell you?" M.J. asked, and then quickly remembered the contract she kept hidden from Dan for months.

"Because after years of believing in his half-baked pot-inspired dead-end business plans I told him I only wanted to hear about the sure things."

"Then he probably won't say anything for two more weeks," Jules said.

"Why? What happens then?"

"If the plants thrive, Paul will be under contract to build living walls for every Cartwright resort in North America. And if those work, he'll get Europe, Asia, and Australia."

"And if they die?"

"He's back on the couch." Jules lifted her gaze to the brightening moon. After a brief pause she said, "It's full tonight. We should be having a meeting."

"We never got our next book," M.J. said, because it was easier than reminding them that they quit.

"It's probably in that secret room," Addie said, with a jazzy flash of her hands and a flippant smirk.

"What secret room?" Britt asked.

"The one in the store."

"Does Verizon know about this?"

"No." Another jazzy-flash. "It's a secret, remember?"

"How long until these Percocets wear off?" M.J. asked.

"Not long enough," she answered.

"I'm your Realtor, Addie, why haven't I seen it?"

"I didn't think I had the key."

"*Didn't?*" M.J. asked. "And now?"

"That night when everyone left their keys on M.J.'s table, I noticed that mine was different." Then with a devilish smile: "Different enough to think that maybe I do have the key."

———

DARKNESS DIDN'T DESCEND that night, it settled slowly, the way a post-op patient might get into bed. Everything in the town's center felt sluggish now that tourist season was over. Sidewalks were empty, restaurants quiet, headlights from the occasional passing car stretched by.

"Welcome to Verizon," Addie said with a listless slur. She ushered them into the sealed-off bookstore, where the smell of ink and inspiration had been replaced by a stale must.

"So it's official?" Jules asked.

"We're in escrow," Britt announced.

M.J. congratulated her as if another sterile, soulless chain store is exactly what Pearl Beach needed because she couldn't call it what it really was: the murder of Liddy's only living child. She couldn't say that, soon, the "first editions" inside these walls will pertain to outdated cell phones, "hard covers" to protective cases, and "characters" to keyboard strokes. It was out of her hands.

Addie flicked on the lights.

Boxes had been packed and stacked along the water-stained walls. The cracked ceiling had been stripped of its dancing bookmarks. And the autographed shelves had been lined up, execution style with signs that read EBAY taped to their backs.

"Is it safe in here?" Jules asked, her gaze fixed on the gaping hole above what used to be the Pride aisle.

"Anything that can fall through already did." Addie winced through a shock of pain as she lowered to sit on a row of boxes marked TRAVEL GUIDES. She closed her eyes. "Including my future."

M.J. peeked at her father's Timex. The airport shuttle would be picking her up in one hour, and Dan was probably one beer into fretting over when she'd be home. "I'm scared I'll miss my flight if we don't get started."

"I'd be more scared of catching that flight than missing it," Britt said.

M.J. could have easily agreed but clung to denial. "Africa is going to be great."

Addie snorted.

"So where y'all hiding this secret room anyway?" Jules asked.

"Back there," Addie said as she handed Jules her purse. "Key's inside."

"Aren't you coming?"

"I'm not allowed. They'll punish me."

"Punish you?"

"I used to spy on their meetings. Put my ear against the wall, hold my breath like a sniper, and listen."

"Snipers hold their breath to listen?" Jules asked as she rummaged through Addie's purse in search of the key. "Why? You can't hear aim."

"It slows their heart rates so they can shoot between beats," M.J. explained. "It keeps them steady."

"Okay, but why do you need to be steady to eavesdrop?" Jules asked Addie.

"Why do you need to pronounce the *V* in eavesdrop?"

M.J. checked her watch again. "Did you ever hear anything?"

"Nah, the walls are too thick. But one time, just before my fourteenth birthday, Marjorie ran out crying. At first, I thought she was a movie star they had kidnapped and she was trying to escape. She was so glamorous, I swear, even her cigarettes smelled different."

"Did you talk to her?" Jules asked.

"No. She just stared at me like I was a dangerous animal she wanted to pet and then she took off. Everyone chased after her and that's when I snuck in."

"What was it like in there?" M.J. asked.

"I remember the lipstick on the martini glasses. That hat box full of envelopes. The four open copies of *Story of O*. One of them had doodles in the margins. A few penises and some boobs, but mostly wings. Same as mine, see?" Addie lifted the necklace from her cleavage, dragged the charm across its chain.

"How have you not mentioned this before?" Britt asked.

"I don't know," Addie said. "Suppressed childhood memories usually do take priority over condemned apartments, job loss, unexpected pregnancy, miscarriage, and hospitalization, so, wow, Britt, I'm not sure."

Jules retrieved the tangle of necklaces, bracelets, and hair elastics from Addie's purse and held it above her head like Lady Liberty's torch. "Let's get in there."

M.J. gripped the fleshy part of Addie's arms and guided her toward the back of the store.

"Tell us about the envelopes?" Jules asked.

Addie looked at her blankly.

"Inside the hat box."

"There were hundreds of them. Some from TWA and others from American Airlines. I also remember the ashtray, like how it was overflowing with butts. One of them was still smoking, so I picked it up and took a puff and . . ." Her voice began to trail, her eyes fluttered closed.

M.J. gave her a nudge. "Then what?"

"I started coughing and that's when they came running in. Except Marjorie. I don't know where she went. But the rest of them?" Another head shake. "They were pissed at me for snooping, and I was banned from the Good Book for a month."

"That was your big punishment?" Britt asked. "Banned from a bookstore? Ha! You must have been stoked."

"More like destroyed. Reading was my life."

Stunned, the girls stopped walking.

"What? I didn't have a lot of friends back then."

"And now?" M.J. asked.

Addie tapped her cleavage. "Now I have wings."

THE DOOR TO the right of the hearth was easy to miss. It didn't have a shiny brass knob or a foreboding Keep Out sign. It was made of the same caramel-colored planks as the other walls. And its hinges—if it even had hinges—were masterfully concealed. If not for the brief interruption in the wood—a chink, about hip-high and shaped like an upside-down exclamation point—the entrance would have been undetectable. And Addie's key fit inside perfectly.

Dark and windowless, M.J. could practically chew the stale cigarette smoke. It filled her lungs and clogged her nose like dust. And yet, she felt a kinship in its presence. How it clung to the room for decades: loyal as a friend, stubborn as a memory refusing to fade.

She found her phone, activated her flashlight, and saw a text from Dan: A reminder that the shuttle would be picking them up in forty-five minutes. A chorus line of emojis followed: the African Flag, an airplane, a glass of wine. She quickly assured him she was on her way and then trained her flashlight app on whatever was blocking the door.

"Addie, will you open that so we can see?"

"The door stays closed," she whispered.

"Why?"

"In case they find us."

"They're in France!" Britt said.

"And they gave you the key," Jules added.

"Still." Addie took the phone from M.J. and used it to find the Tiffany lamp that hung in the center of the room. With a tug of its dangling chain, she illuminated the mirrored table beneath it, which seemed as round and bright as the full moon, and the four *Prim*-covered books that had been laid out like a place setting.

The space was no bigger than a starter office at *City*; something a newly promoted fact-checker might celebrate. And yet, the view was heart-stopping: Hundreds of identical books cloaked in white dust jackets rose from floor to ceiling on every wall, packed on shelves tight as secrets.

"Whoa," M.J. said. "Is this what an acid trip feels like?"

"I had this vision in my head for years," Addie said. "I thought I dreamed it."

"This isn't a dream," Britt said. "It's porn for broken iPads." She pulled a book from the shelf and peeled back its cover. "*My Secret Garden.*"

Jules did the same. "*Lady Chatterley's Lover.*"

Then the others. "*Vox.*"

"*Forever.*"

"*Tropic of Cancer.*"

"*Beautiful Bastard.*"

And so it went until M.J. reached into her crocodile bag, grabbed their once-discarded keys, and released them to the table.

"You saved them!" Jules beamed.

M.J. said she had been meaning to toss them but forgot. Because she didn't have time for sentimental speeches or teary-eyed attempts to keep them from breaking up. Addie was leaving. Dan was waiting. Her future writing career pending. She had to go.

"So now what?" Britt asked. "No one read the book." She slid the cover down to reveal its title, *How to Make Love Like a Porn Star: A Cautionary Tale*, by Jenna Jameson with Neil Strauss. "Can we still read the letter?"

"I don't think so." Jules pulled a sealed American Airlines envelope from one of the copies. It read *For: Addie Oliver* in serious
black ink.

Addie backed away from the table, drew her thumbnail to her
mouth and bit.

"Do you recognize the handwriting?" M.J. asked, and then
wanted to take it back. Only one of those women worked for American Airlines and they all knew it.

But Addie was just standing there, biting. Her body was swaying
slightly from the pain medication.

M.J. checked her watch: twenty-five minutes. She *really* had to
go. "What if you hold it up to the light," she suggested. "You know,
dip your toe in the water . . ."

"And then?"

"If you like what you see, we dive."

"*We?*" Addie asked, suddenly awake and attentive, as if the haze
had been burned off by that one little word. She gripped the back of
her chair and examined the three women for twitches or tics or anything that might signal looming betrayal.

After several minutes, each of which was probably being counted
by Dan, Addie took the envelope, raised it toward the stained-glass
shade, and ripped it in half.

"What the ham?" Jules gasped.

"I can't handle any more bad news."

"How do you know it's bad?"

"It's always bad," M.J. answered for her.

Addie grinned, because it always was.

And that was that. There was no closing ceremony. No turning
keys or crossing bands of smoke rising as one. Just a quick hug when

they dropped M.J. off in the Mini Cooper, a promise to give it back when she returned from Africa, and a pall of sorrow, because Addie and their secret room would be gone when she did.

———————

THOUGH SHE WAS three minutes late, M.J. sauntered into the cottage with an early person's pride. How delightfully smug she would feel rocking on the porch swing—Louis Vuitton steamer trunk packed and final pee taken—when Dan screeched into the driveway. The guilt he'd feel for doubting her. The light she'd shine on his hypocrisy. The window seat she'd demand in exchange for the badgering she endured.

But Dan's bags were no longer by the front door. A sheet of yellow legal paper was there instead. Taped over the peephole and festooned with his semi-legible doctor's scrawl. There was also an airline ticket. Not to Bangui M'Poko International Airport, but to JFK. And the flight was leaving at seven the next morning.

Tears began to gather like a team of first responders, waiting for their orders, ready to react. The ocean thudded and fizzed. Something like a metal fan turned inside M.J.'s stomach; she could feel its blades scraping against her gut, taste the rust. Or maybe it wasn't a fan at all. Maybe it was Fortune's wheel gearing up for another ill-fated spin.

Fingertips cold and heart hammering, M.J. leaned against the door and thought of Addie. How easy it would be to rip Dan's letter in half. Destroy the bad news before it destroyed her. But she had learned to tolerate adversity as if it was a pair of three-inch heels. Now she was one of those girls who was used to the pain. And so she read.

Dear M.J.,

Go back to New York. Sign Gayle's contract. Become the best editor in chief City magazine will ever know. Climb the corporate ladder and don't stop until you reach 35,000 feet. Then wave to the doctor in the airplane. The one blowing you kisses as he flies by. And know he loves you enough to let you go.

You're welcome,
Dan

M.J. called his cell phone. It went straight to voice mail. She sent a text. It went unanswered. She kicked the door. It really hurt.

"I drove today," she cried to a room full of Dans who weren't there.

How dare he make that decision for her—for *them*! She never even had a say. Could he be any more arrogant?

Unless it was a test.

What if he was stalling the flight crew with the hope that she'd come bounding toward him all adorably snotty and disheveled, protein bars tumbling from her backpack, as she pledged her bone-deep commitment to him *and* the Red Cross.

Because she could do that. There was still time.

Or she could unpack the malaria pills and cargo shorts, fill her steamer trunk with black cashmere, board that flight to New York, and wonder if Fortune just spun her a lucky break.

Twenty-Five

Los Angeles International Airport
Saturday, September 17
Full Moon

"MA'AM," SNIPPED THE flight attendant, "your device." He flicked his chin at the window, indicating the passing runway markers, the trails of brown grass zipping by. "We're taking off."

M.J. apologized and turned off her phone, but her attention remained fixed on the screen. Though dead and dark, she searched it for a possible explanation. Something that might help her understand what Addie meant when she texted:

It's bad, isn't it? Must be or you would have called by now.

It wasn't until she woke up from her nap, choked down a rubbery omelet, searched her crocodile bag for gum, and brushed against those two pieces of paper that she understood: Last night, when Addie was beside her in the Mini, or maybe when they hugged good-bye, she slipped M.J. that letter.

THE DATE: May 26, 2016
THE DIRTY: *How to Make Love Like a Porn Star: A Cautionary Tale* by Jenna Jameson with Neil Strauss
THE DETAILS: By Marjorie Richards

This book is about bad decisions, the resulting consequences, and surviving anyway. This book may as well be about me.

Chapter one begins: "There comes a moment in every life when a choice must be made between right and wrong, between good and evil, between light and darkness," and as you can imagine, porn star Jenna Jameson chose darkness. I, however, chose light along with adventure, sex, and freedom. But in 1981 the darkness found me anyway.

I was at the Rolling Stones concert in Los Angeles with some gals from work. We had a seventeen-hour layover, an ounce of weed, and a twenty-dollar bet that said I wouldn't show Mick Jagger my tits. I won the bet *and* lost my shirt—literally. I was waving it over my head and accidentally let go. I didn't care. My friends didn't care. The guys next to us certainly didn't care. But the cops did.

While they were yanking me out of the crowd an attorney from Pearl Beach handed me his card. A Richard Gere type who got me off the hook and into bed, all before my 8:00 AM flight. He also got me pregnant.

My roommate Ingrid set me up with a doctor in Paris who said I'd be out of bed in two days and back in the sack by the end of the month. But I couldn't go through with it. All I could think of was Liddy and Patrick and how badly they wanted a baby. So I decided, what the hell? Why not bake the bun and give it to them when it's cooked?

Of course, Liddy was over the moon, but Patrick had one condition: I had to tell the Richard Gere type that the baby was his so he could bless the adoption. It was the "light" thing to do.

As you might have guessed, I did not get a blessing. I got a proposal from a stranger named Charles Oliver and the promise of a life I never wanted. But what I wanted no longer mattered. I quit my job. I moved back to America. I had nightmares of being buried alive.

Then, just as I was leaving a DBC meeting, you kicked. (The book was *Family Secrets*—how apropos.) Anyway, that kick must have knocked some sense into me because from that moment on I was all in.

You were born on the Fourth of July amid fireworks and the joyful tears of my best friends—all of whom thought they'd never see the day. And Charles, of course. He was elated. Everyone was elated, except me.

I felt detached and disoriented. Like the time Suzette Rodgers and I got our luggage mixed up. I unzipped her bag and didn't recognize a thing. "These are my clothes," I thought. "But why don't I know them? Why do they feel so unfamiliar? Am I losing my mind?"

But with you, Addie, it was different, because you did belong to me. I assembled you in my body, I felt you grow, we have the same green eyes. But none of that mattered. You may as well have belonged to someone else.

I asked Gloria and Dotty if they felt connected to their babies right away. Of course they said yes. And Liddy? She connected with babies who were never even born. So I did the things that mothers do: I cooed and took pictures and strolled around town with a proud smile on my face. But you may as well have been a box of Pop-Tarts. Actually, I felt more connected to those.

I stopped eating and sleeping. It got so I couldn't get dressed or hold you. Sometimes I would leave you in your crib from the time your father went to work until he came home. Forgetting to feed us both. "See," I'd sob into my pillow. "I wasn't meant to have kids."

One day the crying was so bad (yours or mine, I can't remember) I boarded a flight to Paris wearing slippers and a housecoat. Once again, Ingrid took me to that doctor of hers and I was diagnosed with postpartum depression: a mood disorder caused by big drops in hormone levels after you give birth. Who knew?

I flew back home two weeks later, medicated and motivated, ready to make up for lost time. But your father saw it differently. He thought my diagnosis was French for "bat-shit crazy" and filed a restraining order against me.

I called the apartment day and night. I waited outside his office for hours. I even stormed the court during one of his racquetball games. And he arrested me for harassment.

I stopped by the house when your nanny was there and he had me arrested for trespassing. But I was determined. So much so that the girls made me go back

to Paris because the next time—and there would have
been a next time—I'd be sent to prison.

They promised a steady flow of pictures, report
cards, and updates if I promised to stay out of
trouble, get a lawyer, and fight this the smart way.
So that's what I did. But Charles fought, too, and
he always won. But I never gave up. Getting you back
was all I thought about for fourteen years. Because
fourteen was the magic number. When you turned fourteen
you could live with whomever you wanted. And when you
heard what a terrible man your father was, you'd choose
me. You'd choose light.

But the girls refused to let me go through with it.
You were having a hard time fitting in at school (you
were an early bloomer and had been getting teased),
your father's new wife was a twat, and you and David
Golden had just been suspended for smuggling booze
into a dance. They thought even the tap of a feather
would hit you like a ton of bricks and meeting your
"dead" mother was no feather. And so I died all over
again.

I invested the money I had saved for our new house
in Liddy's bookstore. I knew you were a big reader and
I liked imagining you surrounded by the stories and
adventures we never got to share. It's my only legacy,
Addie, and it's all for you. Make it your own or sell
it. It's worth more than the last present you got from
me. Do you remember it? It was a gold wing necklace. I
bought it after I read *Fear of Flying* because I wanted
to wear my freedom where the world could see it. Unlike
Gloria, Dot, and Liddy, flying was never my fear,
landing was. That's what got me into trouble: when to
land, where to land, and what situations were worth

it. I never could figure that out until I had you, and well, we all know how that turned out.

I'm certainly not suggesting that you stop flying. I gave you that necklace so you never would. What I am saying is: look down every once in a while and if you spot something that matters, find the courage to land. And wherever you end up—be it right or wrong, good or evil, light or dark—know that I love you. That you, Addie Oliver, are worth landing for. Maybe someday you'll let me prove it.

> Heart, soul, and wings,
> Marjorie Richards-Oliver
> (Mom)

CHAPTER

Twenty-Six

New York City, New York
Friday, September 30
New Moon

"**Y**OU'RE NOT HAVING second thoughts, are you, Ms. Stark?"

M.J. glanced up from the contract, the tip of her pencil still pressed firmly against the blank line that awaited her signature. "No." She smiled. "Why?"

The Suit removed a pen from his breast pocket, demonstrated its usefulness with a jaunty *click-click*, and then slid it toward her. The Godfather with an offer she couldn't refuse. "My client has concerns." He blinked twice, a nervous tic that couldn't have served the lawyer well in other, more heated, negotiations.

"Concerns?" Ignoring the pen, M.J. leaned back against her rigid chair, gripped the velvet upholstered armrests, and wondered how Louis XIV remained king of France for seventy-two years with such uncomfortable furniture. "What kinds of concerns?"

"That you're going to back out at the last minute."

"Why?"

"They've wanted this for a while now and—" He folded his hands across his ink blotter and managed a *How shall I put this?*

smile. "Let's just say erasable signatures don't exactly scream, 'binding.'"

Blushing, M.J. apologized, though more to her parents than the suit. Had she gone with them to the Montblanc store she wouldn't have needed his pen, her "pencils only" rule wouldn't exist. But that afternoon, M.J. took the gold-plated Parker, and for the first time in three years, used it anyway.

"Well, that wasn't so hard, was it?" He blinked as he placed the contract in his briefcase, snapped it shut.

"It really wasn't," M.J. said. And then, instead of a handshake, she hugged him. Because after months of aimless flying M.J. finally knew where she wanted to land. And he was the only one there when she made it official.

CHAPTER

Twenty-Seven

The Good Book
Pearl Beach, California
Eighteen Months Later
New Moon

HANDS GRIPPING THE sides of the podium, silver neck of the microphone arched toward her mouth, M.J. looked out at the filled-to-capacity crowd, who were finally seated and silent, and blanked.

Why had she been so averse to note cards? Who cares if her sentiments seemed staged? At least she'd be saying *something* right now instead of catching whiffs of her melting deodorant.

M.J. reached for the bottle of Smartwater, lifted it shakily to her lips.

She could always begin with her background: loving parents; the outstanding writing program at NYU; the years she spent at *City* magazine "paying her dues"; Gayle, her mentor, who was kind enough to attend the event and was still doing that restless cross-uncross thing with her legs.

Or she could jump ahead to the rich couple in #5F. How she sold her New York apartment to them last September (even signed the contract in pen!), and used the money to buy the Good Book back from Verizon. And Addie, of course, who, with the help of her mother, Marjorie, has been keeping the store profitable with a tasteful X-rated section (batteries included), so she could reimburse M.J. for the loan.

Then there was Dan, her favorite ex-boyfriend and occasional roommate (he preferred a thatched-roofed mud hut in Central Africa to an ocean-front cottage in Pearl Beach), who flew twenty-three hours to cheer her on. Her dear friend Jules, the lead makeup artist for Goddard Cosmetics, who spent hours perfecting M.J.'s "natural" look for tonight's event. Easton, Jules's boyfriend, who also happens to be the reason why the Good Book has a liquor license and a full-time bartender who responds "As you wish" to his customer's requests. Britt, who folded M.J. into her loving family and lets her babysit the twins each time she and Paul jet off to one of his job sites. Or that little girl inside her who never stopped tugging.

She could ask Gloria, Liddy, Dot, and Marjorie to stand up. Applaud them for coming all the way from France to be with her tonight, and for bravely letting her share their secrets with the world. She could thank them for showing her the power of female friendship, the magic of the full moon, and how to get out from under Fortune's fucked-up wheel.

But M.J., still speechless, couldn't find the words.

She had poured them all into *The Dirty Book Club*: the novel she had spent the past year writing. The one she now held in her clammy hand and would sign after tonight's presentation. Everything she felt and everything she wanted to say was already inside.

And so she opened the cover, flipped past the dedication to

January, August, and April Stark, and then kicked off her book tour by reading the first chapter . . .

"'If Gloria Golden were being honest, she'd say that Potluck Fridays weren't really about making the most of her newly renovated kitchen. Nor were they an excuse to connect with Dot, Liddy, and Marjorie, since best friends didn't need excuses. *Honest* Gloria would say their weekly get-togethers were the one thing she could rely on . . .'"

ACKNOWLEDGMENTS

Did you enjoy *The Dirty Book Club*? Detest it? Either way blame my editor, Karen Kosztolnyik. Without her you would not be reading this. Literally. It took four years for me to deliver this novel (it was supposed to take one), and there was Karen, the skilled midwife, guiding, listening, advising, enthusing, trusting, and waiting when most others would have lost patience and let me bleed out. Karen, you believed in this novel when tequila and I pitched it to you over the phone from Mexico—and you never stopped believing. (Well, maybe you did but you never told me, so thank you.) Waiting along with you, or should I say "champing at the bit," was the publisher of Gallery Books, Jen Bergstrom and the president, Louise Burke; your collective patience tops my gratitude list on a daily basis.

I am also grateful for my editor, Kate Dresser, who pushed it over the finish line, and the associate publisher, Jen Long; subsidiary rights director, Paul O'Halloran; and the marketing crew: Wendy Sheanin, Liz Psaltis, Abby Zidle, Diana Velasquez, and Mackenzie Hickey, who, along with their hardworking teams, managed to let you know this novel existed. Grateful still for the publicity director, Jennifer Robinson; art director, Lisa Litwack; and editorial assistant, Molly Gregory, for connecting us all.

And then there's my meticulous copy editor, Erica Ferguson, who righted every misplaced comma, flagged every continuity error, and let me know that "three inches of exposed butt crack was too much butt crack"; and my production editor, Sherry Wasserman, who made sure it stayed that way. Thank you, Erica and Sherry. My thanks also to Audrey Sussman and Katie Haigler for their indispensable editorial backup.

Thank you always to Richard Abate, my straight-talking agent and friend of fifteen years (FUPM). Thank you to my longtime lawyer, Alex Kohner, for always having my back and for taking the time to craft my margaritas from scratch. Thank you, Hallie Jones and Henri Maddocks, my former assistants, who helped weed through all the terrible ideas, character names, and unnecessary mechanical-bull scenes until I arrived at the right ones.

Thank you to Clay Tarver for spending many happy hours helping me retool chapters, writing *B*s beside the jokes that could be better, and for tolerating my mood swings—of which there were many—while I birthed this labor of love.

Thank you to Rey Anthony for being brave enough to write *The Housewife's Handbook on Selective Promiscuity*. Thank you, E. L. James, for reminding women that sex can be a wonderful adventure with your Fifty Shades trilogy. Thank you, Erica Jong, for your seminal and hilarious *Fear of Flying*. Thank you, Anaïs Nin, for the beautifully written, fearlessly honest *Henry and June*. Thank you, Jenna Jameson and Neil Strauss, for the candid and wildly entertaining *How to Make Love Like a Porn Star: A Cautionary Tale*. And thank you,

Judy Blume, for writing *Forever*. It launched my real-life book club, reminded me of the power of first love and the importance of female independence, and that, like Ralph, all penises should have a name.

Thank you to my Canadian family: the Gottliebs, Coopers, Mom, Dad, and Denise. You are always there to cheer me on, make me laugh snot bubbles when I'm crying, and give me hell for not returning calls. That's love. Thank you to my American family: the Harrisons, Regans, and Foxes for your unwavering support, not only in my professional life but also in my personal life. Talk about gratitude. Thank you, Kevin Harrison, for being my one-stop surf source and for drinking milk with sushi—I couldn't have possibly made that up.

Thank you to my friends who remember who I am when I emerge from the cone of silence, the ones I will guilt into buying this novel whether they want to read it or not.

And a massive special thanks to my sons, Luke and Jesse Harrison. Every day after school they'd greet me by asking how many pages I wrote. And even on those dry days when I managed only a paragraph, they'd hug me and say they were proud. One afternoon we were driving along the Coast Highway and the sun was beating on the Pacific Ocean. I asked Luke to describe it. He said it looked like "raining diamonds." I stole that line and gave it to M.J. Luke, I owe you a bag of gummies.

I'd also like to thank my eyes. Five minutes before I sat down to write the acknowledgments I accidentally spritzed hair spray on my face instead of rosewater face mist. They're still burning, but my vision has been restored. And my lashes? They have a firm new hold that will not be stirred by today's high-wind advisory. So out into the world we go . . . finally!